His move west was supposed to mean he'd be blazing a new path for himself. Alone.

No reminders of his past. No associations that tied him to anyone. But there she sat—looking so alone and forlorn. How could he not offer help when she could leave her past behind, too, and he could easily help her do it?

"You don't know where to run, do you?"

Her hands still clutched the pouch containing the jewelry. "No," she said.

And that one bleak, hopelessly spoken word sealed his fate.

* * *

A Texan's Honor
Harlequin® Historical #1087—May 2012

KATE WELSH

A TEXAN'S HONOR

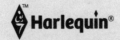
™ **Harlequin**®

TORONTO NEW YORK LONDON
AMSTERDAM PARIS SYDNEY HAMBURG
STOCKHOLM ATHENS TOKYO MILAN MADRID
PRAGUE WARSAW BUDAPEST AUCKLAND

Recycling programs
for this product may
not exist in your area.

ISBN-13: 978-0-373-29687-3

A TEXAN'S HONOR

Copyright © 2012 by Kate Welsh

This edition published by arrangement with Harlequin Books S.A.

For questions and comments about the quality of this book
please contact us at Customer_eCare@Harlequin.ca.

www.Harlequin.com

Printed in U.S.A.

**Did you know that these novels are also
available as ebooks? Visit www.Harlequin.com.**

KATE WELSH

As a child, Kate Welsh often lost herself in creating make-believe worlds and happily-ever-after tales. Many years later she turned back to creating happy endings when her husband challenged her to write down the stories in her head. A lover of all things romantic, Kate has been writing romance for over twenty years now. Her first published novels hit the stands in 1998.

Kate was Valley Forge Romance Writers' first president, and is currently their vice-president. She lives her own happily-ever-after in the Philadelphia suburbs, with her husband of over thirty years, her daughter, their one-hundred-pound Chesapeake Bay retriever, Ecko, and Kali, the family cat.

Kate loves hearing from readers, who can reach her on the internet at kate_welsh@verizon.net.

Prologue

Ireland
May 10, 1843
Midnight

It was officially Alexander Reynolds's twelfth birthday. The mantel clock, in the bedroom he always used on visits to Adair, had struck the final note of midnight. But he was too excited to sleep. At dinner, his Uncle James had told him the book Alexander had been begging for was in the library and his for the taking. He'd also promised Alexander a birthday surprise in the morning.

His uncle, the Earl of Adair, who was very busy caring for the family and its interests, always made time for him and his own son, Alex's cousin, Jamie. Alexander's father, Oswald, spent all his time bitterly complaining that he himself wasn't the earl.

Alex pushed those sad thoughts away. He didn't want to think about his father. He wanted to be happy for one whole day—from midnight to midnight. And he didn't want to miss a moment of it.

Sliding from bed, Alexander crept along the hall, down the back stairs. He carefully opened the door to his uncle's library. Uncle James was there, sitting in the tall mahogany chair behind his desk. He'd fallen asleep there, as he often did. Just as Alexander was about to tiptoe into the room, he heard his father's voice. He couldn't see him and was relieved because if his father saw him he'd be angry, and neither he nor his mother ever angered his father if they could help it. Alex started to back away.

But what his father was saying froze Alex in place. "Wake up, brother. I wanted you to know I'm sending you to your grave. And that sickly whelp of yours won't be far behind. He'll come down with something deadly or maybe I'll arrange an accident. I'll be earl within the year."

"No. Please," his uncle begged.

Before Alex could react, a gunshot echoed in the room and a crimson stain blossomed on the curtains near his uncle's desk. Then Uncle James slumped forward and his head hit the desk with a sickening thud.

Terrified, grieving and sick to his stomach all at the same time, Alexander backed away from the door and crept to the backstairs. In his bare feet, he ran silently back to his room, shaking all the way.

As he made his way to his room, he heard servants rushing through the house. He climbed into bed, shivering and trying to think. He didn't know what to do. If he told someone what he'd seen, would they hang his father? Would that be so terrible? he had to wonder.

But whom could he tell who would be sure to punish his father and save Jamie?

His mother was too cowed by his father. She couldn't even stop him from beating Alex. He just turned on her and she ran away crying. Suppose his father killed all of them? Would that be Alex's fault?

The butler, or the estate manager? No. Not anyone on the staff? No one would take a servant's word over his father's. And if Alex did say something to persons of authority on his own, suppose no one believed him? If his father could kill his own brother and said he was going to kill little Jamie, there was no guarantee he wouldn't kill Alex for telling what he'd seen. He didn't care about that, he realized. Except that it would leave Jamie alone, standing in the way of Oswald's desire for the earldom. Jamie would be at his mercy. Without Alex to help him, Jamie wouldn't stand a chance.

It was too late to help Uncle James, or even get justice for him. But Alex would guard his cousin with his own life.

Alex swore to Jamie he would do just that when the next morning he found Jamie crying in his room over the news of his father's suicide.

That was how—on his twelfth birthday—Alexander Reynolds's childhood had ended, forcing him to keep a terrible secret and a sacred promise.

Chapter One

New York City
September 1878

"Mister Reynolds," his cousin's butler said as he entered the study. Alexander looked up from the map he'd been studying as the tall gray-haired man continued, "A young woman claiming to be a friend of the countess has arrived. She seems a bit...nervous, sir. I thought perhaps you would be kind enough to explain that the earl and countess have sailed for Ireland."

"It is rather late."

"Indeed, sir."

Alex took a sip of his cognac, cautious as always to assume the careless persona he showed the world. Soon he would be free to let go of that facade. Soon that character and everything that had created him would be in the past and he could figure out who the hell he really was.

"Not looking forward to disappointing the lady, Winston?" he pretended to tease. "You never have that problem when I ask you to send a persistent mamma on her way."

Winston stiffened to his tallest, most formal self. "This is different. Disappointing teary-eyed, exhausted females is not my forte, sir."

"You think it's mine?" Alex asked carefully. *Was it?*

"Not at all. But as I mentioned, she seems to be worried. And fretful. I suppose I could awaken Heddie—"

"No. No," Alex said on a sigh. Mrs. Winston worked hard every day and was doing more than usual closing up Jamie's house and with little help. He on the other hand had been doing nothing but marking time until what he thought of as his real life began.

Dammit. Why couldn't this woman have waited another day to show up on his cousin's doorstep? "I suppose I should earn my keep around here."

Winston's left eyebrow rose imperiously. "I believe you did that into perpetuity in San Francisco. You saved the lives of the earl and countess, their child and the lives of the entire household staff."

And all he'd had to do to accomplish that was to kill his own father. Alex knocked back the rest of his snifter of Jamie's best cognac.

The guilt from that night and from the years of hesitation and half measures that had preceded it threatened to crush him. He would have done it years earlier had he known it would come to that. He hoped so at least. It would have saved others endless heartache, his own years of regret and several lives.

"I'd best be off to handle this dirty work for you," Alex joked, forcing his thoughts into the present. "Where did you leave the young lady? Not on the doorstep, I hope."

"Sir! Of course not. I showed her to the front parlor."

Alex forced a grin. Sometimes it was exceedingly tiring to pretend a lightheartedness he didn't feel. "I never thought otherwise. Take a breath, Winston." He stood to go in search of… "The young lady in question, Winston, what is her name?"

"Mrs. Patience Wexler Gorham."

Alex rose. "I should hurry, I suppose. It has been my experience that women named Patience have little of the virtue to call their own."

Winston nodded smartly, then withdrew. Alex strode down the stairs and along the hall of the New York town house. The house spoke of his cousin Jamie's success. But, even more, of his determination to get out from under Alex's father's shadow.

Alex had always pretended to be the carefree one but somehow Jamie had managed to blossom into all that was sunshine and light. He smiled. Seeing Jamie so happy made everything he'd done since he'd turned twelve worthwhile.

Meanwhile Alex had spent years as a phantom and now he couldn't quite find his way out of the darkness. It was his turn to crawl from behind the shadow that had been Oswald Reynolds, just as Jamie had done. The next step on that journey was leaving New York to begin his new life on the Rocking R, the Texas Hill Country ranch he'd bought. He was counting on the completely foreign, totally sunny atmosphere to free him of some of the weight on his shoulders. Of the darkness in his soul.

Because he couldn't seem to do it for himself.

He stepped into the doorway of the parlor, a lovely, light-infused room with Louis Quinze furnishings, gleaming white woodwork and golden brocade-inset wall panels. Three exquisite crystal chandeliers kept it bright even at night.

But the beauty of the decorating paled in the presence of the lovely creature standing near the fireplace. He stared for a long moment at her reflection in a mirror on a side wall. Her profile was delicate, her green eyes heavily fringed with dark lashes and her hair a rich auburn.

Alex's heart bumped in his chest when he cleared his throat and she spun to face him. Disappointment flooded those crystalline eyes. *Winston, you rotter.*

He cleared his tight throat. "I'm sorry, Mrs. Gorham," he said. "I come the bearer of unfortunate news. My cousin, Jamie, and his wife sailed this morning for his estate in Ireland."

"No," she cried. Her creamy complexion went instantly pale. "Oh, no! What am I to do now?" She looked suddenly as if all the starch had gone out of her. Wobbling a bit, she made a grab for the mantel.

Alex knew an overwrought woman when he saw one. The hand gripping the solid surface would hold her upright only so long. He reached her just in time to catch her before she could pitch forward on her face. He scooped her up then laid her on the settee. But she didn't awaken. Not even when he went from patting her hand to stroking the lovely creature's smooth cheek. He looked down upon her and found himself, just for a moment, tumbling headlong into love.

Then he got his head round straight. Lust. This was only lust. And look what pain that had wrought in his life so far! He'd lost all right to the child born of what he'd thought was love, but now knew to have been that baser emotion.

"Oh, dear. I was correct, then. The young thing is more than a bit upset," Winston said from the hall, pulling Alex out of haunting memories.

"I'd say that is the greatest of understatements. Call your wife, would you, Winston? I think the lady may need a woman when she wakes."

"But, sir, what are we to do about her after that?"

Alex sighed. This was a complication, to be sure, but what else could he do? "It is quite late and we can hardly send her out alone into the dark of night. I don't think the earl would mind if we gave her a room till morning if she is in need of lodging."

"I believe Lady Meara's room could be readied in a thrice, sir. Heddie made it up and put the dust covers in place this afternoon."

"I'm as sorry as I can be about having to awaken your wife but I think proprieties should be followed as much as possible."

Winston nodded. "I'll wake the wife and send her along then I'll go and uncover everything. You can bring the young lady up while my wife dresses."

Alex sighed in relief. "Thank you, Winston. I confess I'm completely at sea as to what to do for her. Or to say to her."

"Perhaps you might listen when she wakes, sir."

Alex frowned. Not what he wanted to hear. He could actually feel himself being pulled into a situation he wanted nothing to do with. Yet… "I suppose that means first I would be expected to ask what it is she came here to accomplish." He wasn't sure what good he'd be to her. He was barely any good to himself these days.

He received a reprieve of a sort because Mrs. Gorham—Patience—had not awakened by the time Winston returned. The butler reported that he'd readied the room and that his wife was dressing as quickly as possible.

Not knowing what else to do for the young woman, Alex lifted her slight weight into his arms and carried her up to little Meara's room. He laid her on the counterpane and stepped back.

Looking around the room he smiled helplessly. It held the stamp of Meara, the child he could never claim as his own though he was her true father. Several years earlier Jamie had married the woman Alex had loved. She had given birth to Meara seven months after their nuptials. Alex, absent from England at the time, had had no idea he'd left Iris pregnant when he'd gone off on a mission. She'd died some months after Meara's birth in a fall from a horse. Legally Meara was Jamie's daughter. But more important, Jamie loved Meara no less than if she was his natural child. In fact, Jamie said he loved her more because she was Alex's daughter. Alex shook his head in consternation. The inner workings of his cousin's mind were ever a mystery.

His heart aching for all that would never be, Alex walked to the window and looked out, concerned to see a man walking up and down the street, checking yards and obviously searching for something. He glanced at the bed.

Or someone.

A moan from their guest told him his temporary housemate had decided to join him. He walked to the bed, grabbing a small chair on his way, and sat next to her.

Her eyes drifted open then widened in what could only be named terror. Judging from the way she sprang into a sitting position and shrank away to the other side of the bed, no doubt the person who had her so frightened must be a male. "Who are you? What do you want from me?" she gasped and looked around frantically. "Where am I?"

"At the home of your friend, Amber, in her stepdaughter Meara's room," he told her. "You swooned when I told you the earl and countess had gone from America to Ireland."

She blinked and colored before she took a deep breath, visibly trying to calm herself. "Oh, yes. Of course. I'm so terribly sorry to have caused such an uproar. I traveled all day and I haven't eaten. I won't trouble you further," she added and began to scoot away toward the other side of the bed and the door. "I must get on my way."

Alex wrapped a staying hand around her delicate arm, tilted his head and considered the pretty young woman for a long moment. He took in her frozen expression, as well, and carefully let go of her arm. "Where will you go? You seemed not to know what you would do now that the countess is away."

Tears welled up in her startling eyes, magnifying the multihued qualities of their green color. He had never seen their like. "But that isn't your problem," she whispered as if forcing the words forth.

"But I fear it is of interest to a certain man moving furtively along the street, checking yards."

She sucked in a breath and cast her fear-filled gaze toward the window.

"Perhaps you need help, even if only from the cousin

of the earl?" Alex asked, shocked to his toes to hear himself ask the question. Why could he not learn to mind his own business? He was to leave in the morning.

She blinked and hesitantly leaned back against the headboard. "Alexander? You're Alexander?"

He forced a smile, though he loathed that name having heard it on his father's lips one too many times. "My reputation seems to have preceded me. I hope what you've heard hasn't been all bad."

"On the contrary. Amber calls you a hero. She wrote about the problems in San Francisco and how you saved them all from certain death. I am sorry it cost you so much personally."

Alex pushed thoughts of that night out of his mind. He relived it often enough in his nightmares. "I did only what I had to do. The question is how may I help you? We—Winston and I—already assume you'll stay the night."

She looked at her hands where she'd rested them in her lap. "That is very kind of you but I don't wish to put you out. Or to cause you trouble. My father is a powerful man."

"I assure you, powerful men rarely frighten me. I cut my teeth on a father who probably makes yours look like a petulant angry kitten. We seem to have trouble-some sires in common. So tell me. What is so forbidding about yours that you would flee him?"

She sighed, staring at him as if weighing her options. The expression in her startling eyes clearly put him in the dubious category of the lesser of two evils. Truly, nothing new to him.

"I am a recent widow. My marriage was more on the lines of a prison sentence—though the prison itself was quite lovely." She looked down again as if ashamed of her next statement. "My husband was very disappointed in me as a wife. To spite me, he went through his fortune in his last years. He left me penniless at his death. I had no choice but to return to my father. Father blames me for the problems in my marriage and now has arranged another marriage. Soon."

Alex was incredulous, though why he would be after his treatment at his own father's hands he did not know. Perhaps because she was so utterly angelic he couldn't imagine any man, especially her father, not being softened by that endearing grace. "Your father blamed you?"

"My husband spoke ill of me to Father. And my father also holds a great grudge against me. My husband refused to allow me to travel, you see. Impatient to see her only daughter and how I was enjoying the wonderful marriage my father had arranged for me, my mother and brothers came to visit. She departed swiftly when she saw how unhappy I was. They were killed on their return trip. All of them."

Alex's own father had certainly been capable of such disloyalty. "And so your father blames you for their deaths and not your husband or the driver of the carriage?"

"My husband was a friend of Father's and, as I said, he often spoke ill of me so I would have nowhere to go if I tried to flee my marriage. He claimed I'd grown full of myself and that I'd declared Mother would need to visit me if she wanted to see me. At least she left knowing the truth."

"You said you're recently widowed. For how long, if I may inquire?"

"Three months."

He blinked. He knew Americans were less formal in general than the English but not in the upper echelons of society. Bedraggled as she had been on arriving, she was clearly from that group. "And yet, you said he wishes you to marry again soon."

"The man is another of his friends though quite a bit younger. Mr. Bedlow has long wanted me." She shivered and, though Alex could tell she tried to hide the reaction, he saw nonetheless. "Father told me he has arranged our marriage for two weeks from now."

"Am I to understand you don't wish this man's attention?"

She cast her gaze at her knotted fingers. "I refused the marriage, and more specifically the man, so Father locked me in my room. He told the servants they were not to feed me until I agreed to marry Mr. Bedlow. He made a mistake, though. Amber had come into my life at Vassar." Patience's smile was just a touch mischievous. "She taught me to climb trees. And the tree outside the terrace of my room has grown quite a bit since I lived there before my marriage. It was an avenue of escape. And I took it. I must admit, as afraid as I was of falling, my greatest fear was that if I fell and therefore failed to make my getaway, the fall might not kill me."

Alex was truly horrified at the thought of a young woman preferring death to marriage to the man chosen for her. He wondered if his mother had had similar feelings when she'd been told of the marriage his grandfathers had arranged. And now he knew his father had eventually killed her. Or rather *Alex* had, by sharing the knowledge of his father's misdeeds with her. If only she hadn't found the courage to stand up to Oswald Reynolds over the earl's murder.

If only he'd kept his own counsel.

Just then Mrs. Winston bustled in carrying a tray. "Time enough in the morning to make plans and decisions. Off with you now, Mr. Alex," she ordered. "And here's a bit of a snack, dearie. The husband says you fainted. Nothing a bit of soup and tea won't cure." She pinned Alex with a hard glare when he didn't move. "What is it you'd be waiting around for, Mr. Alex?"

After assuring Patience that she'd be safe for the night, Alex stood and left, cursing his own cowardice. Had he not called upon Jamie's loveable harridan of a housekeeper in the first place, he'd still be sharing a few more moments with their guest. Then he cursed his own stupidity and reminded himself that the only things he felt for Mrs. Gorham were lust and pity and he'd sworn not to let either emotion rule him in the future.

Patience stared after the admittedly handsome Alexander Reynolds as he left, having chivalrously promised to keep watch on the house while she slept. He'd been so kind. And had not even blinked an eye at all she'd revealed.

But really—what had possessed her to blurt out her shameful personal history? She tried to gain solace from the knowledge that she hadn't spelled out the full spectrum of the degradation her husband had subjected her to.

But the question remained. In spite of all she already knew about Alexander Reynolds from Amber, she was unsure if she could trust him or any man ever again.

"You can trust that one," Mrs. Winston said.

Patience jumped nearly a foot and her head instinctively snapped around to stare into the kindly face of the housekeeper who'd shooed Alexander away. It was as if she'd heard Patience's thoughts. Her doubts. "How could you know what—?"

"What you were thinking?" the woman finished, her gray head canted. "Uncertainty is written all over your face, dearie. And I know he's trustworthy because I've seen a lot in the years I've worked for the Quality. Their station doesn't always mean they're good people. The earl and his cousin are. Now, let's get you fed and ready for bed, shall we, Mrs. Gorham?"

That name almost always thrust her back into those humiliating days that had ended only three months ago. No matter how much she managed to block out the memories, those awful days were still there waiting to haunt her when she least expected. She'd heard it said that time healed all wounds, but she was sure anyone who believed that had been given a decent amount of time. Instead, she had more poisonous memories to keep the others company. The newer ones, however, hurt worse because they were wounds delivered by her own father's betrayal.

With slightly narrowed eyes, she concentrated on the older woman, fighting the painful thoughts. After a long moment she managed to say, "I know it is considered a breach but please call me Patience."

The kindly woman smiled, gentle understanding in her warm expression. "Then you should call me Heddie."

"Gladly," Patience said.

"Now that we have that settled, come sit over here,

and eat. I want nothing left on that tray when I come back, hear?"

Patience nodded then let the woman help her to a small sitting area as she fought back tears. No one had fussed over her this way since her mama's death. Had she lived, would her mother have rescued her as she'd promised that fateful day? Patience would never know. Just as she would never know if the accident that had taken her mother and brothers' lives had been an accident at all. She'd always feared her husband had had a hand in forcing that carriage off the cliff. The evidence of the tracks on the road had told the story of negligence at best, murder at worst. But she hadn't been questioned. She didn't believe there had even been an investigation at all.

"Eat up, now. I'm off to find something for you to sleep in."

Patience dug in as ordered. The simple fare was delicious, the soup tasty and warm, the bread crisp and sumptuous. It had been so long since she'd eaten.

Although she'd been taught to take small bites in order to converse with guests throughout a meal, this evening, all alone, Patience fairly wolfed the food down. Her mother would have been mortified. Tears filled Patience's eyes. Penelope Wexler was long gone.

Mrs. Winston returned not long after and dropped a nightgown on the bed. "There you go, dearie. Oh, done already? My you were near starved, weren't you?"

Embarrassed, Patience dropped her gaze. "I'm so sorry. You must think me terribly unmannered to have all but inhaled my food that way."

"What I think is that you were in great need of nourishment. Now let us get you out of those clothes so you can get some sleep. Mr. Alex sent up some brandy. You should drink it. It may help you sleep. Problems can be handled in the morning."

Patience nodded and stood. Heddie helped her undress and put on the nightgown that must belong to Amber, judging from the small size and exquisite quality. Wondering what was to become of her, Patience climbed back onto the bed Mrs. Winston had turned down. The brandy did help and she fell into an exhausted sleep rather quickly, though it was a sleep haunted by the past and future.

She wakened several times with a start, thinking the man Alexander had seen out of the window had somehow found her. Each time she roused she was greeted by a small gas flame glowing in a wall sconce across the room. It illuminated the area enough so she could see that no one but her was in the room.

Hours later the morning sunshine slanted through the bedroom window, rousing Patience from her restless slumber. Though her sleep had been disturbed by nightmares, she had still slept. She hadn't felt this rested since that awful interview with her father when he'd proclaimed her fate and banished her to her room until she capitulated.

She pursed her lips and swung her feet to the floor. He must be furious, surely having discovered her missing by now. And with Amber gone for Ireland, Patience had no one to turn to.

What am I to do?

If only there was some way for her to get far enough away. She walked to the window and cautiously peeked through the airy curtains, wondering if the man Alexander had seen was indeed someone in her father's employ.

Was he still lurking out there? Her stomach knotted. If he was, how would she be able to escape again?

The bedroom door opened slowly and Patience whirled, half-expecting one of the men from her nightmares to be standing there. But it was only Heddie backing in with a tray in her hands. The mixed scents of coffee, warm bread, bacon and fried eggs entered with her.

"Mr. Reynolds asks that you stay in your room until he's taken care of some pressing matters. He wants to make sure it's safe for you to come down. He was quite adamant."

"How can it not be safe inside the earl's home?"

"He said he isn't sure about your rights under the laws here in the United States. Or his for harboring you. He thinks it would be unwise for you to risk being seen until you have a plan and he knows no one can legally force their way inside to look for you."

Her heart fell. She knew the answer to that. She had no plan and no rights with a father as powerful as hers. With his connections at city hall things went his way in spite of the downfall of Boss Tweed and the Tammany Hall political machine. That was why she had run here. Amber's husband, the Earl of Adair, had as much power here and abroad as her father. She'd hoped the earl would be able to help her find a safe haven. She was beginning to fear there was no such place.

"I should dress and be on my way," she told Heddie Winston. "I don't think Mr. Reynolds understands whose runaway daughter he's taken in. I am nothing more than Lionel Wexler's chattel."

Mrs. Winston smiled kindly and shook her head a bit. "You should know Alexander Reynolds isn't afraid of your father, dearie." She frowned thoughtfully. "I don't believe he's afraid of anyone. Considering the man who raised him, I can't imagine there is a person alive who could intimidate Mr. Alex."

She took the tray to the sitting area where Patience had eaten last night. "Now you sit right over here and eat your meal. When you're done, have a good soak. The bath is the door at the end of the hall. I've left a robe in there and I have someone brushing your dress out and fixing the torn hem. She'll bring it up when she's finished and then she'll draw your bath. I'll see she tidies up in here while she waits to help you dress." Heddie turned back and motioned to the slipper chair. "I washed out your chemise and I'm about to iron it the rest of the way dry. Everything will be just fine. You'll see."

Patience ate what she could, no longer as ravenous as last night. Trying not to notice the time passing, she bathed, dressed and let the young maid fool with her hair. Then she paced. Three hours after Heddie Winston left her, Patience had run out of tolerance with hiding in a child's room. She had begun to feel like a prisoner again.

Opening her reticule, she spread the jewelry her mother had brought along on that fateful visit just before the accident that had taken her life. It had been her grandmother's and her mother's. She fingered it now, remembering with a sharp pang the day her mother had given the items to her. And the shame she'd felt as she'd hidden it, guarding it under a loose floorboard in her closet. She'd made sure no one knew she had it, especially after her mother's death and her father's subsequent desertion. For the five remaining years of her marriage, she'd kept it hidden from her husband, at first unable to use it for escape. Following her mother's departure that day, he'd kept her a virtual prisoner.

Finally he'd had a heart attack that had left him so wasted, the worst he'd been able to do was strike her on the back of the legs with his cane as she passed him. She'd learned to wear extra petticoats that made the attacks as ineffectual as he'd been in bed.

He'd blamed her for that, too!

And so she'd endured, knowing she had nowhere to go, hoping Edgar Gorham wouldn't live much longer, thinking she'd be able to use his wealth to build a life for herself once he was gone. He'd lived two and a half years longer, though, and all she'd been able to do was fight against his attempts to crush her spirit. She was unsure of how well she'd succeeded.

She fingered the pieces of her heritage nestled in a handkerchief, hating the thought of selling the only visible tie she had to her mother and grandmother. But she had no choice. She could not enter another marriage to a man she despised. She needed to thank Alexander and be on her way.

Chapter Two

Alex stood at the window of Jamie's study, looking down at the busy street below. He watched as Palmer, his man of business, entered the carriage and drove off. Palmer had given him a good picture of the man their guest was up against. The news wasn't good. Other than Amber and Jamie, Patience Gorham probably hadn't a friend in the world who'd go up against her father.

Or Howard Bedlow.

And she was up against them both.

Dammit!

A noise behind him drew his attention. Reflected in the window's glass, Patience stood in the doorway to the study. "Got impatient did you?" he said and plastered on a grin before turning. Thank God he'd had a bit of a forewarning. The way he felt at that moment he'd have sent the girl scurrying out the front door.

Into danger, no doubt.

Alex cursed under his breath. He'd been wrong. With some nourishment and rest, she was even lovelier than he'd remembered. And more than a bit alluring.

"I'm sorry to disobey your order but I must get on my way," she said. That soft melodic voice that had followed him into sleep washed over him.

At dawn, Winston had relieved him of his watch on the house so he'd gotten a couple of hours of sleep but she'd been there waiting for him in his dreams, with her rich silky hair, those heart-stopping eyes and that voice that got him hard every time he heard it. And this time was no exception. Which left him feeling like the worst sort of cad. The poor thing was terrified of men—himself included.

He forced his mind off his hunger for her and onto her situation. It was good that no one had come pounding the door down, sure she was inside. Now that it was nearly nine in the morning, he was almost sure no one had seen her arrive last night. But he was just as sure there would eventually be an inquiry since apparently Patience and Amber corresponded.

"Disobey my order?" he asked. His heart ached at this window into the kind of life she must have led thus far. He was sure it was the kind of life his mother had been forced to live.

"Mrs. Winston said I was to stay above stairs."

Alex sighed. "You have no obligation to do as I say, Mrs. Gorham. I merely suggested you remain there for your safety. But you may do as you wish."

Though it seemed forced, she gave him an ironic little grin. "Would that that were true. I came to thank you for your hospitality. And to ask if you know of a shop where I could sell my jewelry."

Alex considered her. "A pawn shop? You know you won't get half what it's worth, don't you?"

She clutched her reticule to her stomach looking

pained and sad. "That cannot be helped. I need the funds to get away."

The jewelry means a great deal to her. It couldn't be a gift from her late husband, then. With her desperation so clear in her eyes, she would be a lamb for the shearing to any pawnbroker.

He gestured toward the divan and, breaking protocol, he took a seat in the chair nearest her so she would know he had no intention of crowding her. "I must warn you, that sort of establishment is probably being watched."

She shook her head. "My father has no knowledge that I have it. My mother gave it to me just before her death. I was to use it to get away from Mr. Gorham should I feel endangered."

"As that means you never felt that desperate, I am glad you still have it. May I ask where it is you plan to go? Will you try to follow the countess to Ireland?"

"No. The wharfs are surely being watched. I had thought to make my way out of the city by rail." She bit that lovely full bottom lip with her even white teeth.

He wanted nothing more at that moment than to nibble that lip, as well. The thought made his breath catch.

Then she spoke again. "That is how I got here, but if the wharfs are watched, I suppose the rail stations are by now, as well."

Alex forced his desire for her into the background of his thoughts again. But his resolve to help her had only strengthened in the last minutes. He supposed everyone had a weakness. His was apparently a need to help those being forced into desperate circumstances by ruthless men. He didn't know if it was altruism or if he was condemned to spend his life proving to himself and others he wasn't like his father.

He hated the idea that Oswald Reynolds still had that kind of power and influence over his life. Alex stared ahead, trying to put away the notion of offering more help than he'd already given.

His move west was supposed to mean he'd be blazing a new path for himself. Alone. No reminders of his past. No associations that tied him to anyone but Jamie and his family. But there she sat looking so alone and forlorn. How could he not offer help when she could leave her past behind, too, and he could easily help her do it. "You don't know where to run, do you?"

Her hands still clutched the pouch containing the jewelry. "No," she said.

And that one bleak, hopelessly spoken word sealed his fate.

Winston appeared in the doorway perhaps with a reprieve. "Sir, there is a gentl— A *person* looking for a young lady. He claims she is off in the head." Winston glanced rather pointedly toward Patience when she gasped. "A danger to herself and others."

"I am not…" She popped to her feet, still holding the reticule in a desperate clench. "I swear, I am not anything of the—"

Alex stood and lifted a staying hand to stop her rush of words. She had suffered enough and shouldn't be forced to beg for her very life. To Winston he said, "I will handle this. Is that all?"

"I left him on the stoop."

"That was unusually rude of you, Winston."

"Yes," Winston agreed and Alex would swear he'd nearly smiled.

To Mrs. Gorham, Alex said quietly, "I will send him on his way. As to his claims, I can detect a lie when I hear one even if it isn't firsthand. A lady like you would never invent the tale you have told me. I had a mother who was a lady and all that was kind and gentle. I know you felt diminished by what you were forced to reveal. This is not an order, ma'am, but for your safety, you should go with Winston and put your trust in those trying to help you."

She simply nodded and hurried down the back hall following Winston.

Alex proceeded to the front door. He took a deep breath and schooled his features into that of the carefree lighthearted swell he'd pretended to be for so long. It was another part of his life he intended to leave behind.

A large man with a pinched face and a slightly unkempt appearance stood at the door, a step below. He straightened from his slovenly posture against the rail, looking mulish and annoyed.

Too damn bad, Alex thought as he gazed sardonically down his nose. Leaning on the doorjamb, Alex crossed his arms negligently. "I understand you've come seeking the Earl of Adair," Alex said, making sure that no matter how relaxed he seemed to be he still blocked the doorway with his body.

"I'm with the Pinkerton Agency. We've reason to believe our client's daughter came here looking for the earl's wife. I've been sent to retrieve her."

"Retrieve the countess?" Alex asked mildly, all the while considering the implication of the Pinkertons looking for one lone woman. Apparently Lionel Wexler was determined to get her back and by any means necessary.

The Pinkertons usually worked for powerful corporations against those who threatened their revenues or hunted dangerous criminals intent on menacing their clientele's bank accounts and property.

Alan Pinkerton himself was a ruthless man. A few years ago he'd blown up a home where the mother of the notorious James brothers lived. Their younger half brother had been killed and their mother had lost an arm. Pinkerton denied the arson had been planned from the first but not many who lived by a strict moral code seemed to believe him.

"'Course I'm not lookin' for the earl or his lady," the agent snapped. "I'm seeking Patience Gorham."

Trying to appear just a bit vacuous Alex said, "Oh. I don't believe I know that name. What is this about again?"

"She's off her nut she is, sir. Mr. Wexler wants her back home safe and sound."

Alex pretended to be startled. "Goodness. This sounds serious." Then confused. "When is it you think she would have arrived on my cousin's doorstep? And this Wexler chap is looking for a woman named Gorham but she is his daughter?"

The man's gaze sharpened. "Thought you didn't know her? Why so interested if you don't know her?"

"Don't know her. But I don't live in my cousin's pocket, either. I have my reasons for asking. When would this have been?"

"Yesterday or maybe the day before. Her papa isn't sure when she escaped her room. Climbed down a tree like a child. Shows she's not right in the head. Could've been killed or caused a scandal."

The man had to be parroting Wexler's concerns

because Alex doubted this man had a clue how much of a scandal this would be were it to get out. Unfortunately, it was probably Patience who would be the one tarnished by the gossip this man was spreading. "I think you shouldn't be letting that get out, in that case. I doubt her father expects you to go about damaging the poor daft girl's reputation."

The man had the good grace to look abashed.

But Alex was still left striving to keep his expression one of mild concern and not one of utter outrage. To how many others had this cretin bandied her sanity and good name about like an old society biddy?

Then the full import of what the man had said sank in. If they didn't know when Patience had left, she must not have been given food for at least the two days in question. Nor had anyone bothered to check to make sure she was all right in her pretty prison cell.

It was a wonder she'd gotten this far before fainting. Suppose she'd fallen beneath the wheels of the train at the busy station or the hooves of a carriage team. Alex clenched his hands behind his back.

"This may be very bad," he told the Pinkerton. "The countess added a maid to her staff only yesterday. Can you describe this woman?"

The man checked his notepad. "Uh...smallish. Red hair. Dark red, her papa said. Green eyes. 'Bout all they told me so far. They're working with a printer to make up handbills with her likeness on 'em."

"They? Her parents?" he asked, knowing her mother to be diseased.

"Her intended and her papa."

Alex raised an eyebrow lazily. "Goodness, he must

be a brave man to agree to marry a crazed woman. Or he must owe something to her father."

"*The maid,* sir? There is a reward. And Mr. Pinkerton wants to impress this gent that hired him."

"Well, I am sorry to tell you but the description does put me in mind of the new maid."

The man put his foot on the top step but Alex put a hand to his chest, blocking his advance. "You didn't wait for me to deliver the *bad* news. The earl and his family sailed yesterday for his estate. *With* their staff."

"Where is it? This estate?"

For me to know and you to waste time finding out. If this ruffian worked on a false lead for a good while, Alex could use that time to get Patience out of the city. Let Wexler and the other one pay the Pinkertons to go chasing a wild goose.

Putting on his best, bored aristocratic expression Alex said mockingly, "He's an *earl.* Where do you think his estate is?"

The man cursed roundly, turned away and stalked off down the marble steps without another word. He met with three others a few doors down. Alex smiled as the detective gave his cohorts the news. "You're welcome, you vulture," he said under his breath and stepped back inside.

Now to find out if Mrs. Patience Wexler Gorham was brave enough to consider starting over in Texas.

Patience returned to the study, responding to a summons from Alexander Reynolds. Her nerves were still jittery after hearing the lies her father was willing to tell about her. Contrary to her previous belief, a heart could break more than once. But she had no time to nurse it.

Alexander stood as she entered the room. Heddie Winston trailed after her and surprisingly joined her husband on the divan. Having servants party to a meeting was an oddity but Alexander seemed quite at home with the situation. She rather liked that about him. Actually she liked a great deal about the man Amber had told her about. She wondered if he was really the man she saw and if his kindness was not just a facade, as her husband's had been.

He gestured to the high-back chair where he'd sat during their earlier interview. Patience sank into it gratefully, her knees still a bit weak.

"Thank you for cooperating earlier, Mrs. Gorham," Alexander said and leaned against the desk.

"As you pointed out, doing as you asked was for my benefit. What is it you wished to tell me? Does it appear I can successfully flee?"

"I may have managed to shift your father's search from this neighborhood and, in fact, from these shores for a while. Right now they believe you arrived here in time to escape to Britain as part of the earl's entourage. But that will last only so long."

Patience felt suddenly a bit lighter. "That means it may be safer for me to sell my jewelry to use for train fare."

"Safer but not entirely safe," he cautioned. "The Pinkertons are wily and may still question New York's pawnbrokers. Besides which, it isn't right that you should be forced to sell that jewelry. I assume it's all you have left of your mother."

Patience nodded, any elation gone at the prospect

of selling the pieces to ensure her safety as she had promised her mother. In its place flowed memories and pain at the thought of letting them go.

On nights when her husband's cruelty had been nearly too great to bear, she'd crept to her closet to finger her grandmother's emerald-and-ruby set. She'd close her eyes and remember the Christmases around the tree at her grandparents' home. Nana had always worn the jewels on Christmas, their vibrant colors just right for the occasion.

Standing in her closet, Patience had held tight to her mother's diamond necklace, the one Mama had given her that fateful morning they'd set off for home. "If you need to get away before I can convince your father to intervene, you must use these," Penelope Wexler had begged.

"This isn't about sentiment. It is about survival," Patience said now, repeating her mother's last private words to her.

"Yes, it *is* about your survival," Alexander agreed. "I have an idea how to accomplish that and more. First you should know there is a part of your situation I am afraid you don't know. Your betrothal was announced in the *Times* this morning."

Patience gasped then had trouble forcing the air back out. "I refused. How could he do that?" She shook her head. "Mr. Bedlow is going to be furious when he learns I ran away. He is a man who cherishes his pride. This will make him a laughingstock. He will never give up. Never!"

"If you're willing to take a chance, this additional information may not matter but I felt you had a right to know if you didn't—which you clearly did not. My idea is why I've asked the Winstons to sit in on this talk. I've purchased a ranch in Texas Hill Country. The Rocking R is near a small town called Tierra del Verde. I am to leave for the Newark, New Jersey, train station in less than two hours. From there I am to go to Philadelphia where I will board the earl's private car to travel from Philadelphia as far as San Antonio, Texas. You are welcome to join me."

Patience stared at him—elation warring with fear. Alexander Reynolds, she knew from Amber's letters, had lived most of his life in the pursuit of one thing— seeing to his cousin's safety. But Alexander was also a man. Patience couldn't ignore that basic fact. How could she travel from New York to Texas in a train car alone with a man? Any man? Even Alexander Reynolds?

Mr. Gorham had seemed all that was kind and gentle until their wedding night, when he'd been unable to perform and had blamed her. That night and all the nights after. He'd tortured her nightly, squeezing and pinching her breasts till they'd been bruised purple. Men, once alone with a woman, became animals.

Alexander cleared his throat, drawing her attention. "I know this idea is a shock, but I must urge you think on it. If you traveled alone, you would be at the mercy of any number of strangers. Strangers you would know nothing about and there would be no one with you to assure your safety. Even if you were lucky enough to travel unmolested, you would be in plain view. You are a lovely young woman and will draw the eye of everyone you encounter. That would make you extremely easy to track.

"The Pinkertons are very good at what they do. You will never elude them on your own. And that your father is powerful enough to hire them is even more of a worry for your chances alone. The betrothal announcement speaks to his confidence in finding you and bringing you to heel."

As her heart pounded with fear, Alexander looked toward the Winstons. "And I have a proposition for both of you. It may come to light eventually that we three have aided Mrs. Gorham in her flight. Lionel Wexler, Mrs. Gorham's father, is a powerful man used to getting his own way—as is her betrothed. Neither man will be happy with anyone who has aided her. If Jamie decides not to return to New York from Adair, you will both be released from his employ. I fear you might have difficulty obtaining new employment here in the East."

"The day I let something like that stop me from doing what's right is the day I'll cease to be a good Christian woman," Heddie Winston blustered. "Isn't that right, Jordie?" she said to her husband. Apparently a man of few words, Winston merely nodded. "San Francisco was good to us. We'll just go on back there."

Patience blinked back tears of gratitude to these three strangers. "Please know I am grateful for all your kindnesses to me. But at the same time I am so sorry to have brought this trouble to your doorstep."

Alexander spoke again. "It may be of no consequence to any of us. I have an idea to avoid any and all backlash from this." Still looking at the Winstons he said, "I wondered if you two would consider accompanying Mrs. Gorham and me to Texas to work for me there. We would all travel in the earl's private train car. There is plenty of room. And I think Mrs. Gorham would feel more comfortable with chaperones along. I'm told the car has two staterooms, four berths, a comfortable sitting room and a small dining area. But it is some distance by coach from San Antonio. There is no Indian activity in the area so you needn't fear attack on the way. Still, I will see that men from the ranch are there to act as outriders for us on the rest of trip.

"Before any of you answer, let me tell you what awaits you at journey's end. Tierra del Verde is a small town by any standard we are used to but it is quaint with Spanish influences in its architecture. The people I met while there are amiable and honest. It is hoped the railroad will extend that far and beyond but there is no knowing how long that will take. A while, I think. Which will be good for our purposes."

He looked toward her and Patience found herself riveted by the kindness in his eyes. "There is a need for a teacher there, Mrs. Gorham. I'm sure your education more than qualifies you to fill the position. You could earn a living and begin your life anew."

Patience felt a great spurt of joy at the thought of being a teacher. Then Alexander went on.

"The ranch is called the Rocking R." He looked at Mr. and Mrs. Winston. "I've built a very nice house and need a head housekeeper and, of course, a butler to keep everything running smoothly."

He seemed to have it all figured out, though Patience was nearly sure he would have no real need of a butler and he knew it. Patience wished she could resent his cool head and quick thinking. But he'd solved her problem and might have just offered her a real life. She couldn't turn him down nor could she wait to hear the Winstons' answer. She was sick to death of being a coward. She wanted to be more than she'd become in the last five awful years.

Taking a deep breath, she fisted her hands at her sides beneath the cover of her skirts where no one else could see and said, "I'd be honored to accompany you, Mr. Reynolds. I would love to be a teacher."

Winston spoke before Alexander could respond. "Heddie and I were talking about how much we envy you your adventure, sir. We'd be proud to be in the employ of so fine a man. And if the young lady is going to be with you then it is better that Heddie and I will be going along, as well. Propriety should be observed or she will never get that position as the teacher."

Alexander looked a bit surprised at that last statement. He nodded, somewhat uncertainly. "It seems there were things I had not considered. If we are all in agreement, then, we have quite a bit to accomplish in very little time. I am all packed so I can easily aid you, Winston. Mrs. Gorham, if you would be so kind as to help Mrs. Winston with her things, we are sure to make the train to Philadelphia. We will stay there tonight and begin the trek south tomorrow."

"Oh, my," Heddie said. "Mrs. Gorham is only free to help me because she has no clothes of her own."

Patience blushed. She wasn't sure which was more embarrassing. To place herself further in charity to these good people or to admit how underhanded she had been forced to become in order to escape her own parent. And to further have to admit how weak she'd become for lack of nourishment by the time she'd neared Amber's address.

Unable to look so brave a man in the eye, she cast her gaze at Alexander's feet and said, "I may have some things of my own. I…um…I tore my sheets and knotted them to make a rope so I could lower my portmanteau to the ground. It grew too heavy to carry any farther as I came to the park near here. I hid it beneath a pine tree at the entrance. It could still be there, I suppose."

Alexander moved toward her. She watched his feet grow closer until he sank onto his heels before her. She couldn't help but be alarmed by his nearness but almost against her will, she looked up and stared into his clear blue eyes. In them she read nothing but sincerity. "I find myself awed by your bravery and determination," he said. "You have no reason to hang your head in shame. The men charged with your safety have much of which to be ashamed, however. And more even to answer for. I give you my word. I *will* keep you safe. Even from myself."

He pivoted a bit on the balls of his feet and stood before walking back to his perch on the edge of the desk. "I will try to retrieve your portmanteau before aiding Winston. But I think I will take a sack along to put it in. It wouldn't do for a lurking Pinkerton to recognize the pattern of your bag and grow suspicious."

Alexander clasped his hands together with a snappy little clap. "Shall we get to it, then? This will be a record in readying for so life-changing a trip." His face brightened with a mischievous sort of grin and his eyes sparkled. It buoyed her heart for some odd reason she still lacked the courage to consider. "And think what fun we'll have outwitting them all. I've had a great time so far with Pinkerton's finest."

Alexander strode out but Patience couldn't move. All she could do was stare after him as he moved out of sight.

"What is it, dearie?" Heddie asked.

"He is serious? He finds this amusing?"

"Oh, I doubt that, ma'am," Winston said and stood. "I believe he's trained himself to hide his true feelings. Imagine he had to, considering that father of his. Now, we should get at it. Perhaps, my dear," he said, taking Heddie's hand and assisting her to her feet, "perhaps you could see to the dust covers and Mrs. Gorham could pack your things."

"I have a better idea," Patience said. "Heddie, suppose we unite to do your packing, then we'll work on the dust covers together, as well."

"Oh, dearie, I can't have you doing a servant's work."

Patience shook her head, so many feelings bombarding her she couldn't separate the strands of relief, fear, excitement and sadness from each other. She had allies now. But even they were at risk from her father and Howard Bedlow. She was off on the adventure of her life—about to meld into the vastness of the western frontier. But it was such an unknown. "I have a feeling if I am to become a teacher, I had better get used to doing all sorts of housework. Oh, I cannot wait to be just plain Patience Wex—" She frowned. "I think a new name may be in order, as well, if I am to disappear completely."

"If I might be so bold, ma'am. You could travel as our daughter. As a member of a family, you would cease to be a lone woman to be singled out in the minds of others. You would be the daughter of the butler and maid at the Rocking R."

Patience was touched at the chance he'd taken with his pride. She could easily rebuff his offer because, to society's eyes, his suggestion overreached his station. But she felt only gratitude. She smiled, truly understanding Alexander's mischievous grin. Her father would never imagine she would trade her place in society to become the daughter of a butler and house-maid. "Winston, you're a genius. Patience Winston. I like the sound of it. My monogram handkerchiefs will even make sense. Thank you. What then should I begin to call you both?"

Winston gave her a small smile. "My father was called Papa by my sisters."

"Papa it is, then. I don't call my father that nor do I wish to be reminded of him. Thank you, Papa." She looked at Heddie. "I called my mother Momma. And dear as you are to me for all your help last night and today, I couldn't call you that."

"I understand," Heddie said, laying a hand on Patience's shoulder. "Mr. Alex told me your mother is gone. Hmm… Mother sounds too formal for the child of a housekeeper." Her brow furrowed in thought then seemed to blink back tears. "Would you be comfortable with Mum, dearie?"

"I would be honored as long as you don't feel put upon."

"Put upon? I am more than happy to hear that name. I was blessed with a girl child but she didn't live long. It is the greatest sorrow of my life." Heddie blinked again and sniffed as Winston patted his wife on the back, comforting her.

Seeing the sweet affection the stern butler showed toward his wife, reminded Patience of how empty of tenderness her life had been these past years. She lived with an ache inside her that went so deep she didn't know how there was room left for anything else.

"We haven't another moment to waste if we are to be on time for the train. Let's get ready for our adventure,"

Winston said, then tugged on his vest and straightened his spine. He was back to his formal self.

She and Heddie followed without complaint but Patience had to stifle a grin. The old phony wouldn't fool her again with his cold, stiff demeanor. He was as good and kind a husband to Heddie as any woman could hope for.

Children and a good and kind husband had been Patience's girlhood dream but they were beyond her now. Her new dream was to live her life in peace—mistress of her own future. If the West could give her that, she would ask no more.

Chapter Three

The train station in New Jersey was awash with activity so Alex hung back watching for anyone who might take note of Patience. Apparently, busy men were blind to beauty. No one but him seemed to see her as she walked up ahead of him, between Heddie and Winston.

Alex couldn't help but watch the enticing sway of her hips. This trip was going to be torture. He couldn't help but want her, though he knew full well nothing could ever come of it. He took comfort in the knowledge that once the trip was over she would reside in town and he could avoid her for the most part. Knowing the temptation of her would be removed once they reached Tierra del Verde was his saving grace.

Shamed at the need she created in him, Alex dragged his eyes away. How could he lust after someone so wounded and damaged? Was he no better than his father? He would never forget the pitiful sounds of a young maid his father had cornered in the study before they moved to Adair. He'd been only nine years old and hadn't believed his father when he'd claimed what he was doing was play, but he'd run when ordered. He'd never seen the girl again.

But he had heard that awful sound many times over the years. The move to Adair had changed nothing. By the time Jamie had banished the bastard from his estate, the only maids still working at Adair had been in their sixties.

Alex forced his mind away from the horrors of the past and onto the mission at hand—to save Patience from a man much like Oswald Reynolds. He watched her and analyzed how she must appear to the people milling about the station. Though he supposed she seemed a bit shy it helped her seem much younger than her twenty-six years. And still no one turned a hair as she passed.

It appeared her disguise was a success. Alex had easily found Patience's portmanteau in the park but the contents had been of little help to her masquerade because all of her dresses were too elegant to belong to a servant's daughter. Luckily, Mrs. Winston had remembered that the countess had left some dresses behind in New York. They were from her life as a schoolteacher in Pennsylvania's coal country before her marriage to Jamie.

According to Mrs. Winston, Patience had donned the faded, homemade garments without the slightest hesitation. Determined to become a new person, for anyone within earshot to hear, she'd even begun calling the Winstons "Mum" and "Papa." It was actually a brilliant plan for her to adopt their surname.

The last of her disguise hadn't been as easily achieved as letting out the hem of Amber's old dresses. Patience's hair was too unique to be allowed to show.

But a little boot polish carefully combed into her hairline had altered the coppery strands to drab brown. With the rest of those glorious tresses tucked up into her straw bonnet, she passed muster.

Still staying alert to any notice Patience drew, Alex continued to scan the crowd. No one paid her any particular attention. She was just a pretty girl traveling with her parents, but he did see someone take note of him. His blood began to pound in his head. As casually as he could, he let his gaze slide back past the man intently studying him. It was the oaf who'd appeared at Jamie's door earlier in the day.

A few moments later, Alex stopped and purchased a *New York Times* from a newsboy, allowing the newly formed Winston family to enter the passenger car well ahead of him. He was rather sure no one would think he was a member of their party but the Pinkerton oaf might recognize Winston.

As Alex turned away from the newsboy, the Pinkerton stepped in front of him. "You didn't say nothing about traveling." It was an accusation pure and simple. But since Alex had caught the agent's attention, Patience and Winston had slipped by unnoticed.

Alex blinked then narrowed his eyes in haughty annoyance. "Do I *know* you?"

"I was at your door just this morning," the man said. His tone hinted that Alex either wasn't particularly bright or was hiding something.

Allowing distant recognition to show in his expression, Alex replied, "Oh, yes. Seeking the countess's new little maid, weren't you? However, I must point out—you were actually on the *earl's* doorstep, not mine.

As none of it had a thing to do with me, I dismissed the entire conversation and returned to my packing."

"You didn't say nothing about packing, either. Where you heading?" the Pinkerton demanded, still clearly suspicious.

Alex's heart pounded. He had to knock this hound off his scent. "You bloody Americans are so *infernally* rude. Why should I have mentioned my movements to you? As I noted, you were not at my doorstep but the earl's. This business has nothing whatever to do with me. As I also stated, I owe you no explanations of my personal plans. Now if you will excuse me, I have a train to catch before my trunks go on without me."

He walked off, heading away from the train bound for Philadelphia, where Jamie's private car awaited and toward another one that was boarding. He stopped a passing conductor and asked an inane question so he'd have the opportunity to turn back toward the Pinkerton. Alex breathed a sigh of relief. The man had already passed the Philadelphia-bound train and was moving farther from Alex's position, as well.

He thanked the employee for his help and hurried off to hop aboard the train bound for Philadelphia. He made it just as the conductor shouted a last call for riders to Philadelphia. A quick turn and survey of the remaining crowd showed that no one seemed to have taken any notice of him.

He could only hope he was right and that his ruse had worked.

It was midday of their second day on the rails. Jamie's eighty-foot-long private car was opulent by anyone's standards. On entering from the front of the coach, one encountered two staterooms and two bathrooms along a narrow hall plus fold-up sleeping berths for four crew members. Both he and Patience had tried to give their stateroom to the Winstons, but the older couple had refused and claimed two berths in the crew area he hadn't thought he'd use until Patience almost literally fell into their lives.

A kitchen and formal dining area came next, though he hadn't planned to use the kitchen, either. They took meals from the train's kitchen, delivered by an efficient porter named Virgil Cabot.

Lastly there was a parlor area Virgil had called an observation room when he had shown them around just after they'd arrived. Behind that lavishly appointed section, with its larger-than-usual windows, was a covered observation platform. He'd asked that Jamie's car be the last on the train so the platform promised wonderful panoramas on their way west. None of them had wandered out there as yet, though, preferring to remain unobserved as much as possible for Patience's sake.

Alex looked toward that lovely young woman, her head bent to her stitching as she spoke in soft tones to Heddie. Once again he felt his entire body tighten with need and that need wasn't only sexual. He was deeply touched by her plight and her determination, as well. That was a dangerous combination for him. Because she wasn't just any young widow. She was under his protection and as untouchable as a virgin.

He found himself forever in debt and grateful to Heddie and her quiet husband. It was heartwarming the way she'd swooped in like a mother hen to gather a lost chick under her wing. Winston simply exuded benevolence toward Patience with frequent and surprising smiles.

Unfortunately watching the older couple interact with her was a poignant reminder of the warmth and kindness he'd lost with his mother's death and the loneliness that had never left him since.

Patience laughed at one of Winston's dry quips. My, but she was bright as a new penny today! Thus far she'd spent a lot of her time peppering the Winstons with questions about their lives and devising ways to fit her into their past. Alex couldn't hear exactly what she said as she rehearsed the story of Patience Winston's life but the murmur of her voice kept drawing his thoughts to her. And sparking his curiosity about how they planned to explain where a daughter had been during the years they'd worked in the houses of upper-crust families. He doubted any inquiries would happen but it paid to be prepared.

He found his gaze constantly drawn to Patience even when she was merely reading or hemming another of Amber's discarded dresses as she was at that moment. It didn't seem to matter that she wasn't doing anything remarkable. He couldn't keep his eyes off her. Nor could he help notice the more miles that piled up behind them, the more relaxed and less shy she seemed.

Except around him.

With him she made only the stiffest of polite conversation at meals. It was clear she'd rather he were not there. It was a lowering thing. Most women went out of their way to converse with him. He had to admit her avoidance stung even though he understood it.

But her behavior caused him to worry about more than his stinging pride, too. If the way she acted around him was her normal way around men, all her preparations would be for naught. Because he realized her demeanor didn't come across as shy, but instead as fearful, and when she had to deal with others it would stand out, calling attention to her.

So after a while he had two reasons—one altruistic and the other supremely selfish—to sit across from her in the parlor portion of the car when the Winstons vacated their chairs to sit in the dining area. He had to get her to feel more comfortable around him.

Alex refused to examine too deeply why it seemed so necessary. It could only be to help further her masquerade and he knew it. He wasn't sure a woman could ever heal from the kind of damage her husband and now her father had inflicted on her.

"So how far have you come in writing the life story of Patience Winston?" he asked.

She looked up from her notes, startled.

Afraid.

Then she took a deep breath and squared her shoulders, seeming to reach deeply into the same inner well of courage that had helped her face death in her tree-climbing escape. Again she found enough bravery to look at him steadily. "We plan to tell everyone I was born on a New Jersey farm owned by Heddie's older sister. She was wealthy, widowed and childless."

"And this can fit with the Winstons' lives and personal histories?"

"Yes. Heddie and Winston went there after her sister Esther's husband died. Heddie was expecting at the time but the child didn't live more than a few weeks."

Alex glanced toward Mrs. Winston where she sat toward the front of the car. "That is so very sad."

Patience nodded. "After that, Heddie took up a post as head housekeeper for her sister's home and Winston became the butler. The farm began to fall on hard times because the foreman stole a great deal from Esther."

"It happens," he said in an airy tone that had him wincing. He no longer wanted to be that man who hid his every deep thought behind a wall of careless comments. Patience stared at him, a tiny frown showing in her usually unlined forehead. She was as alone behind her walls as he was behind his. He didn't know her well enough to scale hers or break down his before her, either. Instead he motioned for her to go on.

It took her a short moment of examining her notes before she looked up and began again, all signs of disappointment in his character gone. "Heddie and Winston left in pursuit of income to send back to help pay debts and keep the farm going and to keep Esther in the privileged lifestyle she'd come to expect. The farm was to go to them upon her death except it went for taxes instead. That is where truth and fiction depart."

She looked at her lap, drawing his gaze to her knotted fingers. "The story will go," she continued, "that they left their daughter—me—with *Aunt* Esther to be raised genteelly. *Aunt* Esther had me educated by governesses in her home where she kept very much to herself."

"Good. That will explain your cultured speech and manners. I'd worried." He'd worried about her classic beauty, too, but didn't want to make her ill at ease again by mentioning it.

"The Winstons worried, as well, which is why we formulated the tale this way."

"So, go on with your story. How is it that you've joined up with your parents on a trek to the West?"

"When Aunt Esther died two years ago, I joined them in San Francisco and was hired by your cousin as a governess."

"We had better make sure Jamie and Amber know of this. Amber is an involved parent who still teaches Meara on her own."

Patience nodded. "I have begun a letter to send to Amber so she knows in case there is an inquiry into the Winston family. Heddie apparently took Miriam Trimble's place as housekeeper because Mrs. Trimble was too elderly to keep up with both the staff and act as nursemaid to the earl's daughter."

Alex chuckled. "I would love to hear Mrs. Trimble's reaction to that being said of her—the old warhorse."

A frown crinkled Patience's forehead, her brows pulling together in a *V*. "Warhorse? But she has been described to me as all that is kindness. Amber loves the woman."

Now he laughed. "As does Jamie. She was a mother to him for nearly his whole life. And a better mother no boy could have asked for. Mrs. Trimble was a mouthful for a little tyke. You should know he called her Mimm and still does."

"Oh. Yes. Amber calls her that, as well. Thank you for the correction." She looked down at her notebook and scribbled a footnote.

Alex held tight to his lighthearted facade, refusing to let it crack. "I had another experience with her. She used to call me the spawn of Satan. Even did it once in the presence of the daughter of a British peer. The name followed me in society from that day until I came to America. Mrs. Trimble apologized after what happened in San Francisco, so all is happy between us."

Her eyes softened and he could have sworn she lifted her hand as if to touch him in comfort but she let it fall in her lap. "I am so sorry. I know how much it hurts to be misjudged," she said instead.

Though he wished with all the loneliness inside him that she had found the courage to reach out to him, he shrugged in a purposefully careless gesture. "I didn't care," he lied, feeling a bit like a petulant child denying what was true to spite an authority figure. "I had my way to protect Jamie and she had hers. Together, though very separately, we managed."

She stared at him for a long moment then looked away, withdrawing into her thoughts and leaving him to wish he had admitted that Mrs. Trimble had hurt him with her mistrust.

Keeping his careless facade alive grew more difficult around her than it had ever been. Conversely, he thought he was supposed to be shedding the mask now that he had embarked on his new life, but he couldn't seem to manage it with Patience there. He could come to care for her and her rebuff might actually hurt. Right then, casting off the mask would be too much like casting off an old friend. It kept him safe and protected from rejection and contempt.

Should he have said a simple yes? That, of course, it had hurt? Should he confess that his own mother had been dead? That though he had taken on an adult's role in Jamie's life he'd still been a child himself? That he'd needed comfort and the kind of support only an adult could have provided? He hadn't understood all that at the time, though. Instead, he'd been alone and had felt as if the weight of his corner of the world rested on his shoulders. Especially since then and now he feared his mother's death had been his fault.

Determined to get Patience talking again Alex asked a question with a rather obvious answer, but it was the best his tumultuous thoughts allowed. "So were you supposed to have been in California when Jamie arrived there with Amber?"

Patience shook her head. Why was he insisting on this conversation? It might look casual to the Winstons but she saw determination in his gaze. She almost asked but decided answering his queries was the easiest course to take. And he had been helpful adding one or two facts they'd forgotten to account for. "No. We are to say my parents, the Winstons, were hired by Mrs. Miriam Trimble before the earl and Amber arrived just as they truly were. I am to have traveled there later to meet up with my parents after Heddie's sister, Aunt Esther, passed. I will say I arrived after the fire and became Meara's governess."

She resented her father enormously at that moment. It was his fault she had to lie this way. Resentment warred with shame because she lacked the means to fight him openly instead of resorting to deception.

"Something about this doesn't sit well with you," Alexander said.

How had he known? "You're very perceptive. I was taught to abhor liars. And now I *am* one."

He looked angry for a moment then his gaze softened. He leaned a bit forward and set his forearms on his thighs. It put him at her eye level.

She wanted to scoot off the sofa and run but forced herself to remain still. She didn't want him to see her for the coward she was even though she refused to examine why.

"Your father didn't seem to have the same problem when he began to spread it about that you have gone mad," he told her. "You mustn't let the content of a Sunday sermon on lies endanger you, no matter how much you agree with the sentiments."

She hadn't thought of it that way. If she didn't stick to the plan, her father and Howard Bedlow would win. She set her lips together and nodded before notching her chin upward and straightening her back the way her mother had always done when she'd stood up to Patience's father. "I hadn't thought of it that way. But, still, you cannot argue that I won't be lying. I'll be lying to all my new neighbors and even to the children I hope to teach. I'll be living a complete lie. *I'll* be a lie."

"But you will be keeping yourself safe and you may be giving the Winstons their fondest dream. Did you see Heddie's face that first night in New York when she tossed me out of your room? She was like a mother bear defending her cub. I have been watching the three of you. There is some sort of instantaneous connection between you. I am quite sure they have in mind an adoption of a sort."

She found herself chuckling over the vision that prompted. "I am a bit long in the tooth to be adopted, don't you think?"

"I see no problem with the notion at all." He grinned and sat back, falling into his usual lazy posture. "And I cannot imagine describing you as long in the tooth. You look like a girl just out of the schoolroom."

She fought the need to squirm like an untested girl under his direct gaze. He'd said he'd been watching her with the Winstons. Well, she had been watching him, too.

She didn't think he or his posture were as casual as he pretended. To her, his carelessness seemed studied. As if he, too, had learned to hide who he was. Making her wonder if he was a wolf? Or an ever-protective collie? She frowned at the metaphor, not liking that either made her the pitiful sheep.

"Is there a problem?" he asked.

Called back from her thoughts, Patience realized she'd not only strayed from the topic at hand, but she'd also left the conversation altogether. She cleared her throat. "I do find myself comfortable with the Winstons," she decided to admit. She forced herself to relax into the back of the burgundy brocade sofa. She refused to care if she stepped beyond the strictures of her society. She was no longer a part of all that. And it was just fine with her. It had to be.

"It's an odd thing," she continued. "I am suddenly able to let who I am inside show on the outside. And I am growing to like the feeling. They are wonderful people and it is an honor to be called their child."

"Good." He tilted his head, his eyes so intent she felt exposed. She nearly stood to go and join the Winstons. "Consider this," he went on and she settled back against the seat again. "The Winstons lost a girl child. Judging from their age it was probably about the time of your birth. You must be the fulfillment of their every dream. You have the capacity to give back to them what fate took and be a great joy to them in the gift of yourself."

"I think it is perhaps the other way around. They have become very dear to me in a very short time. So I suppose it is settled." She put a hand to her chest.

"I am Patience Winston, late of San Francisco and points east."

He grinned and inclined his head. "Miss Winston."

Relieved, she smiled at him. "Now that you have salved my conscience, perhaps you could fill me in a bit on your niece. I know from Amber that she is a sweet, lively and bright child. I believe Amber said she is fair with blond hair and blue eyes. Do you know her very well?"

He pulled out the watch and stared down at it for a long moment before detaching it from the chain. "Jamie gave me this the day before he sailed. Set in the cover is a miniature of Meara." Opening it, Alexander smiled. His expression looked a tad wistful and entirely enchanted.

She reached out for the watch when he held it out, careful not to allow any contact when she took it from him. She was sure she'd never want a man to touch her in any way ever again.

The child smiling up at her from the watch's cover was indeed a sweet-looking, blond-haired girl who looked startlingly like her uncle. Patience looked up. "There is a strong family resemblance. Meara could be your child."

Alexander's gaze stilled and widened a bit then he blinked. "But she is Jamie's. We, all three of us, look like my grandmother." He slouched a bit and this time she was sure his careless pose was purposeful. "And we are all thankful to fate that we don't resemble my grandfather. He looked rather like a fat, out-of-sorts troll." His smile was mischievous and irreverent. "Actually, he may have been."

Wondering again what Alexander hid behind the

devil-may-care facade he presented the world, she handed the watch back but forgot to be careful. Her hand touched his. She gasped and dropped the watch, snatching her hand away.

What was that?

Touching him had felt the way she imagined lightning would were it to strike one's person. Dangerous. She had to tighten her abdominal muscles to stop her stomach from its unruly series of somersaults. Her gaze flew to him as he straightened, having bent forward to pick up the dropped watch. He looked haunted but she was sure it was impossible that he had felt what she had.

Men did not fear women. What she'd felt was fear and the need to run.

Stop it! she shouted in her mind. *You're safe here with these people. It's Father and Howard Bedlow you fear. Did Amber's letters teach you nothing of good people? If you continue to tar all men with the same filthy brush, you will go as mad as Father says you are.*

She didn't run no matter how compelled she felt to do so.

Alexander finished settling the watch in his waist-coat pocket then looked at her again. "So now you have a picture in your head of your charge," he said as if nothing out of the ordinary had happened. She could see only kindness and a bit of sadness in his clear blue gaze. And then she remembered.

Spawn of Satan.

She had hurt him just as those other people had. This had to stop. She could not injure others because she harbored unreasonable fears. She forced herself to hold his gaze.

If philosophers were correct and the eyes were the

windows of the soul, then Alexander's aquamarine eyes showed only goodness. She would not retreat in fear. She had to find a way to converse not just with him, but with other men near her age once again lest they see fault in themselves or her.

"Your niece is lovely. Do you think we have woven the tale well enough to fit with the lives of not only the Winstons, but also with the movements of the Earl and Amber?"

"It should certainly stand up to frontier scrutiny." He chuckled. "I now know more about my new employees than I know about most of my so-called friends back in London. And I can say I like the Winstons quite a bit, especially since they are so willing to give aid to someone not of their station."

He smiled and this time it seemed genuine and not that false smirk. "You seem to have quite a bit of influence with the Winstons. Do you think you could get them to spend the rest of the trip at leisure? By Heddie insisting upon making up the berths and setting the table for meals, she is supplanting Virgil, the porter assigned the car. She is also driving me mad with all the dusting whenever we reach a station. Dust is part and parcel of train travel but Heddie refuses to give in to the inevitable."

She tilted her head and sighed deeply. "I have already tried."

Now he sighed as exaggeratedly as she had. "As have I. And I believe Winston refuses to be outdone by his wife. He intercepts the poor man as soon as he steps inside the door with our meals."

"They're what my mother always called a force to be reckoned with. I'm afraid they're beyond me."

Alexander shrugged, an ironic gleam in his eyes. "As you have retired from the field, I shall tip the man handsomely when he arrives with dinner. That way if he isn't to continue on after Chicago he won't be slighted. On my first cross-country trip I learned ex-slaves working as porters live mostly on their tips. I won't be responsible for the man's family doing without."

"That's very good of you."

Shaking his head he spoke at so low a murmur she had to lean forward to hear. "I only have the monetary resources I do because my father embezzled from Adair's coffers. Instead of seeing to the tenants' well-being, he gave me funds to buy a commission in the army. Instead, I invested in Canadian railroads and eventually paid Jamie back but I cannot shake the guilt. No one will ever again do without because of me."

He looked away and stared moodily out the window, making her think he felt awkward for having spoken of his father's illegal activities. Or he felt they'd run to the end of the subject of her new life story, and of his tragic life.

Now that she was free to move away she hesitated. He looked so awfully tortured, though she couldn't imagine how she could help or why she should considering trying. About to get to her feet now that she'd thought through the foolish impulse, he spoke absently with his attention still beyond the glass.

"I've been thinking your Christian name could be a problem." He glanced at her, blue eyes somber, then back at the scenery speeding by. "Changing it could be one, as well. You might not answer to another as instinctively as you should." Again he spared her half a glance as he said, "I think it would be better not to speak it in public until we reach our destination." Again his visual attention drifted out the window. "It could catch the attention of someone who's heard of the search for a woman named Patience. Perhaps the Winstons could use a pet name for you."

"My mother used to read Mother Goose to me." The wistful memory made her smile. "She called me Patty for Patty Cake—my favorite nursery rhyme. I could be Patty to them during travel. I believe I would automatically answer to that."

She was unsure if he'd heard her but was equally sure he was trying to gather the tattered vestiges of his devil-may-care persona. Did he know how unusual it was that he'd learned the porter's name and bothered to use it? Or that he'd given away who he was under the mask once again. "On that last trip across America, didn't you learn that people call all of the porters George after George Pullman? I believe coachmen in your country are all called John Coachman."

Then he looked back at her and nodded, an insolent grin in place. "So, *Patty*, do you play chess?"

"I meant I should be called that by Heddie…no, *Mum*," she corrected before he could tease her for forgetting her role as the Winstons' daughter. She was almost sorry—but not quite—that she'd worried for his feelings. He was a man and men took advantage of any weakness they glimpsed. "I meant *they* could call me Patty. Are you always so impertinent?"

"Oh. Yes. Always," he said and grinned.

"I shall remember not to take you seriously in that case. As for chess, I was the unofficial champion at Vassar for my last two years."

"Amazing." He flipped over the table top between

them. The flip side hid a chessboard. "Black or white, Miss Winston?" he asked and slid open the drawer containing the ivory and ebony pieces.

She took up the ivory pieces and set up her side of the board. At first she played her usual restrained game, allowing Alexander to win. He teased her for losing to an unschooled barbarian, reminding her all men became barbarians when alone with a woman. But they weren't alone and he all but begged for a rousing game. So she played to win and it felt wonderful. She made first one daring move, then another and another.

Watching Alexander try to anticipate her next move brought a strange kind of gladness to her heart. Then she began to recognize that feeling again. It was like learning to ride the bicycle her father had brought from England when she was eighteen. Achievement. Triumph. Victory.

Alexander fought hard, yet he didn't seem to mind when she ultimately won. It was the first time she'd enjoyed chess in years. Against Edgar she'd had to walk a fine balance between losing and not making it obvious she had done so intentionally. The few times she'd miscalculated either way, she'd paid in bruises.

She could admit now that somewhere inside her she'd been elated to see Edgar Gorham so humbled and furious at being bested by the wife he called a failure at every turn. Had she not been so embarrassingly bruised later, Patience might have done it more often. Fear had taken over, though, and it was she who'd been humbled.

"Now what, I must ask myself, is that smug little smile about?" Alexander asked.

Fear poured unchecked through her. Did she look smug? Had she annoyed him? Her heart pounded. The blood drained from her head. Time and place seemed to shift and she was back with Edgar in the mansion in Syracuse. She could no longer hold on to the present.

"Was I smiling?" she whispered, her voice warbling around a lump in her throat the size of New York City.

Then she looked up and her gaze met Alexander's sparkling eyes. His *teasing* smile. And she was back on the train headed west. It was September the thirteenth. Relief replaced fear and she could breathe again.

This panic that washed over her at the unexpected sound of a man's voice was a reflex she had to learn to fight or she was sure to bring notice upon herself. She saw it now. Concern flooded his gaze as surely as the terror had flooded her senses. She could not let them do this to her any longer.

Moving her hand forward, she lifted her remaining bishop and slid it forward till it mated his king. "Checkmate."

Chapter Four

As dusk approached on an uneventful Saturday, the porter entered with coffee and dessert. Alex stood and followed him from the car. It had been three and a half days since leaving Philadelphia. They were due for a layover in Chicago during the night. The farther from New York they traveled the more Alex's confidence rose. It seemed they had pulled off the impossible and gotten Patience away without a hitch in their hastily cobbled together plan.

"Virgil," he called before the man could enter the next car to return to his duties.

The porter turned back and returned across the divide between the cars. "Yes, sir?" he asked over the persistent click-clack of the train's wheels.

To Alex, Virgil looked about his own thirty-five years, though shorter and thinner. Yet he muscled bags and trunks around like an automaton—never slowing, never stopping. It didn't seem right that the railroad paid him a pittance for all that hard work.

"I wanted to give you something for your trouble in case you aren't going through with us to St. Louis."

The porter put his hand up to ward off Alex. "I'm going all the way to Texarkana on this run, sir. 'Sides, it don't seem right takin' money from you. I hardly do a thing for you and yours."

Alex smiled. "And I'm well aware you're not to blame for that. I'm afraid the Winstons are tireless and cannot abide being idle." He slid a one-dollar gold certificate into the porter's hand.

Virgil looked down at the money then back up, his surprise showing plainly in his dark eyes. His expression spoke volumes. At first he was clearly unbelieving, then gratitude shone in his uncertain gaze.

Alex knew it was an extravagant amount of money to a poor man. In Texas an acre of land could be bought for that amount but inequity of any sort bothered him. Living in this land of freedom and opportunity, Alex found it even more troubling to see there were still some left out of America's great promise.

"Thank you, Mr. Reynolds," Virgil said. "You can't know what this is gonna mean to me and mine. You's a good man."

Uneasy as the object of such heartfelt admiration, Alex stepped back toward the door to the car. "You're quite welcome. I had better get in and eat before my housekeeper boxes my ears."

A wide grin split the man's dark face. "She a tough one, sir. Tell her I'll be back for them dishes later."

At about ten the next night, an hour after leaving Chicago, Alex looked up to hear Virgil at the door speaking to Winston. "I needs a word with Mr. Reynolds," Virgil told Winston, worry rife in his voice.

Alex stood.

"Don't trouble yourself, sir. I'll see to this," Winston said.

If something was wrong, Alex wanted it firsthand from Virgil. "No, Winston, you go back to your cribbage game with the family," Alex said, playing to the concocted tale of the mythical Winston family. "I insist," he added when Winston opened his mouth as if to protest.

"Mr. Reynolds," Virgil said as Alex stepped onto the platform of the car, "I thought I should tell you. Somethin' troublin's goin' on. They's two men who got on in Chicago lookin' for a young lady and showin' her picture to the other passengers. Offerin' a reward even. A big one." He paused then blurted, "She look like *your* young lady, sir."

"Damn Pinkertons," Alex growled, not bothering to correct Virgil's mistaken impression of his relationship with Patience. He'd hoped to get her as far as Texas before the detectives discovered she hadn't gone to Britain with his cousin's wife. He sighed and looked toward the heavens. After a moment's thought, he realized there was nothing to do until he learned if the men planned to continue on past Texarkana.

If that were the case, he'd have to have Jamie's car dropped off the train in St. Louis. They couldn't arrive on the same train in San Antonio with the detectives. They were due into St. Louis for a long stopover. He could have them hooked back up for the rest of the trip in a day or so. Perhaps get off sooner than San Antonio and buy horses and wagons to travel overland to the Rocking R.

It wouldn't do to panic, though. Dropping the car from the train could cause more notice of the private car—and its occupants. He would save that as a last desperate measure as it could only buy them a little time.

Which still left the problem of Lionel Wexler wanting to marry Patience off to a man she feared. And there seemed only one solution to that—one he was loath to even consider.

Yet.

Hoping to find a better long-range plan that didn't complicate his new life further, Alex went to work solving the immediate problem. "Virgil, I need to know how far these men plan to go along the Texas Short Line."

"I'll see if'n I can find out about that, sir."

Alex nodded and dug out a half-dollar coin to repay Virgil for his loyalty.

The man shook his head. "No, sir. If I'd of wanted money, I could have gave her up. They offerin' a lot of it, that's for sure. But you folks been right kind to me. Ya'll even bothered to learn my real name so's not to call me George, like my mamma never give me a name. I appreciate that more than I can say. It's lucky I'm the only one who seen her."

Alex sighed. "Lucky indeed. I cannot thank you enough, Virgil. Tell me, how well do you know St. Louis?"

"Real well. St. Louis been my home since right after the war. Why, sir?"

"I have some plans to think over. I'll let you know

if they turn out to be of any consequence. I may need your help in that case."

Virgil nodded, then stepped between cars. Alex was relieved to have an ally who was free to roam the train. A window in the door allowed him to see into the baggage car as Virgil rushed through it. It was good to know the porter felt as he did about the danger of their situation.

Not wanting to face Patience until he was sure of how dire the situation was, Alex stayed there staring between the cars as the tracks blurred by below. The click-clack of the wheels repeated thoughts of what he'd have to do to protect Patience, as well as worries for her safety.

Had he been wrong to bring her along? He shook his head, still seeing no other path for her to have taken. Now, though, it seemed putting half the continent between her and that father of hers might only delay the inevitable. And that was wrong in so many ways he refused to try counting them.

Ten minutes later Virgil returned, clutching a handbill. "Them Pinkerton agents is continuin' on only to Texarkana. They say they got other agents checkin' the other lines just to be sure she ain't travelin' by rail anywhere in the country." He passed Alex the handbill and pointed to it as he lit the lantern on the wall next to the door. "I promised to look through the ladies' car so he give me one."

The description of Patience was spot on and the drawing was good enough to make her easily recognizable. With the five-hundred-dollar reward—higher than offered for most criminals—he had little doubt she would already be in her father's hands had she tried to travel alone. "It's good I asked for Jamie's private car to bring up the rear," he muttered, so deep in thought he'd forgotten about Virgil until the porter spoke again.

"No one should wander back here that's for sure. If you keep those curtains drawn when we stop, no one should even think anyone but you is here. To regular folk it'll look like you headed west alone. You don't got to stay shut up, though. Just the lady and them other two."

"I thought the same." Alex looked at the handbill Virgil had given him. "Do you understand exactly how much money this is?"

Virgil gave Alex a skeptical look, barked out a short laugh and shook his head. "Too much for the likes of me to have." He waved off Alex's concern. "I'd probably get lynched for thievin' if I started flashin' that kind of money." Virgil might act as it he was joking but Alex knew it was an unfortunate truth. "'Sides, like I said, ya'll been kind."

Alex was humbled by this man's integrity and loyalty. And that integrity and capacity for loyalty gave Alex an idea. "Virgil, we're headed deep into Texas Hill Country. I have a ranch there. Think about bringing your family to the Rocking R. A job will be waiting for you if you're interested. I'd like a younger man in the house with Patience and the Winstons when I'm not there. The town's a good place but still a bit wild."

Virgil's eyes widened. "Texas? I'd have to talk it over with my wife. We have a son, too. He's twelve years of age. Maybe he could learn a trade on this ranch of yours?"

Alex rested his hand on Virgil's shoulder and gave it a reassuring squeeze. "Of course he can."

Virgil looked thoughtful for a moment then he too smiled. "Would you be needing a cook? My wife, Willow, is a right good cook. Worked in the kitchens growin' up and she has a position in a big house in St. Louis."

Thinking of the man on the ranch who currently ruined dinner on a regular basis, Alex laughed. "You have no idea how badly the Rocking R needs a cook. I'll be surprised if I don't return to at least one of my men gone from poisoning."

"Lettin' us work for fine folks like ya'll would be a better reward than what them gents up front offered." He pursed his lips and shook his head. "I'd sorely like to take up on your offer but them Jim Crow cars are mighty hard on a woman and child."

Alex tilted his head, sick at heart over this proud man's degradation at the hands of others. "She and your son will be welcome in our car if you can get them to the station and secret them into the car during the time we're stopped." He'd try to give up his own stateroom to reward Virgil's wife for the goodness of her husband, but he doubted they'd accept when the Winstons hadn't.

It was men like Virgil—American men—and their integrity in choosing honest work and self-determined prosperity over inherited wealth and idleness that had kept Alex on these shores after he'd trailed his father here. And nowhere on the continent did that quality hold stronger and truer than what he'd found when he'd visited and fallen in love with Texas. People there didn't care where you came from or what station in life your predecessors had held. They only cared how hard you worked and how much land you commanded as a result. Wealth was still prized, but if your father had been a rag picker or even a criminal and you were an honest man of wealth, then good for you. What a blessing to him considering the reputation he had to live down because of who his father had been.

"I'll think on it, sir. We ain't got much to pack," Virgil said, then pursed his lips as he blinked away tears, clearly overcome. "I'll think on it real hard. Be back in a bit after tellin' them gents I seen no lady like the one in the handbill." Then continually nodding his head, Virgil went back the way he'd come.

Which left Alex alone to worry. The news about the Pinkertons was a deep concern. Though Texarkana was five hundred and forty miles northeast of San Antonio and Tierra del Verde was fifty or sixty miles west beyond there, the search was alarmingly close. The two agents might not search any deeper into the state, but there'd been a Pinkerton operating in San Antonio two years earlier. If that agent was still operating there and if he'd been alerted to look for Patience, their grand plan could easily fail at the end of the Texas Short Line, only fifty or so miles from home. Even if he were gone, they'd still have to move to horse and buggy at the station, exposing Patience to any number of people. Any one of whom, if questioned later, could remember a traveling party that had included a young lady.

There was only one solution that would spike her father's guns for all time. "A *different* marriage," Alex muttered and his stomach flipped over. He took a deep breath. "A *different* husband. Me."

There.

He'd said it, dammit. He'd said it. He raked a hand through his hair. Wexler could hardly marry her off if she was already wed to another. And Alex was the only man available to play the part of groom.

Dammit!

What was worse, he was certainly the only man he'd trust with her welfare. Which was laughable considering what everyone in Britain thought of him. He hadn't even trusted himself with his own child.

Which begged the questions—why him? Why now?

Because Patience needs you. Meara didn't.

The issue that made him waver and dread the task ahead was his vow to never become entangled with a woman again. Breaking it terrified him.

Because this was Patience.

He cared about her.

He wanted her.

And their need to live together would put an end to any chance for a respite from his growing desire for her. He'd expected that respite once they'd reached Tierra del Verde. He'd thought he wouldn't see much of her once she was staying at Mrs. Hampton's boarding house and teaching the children and he was settled into his life on the Rocking R.

If he were to propose and she were to accept, she would be expected to live in his home. Most people would expect her to share his bed but he knew that wouldn't happen for a long, long time. If ever.

No. That could *never* happen. Someday she'd be safe from the men who pursued her. Someday she'd heal and find someone worthy of her. And he would have to let her go. He knotted his hands at his sides. Much as his emotions fought that idea, that was how it would have to be. Still, he saw no other way but marriage to safeguard her. If he could manage to allay her fear of the very idea, he very well might arrive at the ranch with a wife in tow.

Double dammit!

Alex kneaded the back of his neck, trying to stop the ache that was moving toward his head. Maybe he needed to recount all his faults and his own fears before trying to deal with hers.

He extracted his cigarette holder and drew out a Turkish Oriental. Smoking seemed a good excuse for a protracted stay on the platform before returning to the car. It was also the perfect pastime for deep troubled thinking about the prospect of marriage and all its attendant complications.

Marriage.

He'd given up on the idea years ago. He'd been the product of a loveless marriage and had always sworn not to enter into one like it. When he'd thought he'd found love with Iris, possibilities had opened to him.

The loss of Iris had caused him excruciating pain. It wasn't something he ever wanted to feel again. Which had put marriage back into the category of something others did. But never him.

Perhaps the anguish of losing her was so vivid because he'd lost her three times in different and increasingly bitter ways.

The first had come when Jamie had married her while Alex had been away on a long job for his father. He'd reserved his hurt and anger for his younger cousin, not Iris. He'd believed her story that she'd panicked when she'd learned she was expecting Alex's child and had accepted the first offer she'd received since she hadn't known how to get in touch with him. She'd clung to him, begging for his forgiveness and his lovemaking.

But though she'd clearly never loved Jamie, Alex still had and so he'd swallowed his pride and pain and forgiven Jamie…his rejection of Iris complete. All so he could see his own child and his beloved cousin, putting an end to his exile and his loneliness.

Until he'd seen his newly born infant daughter, Alex hadn't fully grasped why he'd forgiven Jamie. Nor had he understood how parental love could blossom for one's child. One cursory glance had been all it took for him to tumble headlong into love, but with tiny Lady Meara this time. He'd kept his visits short, never remaining overnight, fearing Iris would show up in his bed and tempt him beyond enduring. He'd refused to risk losing Meara or, curiously, Jamie.

Then a few months after Meara's birth, Iris had been killed in a riding accident leaving Alex to deal with grief and guilt and a more cutting sense of betrayal from Jamie. Alex had rejected Iris in favor of him and Jamie had refused to mourn Iris publicly. In his anger, Alex had forgotten Meara and the consequence of the rage that had poured out. He hadn't even thought to demand to know why Jamie had made the unusual stand.

They had fought bitterly, even coming to blows, which had caused Jamie to quit Ireland with Meara, leaving Alex behind, unable to see his child and with a resentful father to deal with. A father who bore close watching for all their sakes. Especially Meara's.

The third and final loss of Iris had nearly brought him to his knees and had shown him a devastating truth, as well. By then Alex had grieved for her and for all he'd lost for seven long years. He'd gone to San Francisco to warn Jamie that Oswald Reynolds was still after that damned title by any means necessary.

It had been devastating not only because Alex had been forced to kill his father, but also because Oswald, in a last cruel act, had revealed that Iris had conspired with him to force Jamie into marriage. She'd been on a quest for the title, not for a father for her child.

Alex had left San Francisco a hollow man, numb to life, love and its possibilities. And all because he'd trusted the wrong woman. Though he had attained a measure of peace in Texas, the idea that he'd been so blind and mistaken in his judgment of both her and Jamie still made him second-guess himself to this day.

Alex tilted his head then as an odd thought popped into his brain.

It was a thought that wouldn't be banished.

He trusted Patience Gorham.

Implicitly.

None of the taint of Iris blackened his perception of Patience. With the exception that Iris and Patience shared the same kind of social standing, they were as distant as the earth and moon.

Still, his faith in Patience's goodness and honesty to the contrary, both of them had some hard choices to make in the next few hours. God willing, they'd make the right ones.

Alex stayed where he was, racking his brain, and finally praying to a nearly forgotten God for an alternative. Nothing presented itself. Lionel Wexler's reputation reaffirmed Alex's belief that powerful men were only happy when wielding their power. That belief, and the fact that her father had offered so outrageous a reward to get her back, told Alex the man would follow her to the ends of the earth to get his own way. And there was this Howard Bedlow person. His reputation with women was only spoken of in whispers. Whispers that crossed well into unsavory activities.

Only marriage would keep her safe from both men. Though he didn't want this for either of their sakes, there was something inside him that couldn't let her father win. He'd fought his whole life against tyrannical fathers, and he wouldn't stop now. An impulse no doubt put there by his gentle mother and nurtured by his forthright cousin. And he had to heed that impulse.

Dammit. Dammit. Dammit!

Patience had about given up the idea of reading when the opening door drew her gaze. She looked up to watch Alexander return to the car. There *was* something wrong. She'd worried since Virgil had looked at her with concern before asking for a word with Alexander. And now Alexander had returned a different man. His shoulders were stiff. A brooding look had replaced his carefree demeanor.

Her worry blossomed into fear when he turned the key in the door's lock and checked the curtains as if making sure no one could see out.

Or in!

He stopped at the dining table where the Winstons sat reading the *Chicago Tribune* Virgil had gotten them. Alexander, his expression grave, spoke to them in low undertones that had her straining to hear, but she couldn't make out his words. He nodded and pursed his lips as he rapped his knuckles on the table and turned.

To look directly at her.

His eyes seemed to assess her as he moved toward her. He didn't sit across from her, but took a position on the sofa with her. He left enough room between them that another person could have sat there, but he was still too close for her peace of mind.

Her stomach swirled and her heart began to pound but she held still, forcing herself to breathe in the same rhythm she had instinctively used before he'd approached. She couldn't let him know how she felt lest he once again judge himself wanting. That would be so unfair. The problem rested with her.

She knew she'd failed when he closed his eyes for a moment and sighed. Then he opened them and just watched her as if waiting for her to be the one to strike up a conversation.

She lost patience. "I trust you didn't come to sit by me to distress yourself because I am a coward around men."

Alex pressed his lips together. "I believe I have already told you I don't find anything you've done thus far to be the acts of a coward. I am here because I have troublesome news to report. I hesitate only because I'm loath to upset you."

She felt her back tense while her heart squeezed. She thought again that he could be a very kind man for all his sharp wit. "It isn't your job to shield me from the truth."

He sighed. "You're right, of course."

"Then what is wrong?" she demanded.

He held her gaze. "I'm told two Pinkerton agents joined the train at Chicago. They're flashing handbills with your likeness on them. Virgil the porter gave this to me." He handed it to her. "Virgil pledges his loyalty so you're safe for now, since no one else saw you enter the car."

She glanced down then could only stare in horror,

suppressing a shudder at the frighteningly good like-ness and a more frighteningly large reward depicted on the handbill. She looked out the window on the other side of the car. It didn't escape her that it was the same window Alexander had gazed out of yesterday, tortured over his father's misdeeds. Now it was she who looked at the passing scenery but saw only *her* father's cruelty. Bitterness filled her and she looked back at Alexander. "My. I had no idea I was worth so much as Howard's bed slave."

She felt a momentary shock over what she'd said. Her statement should have put her to a blush. There was no question that it had been inappropriate but her despair was so deep, her fear so great, she couldn't bring herself to care. "I should have known he'd find me." She sighed from her deepest inner being, leaving her deflated and defeated. She stared down unseeingly at the book in her lap.

"He hasn't found you. Not yet, anyway," Alexander said.

Patience snapped her head up to see again the man forced to kill his own sire to save others. The man who felt responsible for the pain his father had caused others. It was as if she could see to his soul—a soul eaten by undeserved guilt.

"Please don't look so guilty," she told him, clutching the book with a death grip. "I was never your problem to solve. It isn't your fault this ruse didn't work. At least you tried to help me."

"It isn't over. You're not going to let them win this easily, are you?" Now she saw yet another side of him—desperate yet strong and determined. She imagined

Travis and Bowie had looked the same way as they'd prepared their men for the final battle at the Alamo.

But those brave defenders had lost.

As would she.

Still, Patience was grateful Alexander seemed to see this was a matter of life and death. She knew in her heart she wouldn't survive a marriage to Bedlow with her sanity in tact. She might not survive it at all.

He'd find her eventually. There was now very little reason to believe she could succeed in her flight. Yet Alexander wanted her to fight on.

"We both know my father will find me eventually and force me to marry Howard."

"You could marry *me*."

She gasped, feeling the blood drain from her head. Had she been wrong to trust him? She'd told him how averse she was to marriage. Why would he suggest such a thing? She looked quickly at the Winstons. They still appeared to be engrossed in the newspaper, taking no note of Alexander's outrageous statement. But she was sure, that like any good servants, they'd heard but refused to let on. She took some small comfort in remembering how Heddie had ordered Alexander from the room the night she'd arrived at Amber's home in New York. She drew even more reassurance, remembering how easily he'd acquiesced.

When she looked back, Alexander looked strained but his intense gaze held her attention. "I know the idea of marriage is shocking. It was to me when the idea popped into my head. It still is. But your father cannot force you to marry this Bedlow chap if you are already wed to me."

How could she explain her terror if he had not fully

understood the implications of what she'd already told him? She felt her cheeks flame in a blush at the thought of having to detail the degradation she had suffered and the fear of the marriage bed Edgar Gorham had given her.

"Please believe it isn't you. There are things that happened in my marriage…." She paused, trying to still the quaver in her voice and to get up the nerve to explain further. "I cannot endure what you'd expect of—"

"The fear I see in you," Alex interrupted, "tells me you were mistreated by your husband beyond what you've detailed." He turned toward her and slid to the floor on one knee. His expression was earnest and kind when he asked, "Am I correct?"

She had to believe he was only trying to find a way to protect her. Still, she couldn't find her voice so she nodded.

His voice lowered a bit more. "Rest assured I would never expect to consummate the union. Which would leave you able to file for an annulment when the danger has passed."

Patience blinked. Could he mean—? "But my mother warned me before my wedding that men have needs they cannot forego."

He offered what she could only term a reassuring smile and said, "Not to disparage that fine lady but she was wrong. Males of all species have those needs but as *men* we are supposed to rise above the behavior of mere animals."

"But—"

"I'm sure," Alexander interrupted, "I can forego animal pleasures until your father gives up his pursuit."

She couldn't keep the blush from heating her cheeks. "I was not about to express doubt about your character, Alexander, but about safeguarding your reputation. If we were to file for an annulment surely that would leave you open to gossip. Perhaps even ridicule."

"And you," he said.

"I have no desire to ever attract male attention. I doubt being…undesirable to a former husband or too skittish with him would harm the reputation of a teacher."

Alexander nodded though he had an ironic glint in his eyes. "And I am made of sterner stuff than to be bothered by gossip or ridicule. Life as Oswald Reynolds's son was of some benefit. Besides, we would simply explain the reasons for our union to our neighbors and friends. You will find most of those who have moved to Texas are very understanding of wanting to leave the past in the past."

"But what would you get out of such a marriage?"

One side of his face twitched in a nearly imperceptible wince and the sparkle faded from his pale blue gaze. Odd that she had so quickly grown to take note of his changing moods. Perhaps it was only the inordinate amount of practice she'd spent needing to detect Edgar's shifting frame of mind.

"Believe me," Alexander said after a slight hesitation, "marriage is the last action I ever thought to propose to anyone. I suppose you could act as my hostess."

"I hardly think that is a good reason to tie yourself to me. It would hold the potential for massive trouble coming down on your head. My father could live for years. Search for years. My disappearance after that announcement in the *Times* will have been dealt

Howard Bedlow a sharp blow to his pride. I don't think I'm worth it to you."

He considered her, his gaze intent. She could almost see him weighing her statement. He answered, "We two are alike in that our hearts have been damaged by the actions of others. I have reason not to wish a love match but I never wanted a marriage without one." He slid back onto the end cushion.

"I still see no way *I* can help *you*. You have just strengthened the case against the marriage on your part. Suppose you *did* find love but I was still in danger."

"You are going to make me say it, aren't you?" His sigh was just a bit theatrical in keeping with his attempts to treat the situation with irony. But he looked more like a man facing a firing squad must. "Besides being sure I will never find love, I have a rather embarrassing problem that having a wife will solve."

Patience had never thought he could be put at a disadvantage by anyone. Though she saw what he was about to say as a ruse, she still felt compelled to lean forward, eager for his explanation.

"I've purchased one of the three largest ranches in the area. It is, therefore, clear I have a good deal of funds at my disposal. Two or three of the wealthier families in the area around Tierra del Verde have marriageable daughters. Those daughters are extremely zealous in their pursuit of me. I am not used to dodging determined mammas or aggressive misses thanks to my father's reputation."

Did he really think it was money and not his tall, broad-shouldered physique, handsome face and sparkling eyes that drew those women? She'd been young and carefree once. She could appreciate how fine-looking he was and couldn't help smiling at how embarrassed he seemed.

"Do not look so amused," he groused. "You will be the pretty new schoolteacher in town."

He thinks I am pretty. The small, careful bit of joy that thought fanned to life was quickly extinguished when he continued.

"You are sure to be as plagued as I by ardent admirers."

Once again terror flooded her. "But I don't want that!"

He grimaced a bit. "Just so. Which means we can be of assistance to each other. Our married state would discourage both persistent young women and hopeful men. And as I said, I'll need a hostess, as I'll be expected to join local society. That would allow you the opportunity to safely socialize. As to one or both of us falling in love with someone else, I'm sure we would face that circumstance cordially if presented with it. I think we can be friends and therefore we would want happiness for each other. And who knows. Perhaps we shall get along so swimmingly we decide to just stay together.

"Another advantage for you I see is that when you told me of your unhappy marriage, it sounded as if you've missed interaction with others. Our being seen as a couple would afford you society with women in the area."

She heard herself sigh before she knew he'd hit upon something she'd felt acutely though she'd not said as much. "My letters to and from Amber were a godsend in dark times. I had no time to speak with anyone when Edgar wasn't hovering and listening to everything I said. The only reason I was allowed to correspond with

Amber was, as a poor teacher living in coal country, she could be of no help to me."

"As my wife you'd be free to visit and invite anyone to our home you wished. Anytime you wished. I'll teach you to ride if you don't know how and to handle a rig, as well. You can also learn the use of a gun so you can defend yourself. I'd only ask that you never ride out alone and that would be only for your safety. And the Winstons will be living in the house so you'd have Heddie's company daily."

She nodded her understanding but not yet her acceptance. She went over all Alexander had said. It sounded so logical yet still so frightening. Perhaps because marriage to Edgar had sounded so right, too, and look where that had gotten her.

Putting a hand to her forehead, Patience asked herself the one question she knew needed asking. Was there a better alternative?

While no other viable option presented itself she still held back, feeling the need to test his character further. "What about the idea of my teaching?"

He shrugged. "I see no reason for that dream to be lost to you. I'll have the ranch. Why shouldn't you pursue something you care about?" He pursed his lips and frowned in thought.

Patience braced herself for the inevitable. He must have thought of a reason not to permit it. Which left her with no hope.

"I have an idea," Alexander said at last. "There's no schoolhouse as yet. If you wish to serve as our teacher, I'll donate a piece of land at the edge of the ranch, bordering town. I'll even throw in the lumber for the schoolhouse."

She looked at her hands, knotted together and aching in her lap, not sure when she'd clasped them. "It sounds so easy. Nothing's been easy for so long, I find it hard to believe this could be." She shook her head. How could it be that her life—the nightmare it had become—could be fixed so easily?

And by a man?

Then again, marriage would not be easy for her. Trusting another person—a male person—was the very opposite of easy.

"I should get off in St. Louis, pawn the jewelry and run as far as I can. I could join a wagon train to Oregon or go on to San Francisco by rail."

"As much as I wish for your sake that were possible, it isn't. Please try to think that through. The railroads have shrunk this vast country, making few destinations unreachable. And they're already checking all the train lines. As for your other idea, I'm afraid a single woman could never join a wagon train. If you tried, the wagon master would present you with all the single men and you'd have to choose one to wed. At least you know me somewhat. You have my pledge not to push you into a physical union. You know I can offer you a comfortable existence.

"I don't wish to pressure you but you must decide before we reach St. Louis. We'd need to accomplish the marriage there to get the safeguard in place."

Something surged in Patience as it had when she'd decided to come west. She sat straighter, separated her fingers from each other and fisted her hands. Alexander was the one with the most to lose. At least she was sure she would never fall in love. Her trust would never extend that far. If he met someone he thought he could love, marriage to her could easily destroy his chance of even getting to know that lucky woman. If he could willingly offer to do this for her, who was she to treat him so shabbily as to doubt his character, all but throwing his gesture back in his face.

"I've already decided," she said. "I'm sick to death of being afraid. I want to outsmart my father the way I did when I climbed out my window. I want to live my life *my* way. You're right! I have few options but I can at least accept your kind offer. This is *my* choice. Thank you, Alexander."

He nodded. "I promised you last Wednesday I would protect you. I'm sorry there seems to be no other way than this. I'll prove worthy of your trust."

"It's hard for me to trust but you've already earned mine." She gave him a small careful smile.

When he smiled back, his eyes sparkled like the sun on clear water. "I find I trust you, as well. That's not a bad place to start, is it?"

Her stomach dipped again in that odd dizzy way only he had ever caused, but she managed to say, "No, it's not."

Chapter Five

When Virgil returned, Alex opened the door. "Virgil, join us for a moment, will you?" he said and gestured to the three chairs across from the sofa. Alex returned to his seat on the sofa with Patience. "We've been planning something and I hope you can render us some aid."

The Winstons were already seated in the other two chairs. Virgil bowed slightly to them in a deferential greeting. "I'm more than willin' to help any way I can. I decided to take you up on your offer, sir."

Alex gestured to the chair again. "Please sit. We'll all have upset stomachs if we continue to watch you swaying above us while we plan."

Virgil perched uneasily on the edge of the brocade smoking chair's cushion.

"I want to reiterate how much we appreciate your loyalty and your continued help," Alex began. "Do you know a minister in St. Louis who might marry us? I'm sure we need a license, too. Do you have any ideas how to smuggle my young lady out of the car unnoticed so we can take care of all this?"

"We pull into St. Louis 'bout daybreak and leave at ten in the mornin'. Sharp," Virgil said. "I ain't sure city hall even opens by then. 'Sides, with them Pinkertons sniffin' 'round you ought not let the lady go nowhere." He fell silent then. Engrossed in his thoughts, he pursed his lips.

Alex's heart plummeted. He refused to believe he was disappointed that the marriage, which could tie Patience to him for a long time, could not take place. No. Surely, it was the danger her unmarried state posed worrying him.

Of course that's all!

After a long silence, the thoughtful frown left Virgil's dark face and his eyebrows rose nearly to his hairline. His black eyes lit with what could only be called glee. "There's this judge. Got waylaid by a bunch of thievin' thugs one night 'bout two years ago. My friend and me stepped in. Chased them devils off. Judge Appleby said if I ever need anythin' I should go to him. Well, with us comin' to Texas, I got no further use of a Missouri promise. And I expect the judge'd handle the license *and* say the ceremony for ya'll. He was right grateful, you see."

"Do you think he'd keep our confidence?" asked Winston.

"I hear tell he's an honest man. I'm thinkin' you could trust him."

"Then we will. But if you plan to contact the judge, how will you have time to speak to your wife and son about coming along to Texas? Surely they'd not be able to make the train?"

"Our home place is near the tracks. I can stop and send them here, then light out for the judge's house.

Willow can get Jerome to the station. Not much to bring along that matters more than a better life, now is there?"

"Are you in agreement, Patience?" Alex asked. "Or would you prefer a minister perform the ceremony? A rushed wedding in a train car is hardly what a young woman dreams of."

Patience looked surprised, then sadness entered eyes that should have seen only joy. It seemed to him that once her father had deemed her ready for marriage, she'd been given few choices in how she'd live her life. And this marriage was not much different, he thought ruefully. He understood how she felt much better than most men could.

His childhood had been fraught with fear and his life with a kind of captivity to duty because of his father. But Alex was a man, and once of age men were free to make their own choices. Protecting Jamie against Oswald Reynolds had been Alex's choice. And frankly so was this marriage and the protection he'd already extended to her. He'd always been free to wash his hands of the entire affair.

Patience was not so fortunate.

Her deep breath pulled him back to his unanswered question. She nodded at last with a small gracious smile tipping her Cupid's-bow lips upward. Her expression said she understood why he'd asked. "I *had* the dream wedding, Alexander," she said. "That ceremony turned my life into a waking nightmare."

She looked toward Virgil. "Do you think the judge will agree to this? We are strangers to him, after all."

Virgil nodded from his seat across the aisle. "I surely do, ma'am. He's a good man."

"Then I'd say we have quite an effective plan

arranged," Winston chimed in, clearly taking to heart his duty as father of the bride. "It is as if this were preordained. Thank you for you assistance."

The porter stood then to return to his nightly duties and Patience said, "And thank you for including me as more than a spectator, Alexander. I had not expected that. But then again you've surprised me from the moment we met." She gifted him with another stunning smile.

It had to be a trick of the light but the space seemed to brighten appreciably. Which meant he was in real trouble here. As, by default, was she.

Alex took a chance that his worry was unfounded and reached out to clasp her hand lightly in his. She didn't pull away, which heartened him. He felt a distinctive thud low in his gut, which didn't. Continuing the conversation as if it was all he'd been thinking of, he said, "Of all the injustices you've suffered, having to bow to the wishes of others against your own better judgment must have been one of the most difficult to bear. The circumstances of our marriage will be the last time anyone forces your hand in anything. That, I promise you."

Patience cocked her head to the side and slid her hand back into her lap.

Feeling the loss, Alex looked away from her and noted Virgil quitting the car, then Winston locked the door and sat across from Heddie at the dining table. Their absence increased the intimacy of the moment between him and Patience, making Alex rather sorry he hadn't been quick enough to prevent the Winstons from leaving the parlor area.

Had his mind been where it ought, he'd have fled himself.

When he glanced back to Patience, she was considering him closely. He nearly squirmed under her direct assessment. The feeling reminded him of how he'd always felt when Jamie's nurse had stared at him this way—as if she were reading his soul. He'd always been found wanting and had no doubt he would be this time.

Even though his discomfort mounted, Alex still found himself rejoicing that Patience dared to demand his attention so boldly. "May I ask what has become so fascinating about my nose, ma'am?"

She blinked, startled. "Nothing. Truly, I was lost in thought." She colored up and became flustered, leading him to dangerous territory as he wondered where those thoughts had taken her. He was a fool. No good could come of thoughts like that. She was a scarred young woman who deserved his protection, not his lustful hopes.

Even more nonplussed than she, he continued, acting nonsensical to cover his discomfort as he usually did in situations that might reveal his true self—whatever that was. "Thoughts about my nose?" he asked, grinning. "I assure you it is a quite ordinary one. A bit crooked I believe from the fist of a detractor. Took exception to my claiming the last of his fortune." Her eyes inquired after the circumstances—which he supposed he'd more or less expected. Why throw up a smoke screen in only half measures. "The man in question foolishly wagered said fortune at a faro table in a London gaming hell."

She swallowed. "Did you hit him back? And you still took the money?"

"Take pity on a fool? That isn't how it's done, my innocent. Were I to have done that all fools in London owing me blunt would have expected forgiveness of their debts. No. The guard at the gaming hell tossed his highborn bag of bones into the street and I added substantially to my fortune. A fortune you will now share."

She popped to her feet, a look of horror she desperately tried to conceal reflected in her crystalline-green eyes. "I should go to bed. Thank you for all you are trying to do for me." That and a quick curtsy and she was gone.

He wanted to take back what he'd said and cursed under his breath. Had he become so base he didn't know how to speak around a lady? To a lady?

And then he'd compounded his bad behavior with a lie. A lie of omission but a lie nonetheless. He rarely lied because his father had rarely told the truth. Alex saved that particular vice for those rare occasions when it was necessary to prevent hurt feelings or to save lives.

Dammit!

When he'd learned there was a wife and children involved, he'd returned a sizable portion of the problematic winnings to the feckless baron's clever wife to keep to herself and use as she saw fit. But that transaction had been between him and the lady. Consequently, Alex had promised to keep her confidence.

He had never to his knowledge broken his word to himself or anyone else. He couldn't do it now even to elevate himself in the eyes of his soon-to-be bride. If a man did not honor his word, who was he?

And now the damage was done. He'd instinctively

said the one thing that deep inside he'd known would send her, if not running from him, then wishing she could.

It had been reflex. He would swear it had been.

Dammit!

He was aware enough of his own emotions to know why he'd done it. He'd begun to care for her. Worse, to want her. And that wouldn't do.

Because she could hurt him—could reject him as Iris had.

Or she could be taken from him as his mother had been.

And there was the possibility that he could hurt her—destroy her as his father had done with anyone he'd ever gotten close to.

Avoiding pain and loss had ruled Alex's life for so many years it must have become second nature. As had pushing people away for fear of hurting them. He would have to find a way to fight all three instincts. If it meant not hurting the young woman fate had placed in his care, then by God he would more than fight. Somehow he'd find the courage to win. Patience thought herself a coward. But Alex, a man with the wealth and freedom to go off and make a new life for himself, had shown himself to be the true coward this night.

For the first time in years he was utterly ashamed of himself.

Alex woke to the sound of light knocking as the door opened to the stateroom he'd taken for his own. "Sir," Winston called quietly, "we are pulling into the station at St. Louis."

How can it be dawn? Alex sat up. His head felt as

if someone had stolen in while he slept and stuffed it full of cotton before returning it to his shoulders. He shouldn't have had that last snifter of brandy Winston had suggested. He turned his head to focus on the older man and upped that wish to include the last several snifters.

"How can you be so lively, Winston? You drank as much as I did."

Winston arched an eyebrow. Alex had admired that ability of Winston's but this morning he found it extremely irritating. "It is a gift to be able to drink and suffer no ill effects, sir. One I must assume you do not possess."

"Apparently not," Alex replied. He never over-indulged. Never. But with sleep annoyingly elusive, he'd let Winston talk him into turning to brandy.

One in a growing line of *firsts* in his life he could lay at the feet of the lovely Patience Gorham—soon to be Reynolds. Being pursued by the largest private detective agency in the world had been the *first* of the *firsts*.

No, having a lovely young lady pitch over in a dead faint within moments of meeting him had been that.

Alex grinned. At least their acquaintance wasn't boring.

The low murmur of voices from the other stateroom reminded him of the reason sleep had been so diffi-cult to achieve last night. His grin faded and just that quickly, his thoughts were back where they'd been when exhaustion had claimed him only a few hours before.

Back to the shame he'd felt for sending Patience running from him. He couldn't recall scaring a young woman out of his company before. Two more *firsts* there if he was of a mind to keep count. Alex sighed and scrubbed at his face.

After he'd stupidly pushed her away, he'd avoided thinking of her by trying to become fascinated with a book from the car's library but that had failed miserably. And so he'd thought about what he'd done and how to fix it. He honestly hadn't been able to think of another recourse that didn't include confessing his lie.

Then Winston had arrived with that dammed brandy decanter and Alex was off to completing another *first*. God, had he really ended the night calling Winston Jordie? And confessing to his growing feelings for Patience? Plus his total unworthiness as a husband, however temporary the position was likely to be. *Dammit!*

He wanted to dress as quickly as possible that morning but Winston would have none of it. "It is your wedding day," his self-selected valet fussed.

"Really, Winston, I don't employ a valet. I'm more than capable of dressing myself."

But Winston was having none of that, either. "A gentleman should have a valet. And a bride has the right to have her groom appear *well*-groomed. It is our Patience's wedding day. The least you can do after upsetting her last evening is play the part of a besotted well-turned-out swain."

Alex's problem was that he could easily be just that. Again Winston's damned eyebrow rose, awaiting one confession or another. Alex refused to repeat either of them sober.

Winston shook his head as if despairing of him and turned away to go about his self-chosen chores. He decided Alex was to wear a charcoal-gray swallowtail coat, black trousers and a pearl-white brocade waistcoat. He all but shoveled Alex into his clothing, while prescribing upon a groom's correct conduct at the ceremony. Did the man think he was a total heathen? Alex decided not to dwell on the answer to that and set his mind to his appearance.

Between the two of them they got his wide black tie knotted perfectly, according to Winston, a pearl stickpin sitting exactly at its center.

Alex left his stateroom. To get out of the ladies' way, he moved to the parlor at the rear of the car and settled down on the sofa. "So what comes next, Winston? You seem to be in the know this morning."

"Virgil decided his wife should begin cooking when she joins our party. He said something about obtaining groceries for the car's kitchen while he's out. He worried someone would notice the copious amount of food coming in here as you're supposed to be alone. It could alert the wrong persons to our growing company of travelers. Oh, and he did bring a bite to eat for all of us as he planned to be off the train before it stopped completely. He expected it would save him quite a bit of time as it would put him closer to his home."

"So all we can do is wait?" Alex stood again. "I detest sitting around waiting for someone else to do something I should do for myself."

Winston, Alex could see, fought a smile, though his posture was as severe and unbending as ever. "I'm sure we have all noticed that, sir. Perhaps you should try to choose ever more helpless companions. That would fill your days better. Alas this new friend of yours is a poor choice to be sure as he seems to be rather quick-witted and resourceful."

"Point taken," Alex said and chuckled as he settled back into his chair. "I've become friends with an ex-slave. Lovely. My father would have had apoplexy. I believe you have lightened my spirits, Winston."

"It's bad luck," he heard Heddie say a moment later. "Please, you must stay in your stateroom until the judge is here." She sounded as exasperated with the bride as her husband had with the groom. These two acted as if this was a real marriage.

"I didn't see my last husband until the altar," he heard Patience say. "I assure you that marriage could not have been less lucky for me had I paraded before Mr. Gorham in my wedding gown twice every day for a month prior to the ceremony."

"Very well, dearie, do to suit yourself."

There was a long silence before Patience sighed. "Would that I could, but that isn't the way it's going to be, is it?"

All of Alex's amusement and good humor fled. Was she simply nervous or had he made today worse for her? He must have given her an even greater distaste for him than she'd already felt because of his gender. A problem he'd thought they'd gotten past—at least partially, until he'd instinctively tried to push her away.

He needed to fix this.

Not for himself—he deserved her disdain—but for her. He didn't want this day—or any of her future days—to bear any similarity to her old life. Apologies to the baron's wife, he planned to tell Patience the truth about his gambling win.

Patience stalked out of her stateroom wearing her favorite dress. Though it was four years old, it was still like new. That, of course, was because she'd only been able to wear it since Edgar's death. He had deemed it immodest and seductive and had forbidden her to wear it. As such, it felt like the perfect choice for this wedding that was supposed to assure her freedom.

The bodice was fashioned to resemble a short-sleeved, jewel-neckline blouse made of fine embroidered lace. It had a strapless silk under dress that was just a tad bluer than the very pale blue lace overlaying it. Its delicate three-tiered, embroidered lace skirt fell in cascades to skim the floor from her waist, cinched with a blue silk sash, which was tied in a bow at the back. A bow Heddie had fussed over for an agonizing length of time.

The dress was more than a statement of freedom. It was also one last test of Alexander before the ceremony. She glanced uncertainly at him, watching for his reaction to her costume. And wondering again why he'd told her that awful story last night. She wondered if the baron had had a family to support. If so what would have become of them? She didn't think she'd be able to watch Alexander spend a dime on her, knowing children could be hungry because of her. The sparse wardrobe she'd brought along, augmented by Amber's old dresses and skirts, would have to do her until the school was built and she could earn a salary.

Alexander approached her from the back of the car but he didn't seem to be affected one way or the other by the dress. He seemed distracted and on edge. Apparently neither feeling had anything to do with her attire. In fact, his eyes hadn't drifted from hers.

Perhaps he couldn't see her well. It was quite dark with all the curtains drawn. But disappointment still warred with consolation in her heart because he didn't seem to notice or want to dictate the manner of her dress. That thought pulled her up short.

What is wrong with me?

She didn't want Alexander to object to her mode of dress even one quarter as strongly as Edgar had, nor did she want him to confirm her late husband's objection to the dress by being overtaken by lust upon seeing her in it. She couldn't want him to admire her. That was impossible! She was disappointed in him. Why should she care what he thought?

"Could we speak a moment?" Alexander asked.

Her ire restored, she replied, "I don't know that there is much to say. Unless you've decided to withdraw your offer to protect me through marriage."

Alexander gestured to the sofa. She crossed to one of the chairs instead. He sighed and sat across from her. She didn't know why she'd been so defiant. He wasn't like Edgar or her father, demanding she acquiesce to his every gesture. But now she understood he was capable of harsh and if not illegal then immoral actions. Still, she couldn't say she feared him the way she did men of her previous acquaintance.

Perhaps it was simply that he seemed to fill any room by just entering it and she resented that. All she knew was she hadn't wanted him too close. Unfortunately, he felt too close even sitting across from her.

"I had thought you might have changed your mind about marrying me after what I said last night," he said.

"Last night?" she asked, pretending nothing was amiss between them. She owed him. He'd offered to protect her, and now was offering marriage to make that protection stronger. Thus far he'd asked no favors in return. For her it was not a case of "Better the devil you know than the one you don't." Her heart seemed to sigh within her chest. She might not know Alexander very well but even if he had taken another man's fortune, he was miles better than Howard Bedlow.

"I'm speaking of the incident that sent you running to your stateroom last night," he reminded her.

She opened her mouth to deny his assessment but he put his hand up, clearly unwilling to ignore what had happened. "Don't deny what we both know to be true, Patty."

She fought the grin at his impudent use of that nickname. He could wring a smile out of her so easily it was embarrassing. It made her feel a bit ashamed. He was so very nice to her. "I'm sorry. It's certainly not my place to judge. You must think me very unsophisticated. I'm sure men take each other's fortunes all the time in business. Why not at a faro table?"

"I'm not trying to defend myself. Nor am I looking for an apology. I had reasons for what I did and wouldn't undo it if I could. But I should not have tried to elicit your reaction."

"You hoped to upset me?" Then the truth dawned. "We need not go through with this marriage idea, Alexander. You clearly would rather not."

"Let us not get into wishes. Or reasons. We have set this course and need to continue on it. I only wanted to explain something I omitted. It was an important fact. One I don't feel comfortable revealing even now. But if you pledge to never repeat what I tell you, I'll explain further so you'll know I am not a heartless beast."

What could she say to that? That she had not thought him heartless when they both knew she had. So she addressed her part of this. "We are going deep into the West. Who would care enough about an English baron to listen if I were inclined to break a confidence? Which I am not, by the way."

He huffed out a breath and squeezed the bridge of his nose as if he were suffering a headache. "Of course you wouldn't. It was insulting to infer you would. It's just that I gave my word and I never break my word. Ever. That night I hadn't stopped to think he might have dependents. Then I learned he had a wife and children. So I begged an audience with the lady and returned to her keeping a substantial sum. I offered it with the stipulation that she manage the money on her own for the good of herself and her children. She took it after I promised no one would ever know she'd accepted it. Her name would have been ruined were it known she took money from me."

"You must allow me to apologize, Alexander."

He winced a bit. "Only if you will accept mine for beginning this contretemps in the first place."

She nodded but noticed he hadn't explained why he'd tried to push her away, nor had he denied wishing he could retract his offer of marriage. She now had two reasons to be thankful for him leaving the idea of an annulment open. For her part, she never intended to allow any man to have power over her. His promise of freedom in the future was unnecessary. Indeed, so far it appeared she would have more freedom *in* this marriage than out of it.

"Then suppose we go see what Virgil left us to eat and await the future together," Alexander said instead.

She nodded her agreement, ever so glad that at least he'd said future and not fate as if he faced the gallows. That would have been more guilt than she could bear.

Chapter Six

San Antonio, Texas
September 18, 1878
Half-past 9:00 p.m.

"I agree, sir. That delay between Columbus and Schulenburg this afternoon was most fortuitous," Patience heard Winston saying. She assumed he was speaking to Alexander, as he was the only person Winston ever addressed as "sir." Which meant they had returned from their mission to check the lay of the land, as Alexander had put it. Hopefully not only had they found the wagon waiting, but they'd also found no Pinkerton agents standing watch as the train emptied.

She had to agree that the delay earlier in the day had been a saving grace. They'd been due into San Antonio before twilight, which would have left her exposed to watching eyes as she left the car. But the train had needed to stop to let a huge herd of cattle lumber across the tracks. Alexander had estimated the herd to be as much as two miles wide and fifteen miles long.

The slow crossing of the beasts had delayed them over an hour.

It was as if God himself had tried to throw down a blanket of protection for her, because now it was fully dark. Even the moon, only a tiny sliver in the black, diamond-sprinkled sky, was her friend.

In the stateroom, Patience folded the last of her things and closed her portmanteau. She looked around the small but luxurious stateroom where she'd come to feel so secure during their trip west. She would miss it and the feeling of being cocooned in security. Reluctantly bidding the pretty chamber goodbye, she dragged her bag out to the short hall where Virgil's young son, Jerome, eager to please, rushed up and dragged it away. The time had come to leave the safety of the train.

Fear and anticipation waged a battle within her, making her heart pound. Then Heddie approached. "Jordie says it's a might chilly. And Mr. Alex thought your cape would be a good disguise we can use now that the train has delayed us."

Unable to find her voice, Patience nodded and turned so Heddie could help her into her cape. She found herself facing the full-length gilt-framed mirror that hung in the dining area. To stall for time, she made a production of fastening the horn button at the neckline and making sure it lay just so.

When she let her eyes drift upward, she caught sight of her reflection. She looked so pale. So worried. Which she was. She was also nearly sure it was a waste of energy. Alexander had designed the move to the carriage with the greatest of care.

With nothing left to do while the last of the supplies and luggage was transferred to the waiting wagon, she stared at the stranger in the mirror. She had changed since the day her father had shoved her into her room, pronouncing she'd stay there until she agreed to his demands.

The change was reflected in her eyes.

She hadn't been playing to Alexander's sympathies when she'd said she'd been prepared to die while climbing down the tree to escape her father's home. Her eyes in the mirror that night had been flat. Dead. She really hadn't cared one way or the other that she might fall.

This night, though she was terrified of being recognized, at least her eyes looked alive. She might be anxious over the path she'd set her feet upon but she'd made the decision to forge ahead toward life. She wanted to live. Free.

Maybe she felt that way because, unlike the mouse who'd hidden her every thought for five long years, now she had no one telling her how to think. How to act. How to speak. It occurred to her that she barely knew the woman reflected in the looking glass and yet she felt familiar—like an old friend who'd returned after a long absence. She was becoming the person she used to be. Her true self.

Suddenly Alex stepped behind her and held her gaze in the mirror. "You *will* get to know her again," he said quietly, leaving her to wonder how he could know her thoughts so well. "It may take a while but you're well on the road." He grinned as he raised her hood from behind and laid it over her head before resting his hands on her shoulders. "I expect to be henpecked within months." A little more than a week ago his touch—any touch from a man—would have sent her into a spiral, back into the nightmare world of her marriage.

"But for now," he went on, "let's keep you under wraps, shall we? Like Helen of Troy, you're infinitely memorable. I don't want to launch a thousand ships—or inquires—over you." He pulled the hood forward to cover her hair completely and shadow her face. The plain serviceable cape changed her appearance so much she'd look like any anonymous working-class passenger.

But if her identity had changed, his had, as well. She was shocked by how much. In the full-length mirror, as he stepped a bit to the side, she was able to take in his cotton-twill, collarless shirt, the leather vest over it and the rough black canvas trousers he wore. He was a far cry from the elegant gentleman she'd met in New York. She'd read enough news accounts of the West to know the way he'd dressed then would have labeled him a dandy now they were in Texas.

This husband she was surprisingly tied to was no dandy. From the black, wide-brimmed hat that cast a shadow of mystery over his pale blue eyes right down to his square-toed, narrow-heeled riding boots, he was as tough and dangerous as the gun at his hip.

Oddly, she wasn't afraid of that. Perhaps because Edgar had been such a coward. One night they'd been accosted outside the opera and Edgar had shoved her at the ruffian and darted back into the theater calling for help. He'd lied, claiming the man had grabbed her, but a witness had exposed his lie. So he'd beaten her unmercifully that night as if trying to repair his damaged pride.

He'd looked like such a gentleman and had turned out to be nothing but a bully. The man in the mirror didn't need to bolster his pride with false shows of strength. He was strong enough in his own right.

"Try to relax," Alexander said. "I saw no one loitering about the station or on the street. There's every chance the Pinkerton who worked in this area is either gone from the city or he wasn't alerted to look for you. When I wired my men from St. Louis I asked them to bring the landau and have the top up. It's waiting at the end of the platform. Anyone who looks at it will see nothing more than the silhouettes of three females and one male in the darkened interior."

He turned, gestured toward the doorway and her fellow conspirators. "Are we all set then?" he asked.

They all nodded. "All right, then," Alexander said. "We should be able to slip out of San Antonio relatively unnoticed. I doubt I am the first or last man to come through here with his household in tow. Shall we be off?"

She took a deep breath. This was it.

Patience followed the others toward the exit, sure the pounding of her cowardly heart could be heard by the entire group. But if anyone noticed, they didn't mention it.

At the doorway she found Alexander waiting at the foot of the stairs. He reached up to help her down the steep steps then gave her hand a gentle, reassuring squeeze before he let go and stepped back.

She put one foot in front of the other, telling herself if they got out of town unchallenged, it would be worth the chance she'd taken with this marriage. She'd be able to live free of her past as Alexander's wife and Tierra del Verde's new teacher.

There was just enough light that she could see the six men he'd said awaited them. They were all mounted, surrounding the carriage. Once again Alexander had protected her as he'd been doing ever since they'd met. Heddie had told her he'd thought he wanted to start anew in Texas with no one dependent upon him, but she really thought he needed the opposite. Patience thought the same. From the moment Patience had met him, he'd been gathering up chicks—one after another—to bring along. It was clear from what little she knew of Alexander from Amber's letters that he needed all of them as much as they needed him.

How long it would take him to realize he'd created a new family for himself, she didn't know. But she saw it and thought that perhaps Heddie Winston had, as well.

As they all walked along the wooden station platform, their shoes clopping along the boardwalk, Patience's mind went back to the short precise wedding ceremony that had tied her to Alexander while at the same time promised to set her free.

They'd talked it over and had decided to tell the judge the absolute truth. Alexander didn't want the judge to feel they'd taken advantage of him or lied to him if he was questioned later. A kindly man and the father of three daughters, the judge had been appalled that her father had tried to force her to marry a man she feared, especially after having chosen so unwisely for her the first time. Judge Appleby had promised to make sure the recording of the marriage was difficult to find and wasn't published in the paper.

Alexander had lied about one thing, though indirectly. He'd spoken his vows as if he actually meant to love her. At least she hoped he'd been pretending. She had no wish for him to have feelings for her and therefore decide he wanted to exercise his husbandly rights.

So far, though, since the ceremony, Alexander had

only spoken to her casually and with a friendly relaxed manner that was more reminiscent of a brother than a lover. She knew firsthand about brothers. She'd had brothers but had never had a lover. Her husband—her *first* husband, she reminded herself—hadn't been her lover. He'd been her torturer. Her jailor.

She really had no idea how a husband should act. Though she'd always believed her parents had loved each other, they'd been very formal and proper as a couple. Alexander didn't seem to have a proper bone in his body. He was flippant, irreverent and mischievous when he wasn't being the kindest man she'd ever met.

Unprepared, she started in fright when Alexander suddenly appeared at her side and wrapped his arm around her shoulders. She hadn't even known he was close. She put a hand to her thundering heart. "Don't sneak up on me like that. How can you walk so quietly?"

"Practice. I'm sorry. I should have realized how terrified you must be right now."

Striving to put a thick air of irony into her tone in the hope of hiding her fear she said, "I must point out you are *still* holding on to me."

He gave a little chuckle. "For two reasons. One—no one is looking for a happily married couple. Were someone to look out a window that's all they'd see. Your father and certainly not Howard Bedlow would ever think you would have married this quickly so our very silhouette would throw him off our trail."

She nodded. "Oh, you're right. And the other reason?" she asked, praying he didn't say that he wanted her near.

"Because we cannot use the pretense that you are merely traveling with your parents as we did in New

Jersey or at Penn Station in Philadelphia. You are also my wife. As such, I would lay down my life to keep you from harm. I'd like the men to see us as a couple from the very start. They are another part of the web of protection I intend to weave about you. I would have them know you are important to me."

Patience nodded and kept her eyes straight ahead, looking neither left nor right. No one accosted them or even came near their little group as they approached the wagon and carriage. Alexander, once again without warning, scooped her up into his arms and set her into the carriage with Willow and Heddie. She was breathless as she sank into the soft leather upholstery. This time she was nearly sure her pounding heart had nothing to do with the fear of being recognized.

This time the fear was about Alexander. Though when she looked carefully at his actions toward her, she didn't understand why that was. She didn't understand it at all.

No one spoke as they rode through the streets. Alexander leaned down once and pointed to the Alamo. Though the building was now a warehouse and retail space there was still a quietude about it—almost an unspoken reverence flowed from the area.

He pointed out the Menger Hotel next to the Alamo and the Menger Brewery across the road. He told them William A. Menger had founded both but it was his widow, Mary, who currently ran them. "In Texas," he said, "a woman can be respected and prosper on her own." Patience knew he'd said what he had for her benefit. Almost like a promise.

A while later the sounds coming from the last building they passed—a noisy tavern—faded behind them.

For the first time since walking into her father's library and having Howard Bedlow introduced as her next husband, Patience breathed a sigh of relief.

Alexander once again seemed to read her thoughts. He rode close and said, "So, Mrs. Reynolds, are you beginning to believe you've made your escape?"

She couldn't help but smile. "I do believe you are a miracle worker, Mr. Reynolds."

After about two hours' travel, Alexander's foreman—Michael O'Hara—declared that riding farther in the pitch-blackness was a bad idea. They made camp. Though a couple of the men grumbled good-naturedly about troublesome women, they took enough of the baggage and supplies out of the wagon to allow the women to sleep in it and off the ground. Patience was grateful, as were Heddie and Willow, though Willow said she'd slept in worse places than the ground around a friendly campfire.

It was heartening to see how easily the cowboys accepted the family of ex-slaves, although after dinner on the second night, O'Hara warned them that frontier justice wasn't always distributed as equally in large towns and cities like San Antonio and Dallas as they'd find it in Tierra del Verde.

Virgil chuckled but there was a bitter edge in his voice when he said if he never went farther than the ranch or Tierra del Verde for the rest of his life, he'd be a happy man. He just wanted peace and respect, and the closed society Alex had described at the Rocking R sounded like heaven.

He also mentioned his wish that his child learn to read as he and Willow had never been allowed. After that, Patience started teaching them all as they rode toward their futures.

* * *

Alex stopped at the top of the rise and looked down on sleepy little Tierra del Verde. He'd ridden ahead, anxious for the earliest sight. For the first time in his life somewhere felt like home, even though he'd only spent six months there building his future. And making friends.

Surrounded by the rolling green hills of Texas Hill Country, Tierra del Verde's adobe buildings, so indicative of Texas's shared history with Mexico, were nestled around a small town square and park and mixed with some homes that looked as if they belonged in Germany. The square was the hub of much of the town's activity.

The town hall on one side of the square shared the building with the sheriff's office, jail and courtroom. Across the square sat the hotel.

Reiman House, built in the same style as the classical Menger Hotel, while not as grand, was well-appointed and rather formal for a town as small and remote as Tierra del Verde.

When Alex had first ridden into town in search of a woman his cousin felt indebted to, Adolph Reiman had been the first person he'd met. Serendipitous was the only description for that meeting. Reiman had been anxious to sell the Rocking R because his wife preferred town life. The meeting had changed Alex's future, giving his formerly rudderless life purpose.

Now, anxious to show off the little town to Patience, he wheeled Big Boy and rode back to the wagons. O'Hara intercepted him. "It being Saturday night, the men are anxious to blow off some steam and be doin' some celebratin' with the girls over at the Golden Garter. 'Tis also Founders' Day tomorrow," he explained. "Most of the rest of the men'll be comin' in tomorrow. There's the big picnic after church. A big shindig after dark at the barn on the Shamrock."

Alex nodded. "Why don't we all stay then? Maybe sometime tomorrow I can talk to the mayor and the town council about the school. And I need to talk to Sheriff Quinn." The sheriff needed to know the true story for the same reason Judge Appleby had. Her safety lay in the truth.

"The ladies'll get to rest before undertakin' the house," O'Hara said.

Disappointment shot through Alex. He'd wanted her to see her new home in its best light. "You wrote saying it's done."

O'Hara nodded. "Done but there's all that furniture and such you had shipped. It only got here a few weeks ago. The first floor has the look of a warehouse. My wife didn't think it was our place to uncrate and arrange. It'll all have to land where your wife wants it, anyway. Mine gets pure pleasure out of rearranging. And her pure pleasure is pure hell on me back."

Alex chuckled, his heart a bit lighter. Patience might feel more at home, more respected, if she directed the placement of the things he'd had shipped from New York City.

"Reiman House it is, then. Perhaps we'll stay on the Shamrock with Mrs. Kane tomorrow night and head home from there," Alex said and nodded to his foreman, who wheeled his horse around and rode back to tell the men the good news. Since the carriage was in sight, Alex sat waiting for it to catch up to him.

"We'll stay at the hotel for tonight," he said as they drew up to him. "Apparently you are going to have some work to do on the house to make it a home, sweetheart. Right now O'Hara tells me it looks like a warehouse."

Patience smiled broadly, and sat forward, excitement alive in her tone when she said, "I've never gotten to do anything like that. Are you sure you trust me with your home?"

"My home? It's your home, too. And lovely as you always look, I know it'll be a home I'll be proud of."

She put her head down, "Oh, I—" she choked out.

He'd made her cry. Damn. When had he become so clumsy with women? Driven to change her mood, Alex reached down, leaned into the uncovered carriage and scooped her up onto his lap with one arm while holding on to the pommel of the western saddle with the other hand.

Her swift intake of air showed he'd surprised her but then he noticed how stiff she was in his arms. He would have set her back in the carriage but with the men cheering and good-naturedly teasing them he was well aware they had an audience.

"I should have this written on my forehead for all the times I have to say it to you," he whispered. "I promise to never knowingly hurt you."

"I'm sorry," she said, head down and still sniffling. "You surprised me is all." He felt a shiver go through her then she relaxed against him, but he knew she'd forced it by sheer will.

It has nothing to do with you and everything to do with fear as instinctual as a cornered animal's. That's to be conquered another day.

"I didn't mean to scare you or to make you cry. Somehow I put a foot wrong."

"Oh, Alexander, what kind of women have you

known? We are often silly ninnies who cry when happy and scream and rant with anger when hurt. I forever perplexed my brothers before I left home to marry. I am simply overwhelmed with happiness."

That he'd not considered. Perhaps he had helped Patience recover a bit if she could react as other women did—as she used to. Perhaps soon he could tell her he hated it when she called him Alexander.

It was his *before* name. *Before* the final showdown with his father. *Before* he'd killed him to save Jamie. *Before* his new life had begun.

But that was a problem to solve later. He had a bigger one right now. He shifted her in the saddle and pushed against the saddle horn, desperate to hide the reaction he was having to her bottom pressing against him. He cleared his throat. "I wanted to show you something I thought might gladden your heart," he said and smiled. "Apparently it'll only gladden it some more."

Then he heeled his horse's side, hoping a jostling uphill ride would tame his need to be more to her than a husband in name only. He cursed the errant thought. He couldn't begin to wish this were a real marriage. Or even that it could progress there in the coming days. He was unworthy of such a gift, but hope was a difficult thing to smother.

Scant minutes later they were on the hill overlooking Tierra del Verde. "There it is."

She gasped and it sounded to him like a happy sound. "It's like a picture postcard. Amber sent me one from the International Exhibition in Philadelphia. But, oh, this is just so much lovelier because it's real. And as green as its name promises. Is it as friendly as it looks?"

"For the most part, yes. The first time I saw the town

I sat right here on Big Boy's back. Over there on the other side of that hill, do you see the stream? That's the edge of the Rocking R. We can build a little bridge for the children to walk across. I thought in the shade of that big oak would be the perfect place for your schoolhouse. Can't you see swings for your students hanging from its branches? What do you think?"

He held his breath. Waiting. Praying. And then she said exactly the right thing, to lift his heart. "Oh, it's perfect. It's all so perfect." She breathed the words, tears flooding back into her voice. This time, though, he understood them. "It really is home, isn't it?" she went on in wonder. "It's *home*."

"That was my first thought the day I arrived on this hill. It made no sense, but there it was," he admitted, daring to open his heart to possible ridicule. If she could be brave enough to let him hold her, how could he be so cowardly as to pretend this meant no more to him than a pretty scene? But opening himself to those feelings left him fighting a sudden stronger surge of desire flooding his blood. He more than wished theirs was a real marriage. He wanted it. And her.

Determined to ignore that, at best to hide it, he continued as if he weren't on fire for her. "I had a letter to deliver to an acquaintance of my cousin," he explained. "I rode down there full of hope for the first time in years and my life changed within minutes."

"We're both refugees from the world of our childhoods, you and I, aren't we?"

He shrugged, taking the cowardly way out, again. "It's what the West is all about. Forgotten pasts and new beginnings."

The carriage drew even with them and he pivoted Big

Boy so he could set her down in it. He thanked God it had arrived at that moment because his arms had been about to give out. And if they did, she wouldn't miss the difference between the feel of the saddle horn and the unmerciful hard-on he'd developed in those last foolhardy minutes.

What the *h-e-double-l* had he been thinking?

Chapter Seven

Alex rode into Tierra del Verde ahead of the wagons and dismounted in front of the Reiman House hotel. For the first time as he rode into town, he hadn't felt the need to trace the rooftops of the town with his gaze. Or take a long moment to absorb the color of the buildings or the sound of water as Johnson Creek rushed by behind the hotel. There was no need to store it all away for a day when he was surrounded by the hustle and bustle of life in San Francisco or New York.

Because this time he was there to stay.

So instead of storing memories, he stood anxiously waiting for the landau to draw even with the hotel. He wanted Patience to feel the way he did about the place he'd chosen to begin his new life. And now, by default, hers. He wanted this to be a place where she felt happy. And safe.

After Virgil brought the carriage to a stop, Patience stood to alight. Alex rushed forward. She still wore the same happy smile she'd worn atop the ridge. Rather than hand her down, he lifted her by her slim waist.

The soft twill of her traveling skirt swirled about his legs as he swung her to the raised boardwalk. And as always happened whenever she was close, a sensual flood rushed through him. It didn't matter that there were several layers of crinoline between them. How could he feel so much for so little reason?

Had he learned nothing up there overlooking the town? Honest to goodness, he was acting like a besotted, overly poetic fool. At least he wasn't so foolish as to let her body slide down his. Though his body, which had apparently developed a mind of its own in the last week, thought that was a wonderful idea.

Dammit, he was no green boy. He'd had a great deal of practice managing the part of him currently being ruled by runaway desire. With considerable effort, Alex managed to keep physical need from ruling his mind. From betraying his developing feelings.

He set her on her feet, but she felt so damn feminine under his hands he couldn't make himself let go of her.

Until she looked up at him.

At that moment he witnessed the awful sight of her happiness being drowned by fear. Deeply regretting those extra seconds he'd held on to her so greedily, he dropped his hands immediately, ashamed for scaring her. He would *not* be like his father.

Nor would he let her know what he'd seen in her eyes, thus placing blame on her. And so he turned back to help Willow to the ground. Slender as Patience but tall for a woman, she hardly needed help, but he lifted her from the carriage, too. With any luck Patience would now think he'd meant nothing but to be helpful.

"Mr. Alex, that was hardly necessary," Willow said, breaking into his thoughts.

He had to think for a moment what it was that hadn't been necessary. Oh, yes, the lift down. No one seemed to want his help, did they? He grabbed for his heart. "It seems chivalry is truly dead," he gasped, then reached for Heddie, intent on aiding her the same way. She smacked his hand.

"Alas, three for three," he said in pretend misery. "I am so deeply wounded I may not survive."

"Scamp. What wouldn't survive would be your back!" Heddie cried. "It'd take you and Jordie both to lift me down. Now grab hold of my hand and quit flirting. Your charm won't work on me or Willow. Patience may be another story. You talked her into marriage, after all."

Willow, and then blessedly Patience, tittered behind him, thus lightening the moment. Alex laughed, grateful Heddie had known exactly how to relieve the tension that had hung in the air.

He honestly didn't know what to do to help Patience get past her fear. It was as if it held her as captive emotionally as her husband then her father had physically. It was the kind of fear he knew was ruled by instinct. He hated seeing her frightened. Especially since her fear was so overwhelming that though she tried to hide it, he saw it easily.

He wished he had someone to talk to about it. Or that she did.

"Alex Reynolds. Is that you finally home from New York?" a female voice asked.

Alex turned toward the woman whose presence in Tierra del Verde had drawn him there. His closest neighbor and a force to be reckoned with, Helena Conwell Kane ran the third largest ranch in the area. Single-handedly, as she was sadly estranged from her Texas Ranger husband.

Then he remembered Helena's story and her connection to Patience. Without another thought, Alex rushed up the walkway and scooped Helena into an enthusiastic hug. "Yes. Yes, I'm home. And I've married," he whispered and quickly outlined her connection to Amber and that Patience desperately needed a friend.

Helena once had been in slightly similar circumstances and was a person who might be able to teach Patience how to leave the past where it belonged.

In the past.

Patience watched from several yards away as Alexander hugged the woman who'd called out to him. She had to wonder if her problems had conspired to force him to put aside plans with this pretty woman for whom he obviously cared. Had he lied about that?

Giving her head a slight shake, she berated herself. While on the trail she'd begun to speculate on Alexander's needs and expectations in spite of all he'd promised. What would their bedroom arrangements be at his home? How would they hide the fact that they didn't share a bed from servants who might talk? Had that been his plan all along, to force the issue?

She'd gotten more and more on edge the closer they'd come to Tierra del Verde and the Rocking R. And only moments before, when she'd stiffened at his touch, he'd probably heard that awful title—spawn of Satan—echoing in his mind.

She should have stopped dead on the platform back in San Antonio and demanded to know what he'd meant when he'd said he wanted everyone to think theirs was a love match. When he'd said he wanted to weave a web of security about her, the image of an insect struggling for freedom from a web, while the spider approached, had flashed into her mind. It was an image she could not yet banish.

Alexander had whispered something before he'd stepped back from his lady friend, as if realizing how scandalous their public display of affection could appear. He seemed to have forgotten his plan to portray them be a love match. Instead he looked at this woman as if she were an answer to prayer.

"Helena Kane, please greet my wife, Patience. And Patience, I'd like you to meet the reason I came to Tierra del Verde and made it my home."

Patience's heart sank and she stifled a deep sigh. So she'd been right. He'd lied.

"I'm so pleased to meet you," Helena Kane said with a wide welcoming smile. "You must forgive your clumsy-tongued husband. What he meant is his cousin, Lord Jamie, insisted he hand-deliver a letter to me. Alex and I became friends but that hardly makes *me* the reason he settled here. Now tell me all about you two. How did you hog-tie this confirmed bachelor into marriage?" She beamed another sunny smile Patience's way.

Confused, Patience tried to process all the information Mrs. Kane had given. There was something just out of reach, evading her. Unable to grasp whatever it was, she switched tracks and focused on the one revelation she'd managed to decode.

Patience had no reason to feel guilty about separating lovers. No *added* reason. She was still guilty of—what had Mrs. Kane called it?—hog-tying Alexander. He'd even tried to scare her away the night before the ceremony. No matter how attentive he seemed it was only unselfish kindness on his part. She'd taken the freedom he'd apparently prized. Most people would think the least she could do was give him her body as payment. But just the idea of that threw her into a breath-stealing panic.

"I have a wonderful idea," she heard Alexander say. "Why don't you two ladies go have tea in the hotel dining room while the rest of us get signed in and settled. You can talk of fashion and mysterious woman things. And, Helena, you can explain to Patience all about tomorrow's festivities."

"Alex tells me we have a friend in common," Helena said. "A school friend of yours. Amber Dodd... Oh, no. It's Reynolds now. Or more importantly, Countess Adair. Did you ever hear such a romantic story as theirs? It's like a fairy tale." Helena frowned slightly as if considering something deep. "Except, of course, there was no wicked stepmother or dragon and her prince is really an earl." She laughed as she held out her hand but the sound was tinged with sadness. "Come. We simply must compare notes. Your arrival is the most interesting thing to happen around here all summer."

Patience saw little else to do but to let the young woman pull her into the unexpectedly elegant hotel. And to call her Helena as she insisted.

The dining room was lovely. Classic features of bright white woodwork, coffered ceilings and rich brocade cushions reminded Patience of the beautiful, safe train car.

"So. Tell me how the romance is going," Helena said as they were seated at their table.

Patience could only stare across at her. What to say? "I don't think that is any of your—"

"Oh, goodness." Helena put a hand to her heart. "I haven't forgotten my manners that much since arriving in the West. I meant Lord Jamie and Amber's romance. I have a vested interest in their being tremendously happy since it's my fault they married in the first place."

It took Patience a moment to finally make the connection. This was *the* Helena—Helena Conwell. The woman Amber had been impersonating when she'd met Alex's cousin Jamie aboard a clipper on the way to California. Patience supposed it was a symptom of her life and her desperate circumstances that this subject had never arisen between her and Alex.

Thinking of Amber, Patience smiled, wanting to tell the happy news from Amber's last letter. She began carefully. "Amber hoped she was about to add to her nursery again this year but she sailed for Ireland before it was certain. I met Alexander while working as governess to Amber's stepdaughter."

"Alex whispered of our connection through your friend," Helena said. "Also that he hopes we can be friends. I'm so glad you and Alex fell in love."

Patience blinked. How had Helena gotten that idea? Perhaps because it was what Alexander wanted everyone to think. "Not all marriages are for love. Some are out of obligation," she said, vaguely needing to interject some truth into the conversation.

Helena tilted her head then wistful sadness swept across her face. "Marriage should *only* be about love."

From what Amber had said in her letters, Patience knew they were both a few years older than Helena, but in experience, Patience felt like a backward girl who'd never been allowed out in the world. While the years of her marriage to Edgar made her feel old and tired and used. She sighed. "It would be a happier world if love was all that mattered to anyone, wouldn't it?" she said.

Helena nodded. "Indeed," she agreed with determined cheerfulness. "Now, I am supposed to tell you about the celebration tomorrow. You're going to love it here."

Leaving town the morning after the Founders' celebration was a relief. Alex simply couldn't wait to see the house. Patience seemed glad to be on the road, too. Being out in the open among strangers the day before had made her anxious. He'd noticed her eyes were never still when they were in public. Her hand on his arm would tighten if a man passed them on the street. The picnic seemed to be particular torture for her. Seeing her so tense, he'd suggested they skip the dance at Helena's and rest up for their first day of work at the new house. He was confident she would eventually face her anxiety head-on as she had every problem thus far. Until then he'd be there to smooth over her transition.

The informal meeting with Mayor Angelo and the rest of the town council had gone well. As he'd hoped, the men were so grateful for the pledge of materials to build the school and the land he'd loaned the town, they didn't even mention checking Patience's credentials.

Half an hour after leaving town on Monday morning they turned off the main road between Tierra del Verde and the next town, Mountain Home, onto the main trail through the Rocking R. The road began to climb almost immediately to the newly built heart of the ranch. "We're almost there," he told everyone in the carriage. "I hope it's right."

Patience smiled up at him. "Alexander, you've been acting like my brothers did on Christmas morning. Mr. O'Hara said the house is exactly like the drawing. Wasn't the house nearly finished when you left?"

He winced before saying, "There were elements that hadn't been added yet."

"Elements?"

"A porch and the second-floor gallery above it. Though I did see the decorative iron work that was to be used as railings."

She tilted her head and looked up at him, smiling in a way that seemed indulgent. Better than fear. Infinitely better. Then she said, "Why don't you ride ahead?"

He wanted to but he knew he shouldn't. Still, she'd brought it up. "You wouldn't mind?"

Heddie snorted. "It'd be better than watching you ride ahead then turn to race back. I think you've covered the territory since we left town twice. You're worse than a child with a yo-yo. Up. Back. Up. Back. And that horse of yours is a far sight bigger than one. Go!"

Alex didn't need to be told twice. He wheeled Big Boy then urged the gelding into a canter along a trail through a dense thicket of pecan, mesquite and madrone trees.

After a few minutes the trail twisted left then right. It led him to the cluster of buildings off to the left at the bottom of the hill. The stable and log bunkhouse had been there when he'd bought the ranch but that was all. The first building he'd added was a foreman's cottage for Michael O'Hara and his wife. Next had come the carriage house with the upper-floor living area where he'd stayed on his visits there. The lower floor had sheltered the building materials for the house, but was now the home of the landau and the gig. There was still an empty cottage where he would put Virgil, Willow and Jerome.

And up on the rise, in the shade of two ancient live oaks and one huge madrone, sat the completed house. It looked wonderful. Perfect.

Alex sat back in the saddle and let out the breath he hadn't even known he'd been holding. It was a home to be proud of. Smaller to be sure than Adair had been, but that place had never been home. It had been the stuff of nightmares and Alex never wanted to step foot there again. The murders, the close calls with Jamie's life, the beatings for them both.

It was all there in the cellar of his soul, always lurking, waiting to emerge and torture him. That place would dig it all up and swallow him whole. No, if he never saw the gray stone of Adair or even the white cliffs of Dover, it would be too soon.

"Alexander," he heard Patience call and realized it had happened again. The memories had come to the fore, ready to spoil what should be a happy event. He wouldn't let them. No. He wouldn't let *his father* win. Nor would he spoil Patience's day by explaining how much he'd come to loathe his given name. His mother had never called him anything but Alex, nor did Jamie anymore, either. Alexander had been his father's name for him.

Shaking off the specter of the past, he turned in the saddle and plastered on a smile. Then her gaze rose to the house and the genuine smile that tipped her lips changed his to a smile he truly felt. How could anyone hold on to a nightmare when a dream sat before him? What a gift having her stumble into his life had become.

He turned back to the house. And stared, shocked. Though he cared about this place, whose every board and stone he'd helped choose, that feeling paled in comparison to what he was beginning to feel for her. But only beginning, he assured himself. It was only desire and wanting to see her happy and secure. That was all, he assured himself.

One more day and you'd have missed even meeting her.

The thought was almost frightening. But for her. Not him. He could have done without her. Of course he could. He wanted her. That was only natural. She was a beautiful woman who had become his wife. That was all there was to it.

But in a small secret corner of his heart, he wished it could be more.

"Shall we proceed?" he asked her.

Patience nodded. "It's so lovely, I cannot wait to see the inside." But he couldn't help noticing how tightly clasped her hands were. Did that display excitement or terror? Or had she seen into the darkness of his soul when the past had grabbed his thoughts?

Unsure, he pivoted Big Boy, urging him into a gallop. Minutes later he dismounted and hurried up the walk to the porch then unlocked the door. The air was stuffy and the place did look like a furniture warehouse. But the temperature was relatively cool thanks to the thick limestone walls. That coolness was the only hospitable thing about the interior unfortunately. He walked through the first floor, skirting crates, opening the windows and the double doors that led from the parlor onto the porch. He did the same in the dining room. The French style made this house different from Jamie's house in San Francisco, just as he'd planned.

Fighting the memories of that fateful night of fire and death, Alex shook his head. When he'd come to the Rocking R, he'd been running from more than his reputation in England as Oswald Reynolds's son. He'd been on the run from those new memories, too.

He hadn't wanted his own home to remind him of that night. This one didn't. He looked toward the jangling sound of the harnesses and hurried back out and across the porch to meet the landau.

"It's wonderful," Patience called as he trotted down the front walk.

"The architect calls it French Second Empire."

"The roof line is quite singular," Winston said as he climbed down and turned to help Heddie alight on the far side. Willow bounced down after her to go and hug Virgil in obvious excitement, leaving Patience staring up at the house, still in the carriage.

"He called it a mansard roof," Alex told the elderly butler. What the hell was he going to do with a butler, anyway? He'd never had any servants of his own before and now he had a house full. Oddly even that felt right. Perhaps sometimes in life one got what one needed, not what one thought they wanted. He certainly hadn't thought he needed a wife or a house full of adoring servants, just as, until arriving in Tierra del Verde, he hadn't known he'd needed a home or a cattle ranch. Yet all of it felt right. Once again came the unbidden thought—*Patience feels right.*

Patience is temporary, he told himself.

"The roof certainly is unique," she said, still gazing upward, then she added in a dreamy voice, "Oh, and

look. There are dormers on the third floor. I always
wanted a window seat in my room when I was a child.
May I make my room up there?"

He had to wonder if she'd made that request so her
room was as far from his as possible. "You may light
anywhere you wish but that floor was left open for
parties and such. Besides that, even though the house
is shaded and the limestone tends to keep the inside
relatively cool, the third floor can get awfully warm in
summer."

Texas, even in Hill Country, was much warmer in
summer than England or Ireland, but the mildness of
the winters more than made up for the few months of
ninety-degree summer days there in the hills. The tall
arched windows on the first and second floors would
ventilate the house well during the hot summer months.

She bit her lip. "I suppose. Is that why all the windows on the first and second floors are so large?"

He nodded.

"Well, I think it's a right fine house, Mr. Alex,"
Heddie said.

"It is, Alexander," Patience added. "It really is quite
lovely. I think my favorite thing so far is the fretwork
on the porch and the way it mirrors the arch of the
windows."

"That's the cast iron I spoke of earlier. I'm actually
partial to the inside."

"I cannot wait to see it," Patience said and stood to
alight, her hand gracefully gripping one of the steel ribs
to the folding top.

Alex grinned and stepped in front of her, looking
up into her grass-green eyes. They fairly sparkled. She
seemed to have forgotten her nervousness in her excite-

ment over the house, endearing the place to him further. "O'Hara didn't exaggerate. There is a lot to do in there."

She put her hand out to him but he shook his head as he took note of the others proceeding into the house. "We can't know the future. Suppose through some miracle we find common ground and manage to build a future together. I can't stand the thought that if we succeed, one day you'll look back and regret missing all the special parts of a new marriage. So, please, allow me to carry you over our threshold."

She reached out both hands this time and settled them on his shoulders. "You have a real problem assuming guilt for things that aren't your fault," she told him when he lifted her down and set her before him on the ground. "You didn't wed me to fulfill any romantic illusions about marriage, but to save me from the reality of a terrible one."

Alex nodded, sad for her. And for himself. What a pair they were!

Chapter Eight

Patience marveled that Alexander could carry her along the lengthy walkway, then up steps and across the porch without becoming even a little winded. She'd acquiesced to being carried across the threshold but not because she cared for the sentiment. It had happened after her first wedding, after all, and had merely signaled the beginning of five years in hell.

Alexander had sounded so sad, though. So she hadn't had the heart to deny him this small symbol. Now she was glad she hadn't. It was little enough, considering all he'd done and still planned to do for her.

With so much going on around them—their baggage being unloaded, Virgil taking the landau off to the carriage house, Heddie fretting about how much had to be done to put the house to rights—Patience had little time to feel much of her usual nervousness at Alexander's nearness.

She looked around as he set her on her feet inside the house in a wide entrance hall. She couldn't help but laugh at his chagrined expression. "Oh, you're right," she said. "It does look like I'd imagine a warehouse would. But think how much fun the unwrapping will be. It is like Christmas today, after all. You were right to be so eager to get here."

Beyond the stacks and stacks of crates she could see light-colored walls. There was a parlor to either side. Surprisingly, they were painted not papered. Though paper was all the rage in New York and London, she shouldn't be surprised Alexander would eschew current fashion. Look how easily he'd switched from up-town gentleman to rough-and-ready rancher. He clearly cared nothing for convention.

The more formal parlor on the right was done in shades of gold like the hall. The less formal parlor was a happy green. Each room had wide elaborate moldings set against the fourteen-foot ceilings. The more formal room had gleaming white woodwork but in the less formal one, like the hall, the woodwork was a darker wood like walnut.

And the windows, framed with the same shining woods, were nearly floor-to-ceiling and also had very unique and regal-looking cornices. She sighed. "It's beautiful, Alexander."

Alexander smiled but it looked a bit tight. She supposed he was upset that it wasn't quite ready to be occupied. "It turned out rather well. Not the least like a wedding cake," he muttered. He seemed to read her confusion. "My cousin's San Francisco house does, you see. Looks like a dammed frothy wedding cake. I wanted something else. *Anything* else."

He looked left then right. "Gawd, this is a mess, isn't it? There's a good deal to do, isn't there? O'Hara went to round up some of the cowboys to help." He looked around again. "It's hard to know where to start."

"A crate at a time," Heddie called from somewhere within the mass of towering crates. "Take your missus on a tour then come back ready to roll up your sleeves. We need to get to work on this if we're to live civilized."

Alexander laughed. "Yes, General Heddie," he called out then and took Patience by the hand. "Ready to inspect your home? You do need to know where all this must land. Otherwise, in spite of our energetic general, I fear we're doomed to live in a forest of crates."

He took her through the house, past the two parlors to the dining room. Next, in its own wing, came the kitchen, which kept the house cooler and allowed cross ventilation to keep the kitchen cool, too. It was modern, well-stocked and ready for Willow, who exclaimed over every corner before she went to work on a noon meal.

Patience learned they had running water thanks to windmill-powered pumps and gas to light the house because there was a gas well on the property, accidentally found as they'd drilled for water.

Impressed, she followed him from the kitchen past the back stairs that led to a wing where the Winstons would live. Virgil, Willow and Jerome would have a cottage to give the little family privacy.

When Patience exclaimed over his wonderful house, she noticed again that he had difficulty accepting compliments. They seemed to embarrass him and he said it was all owed to Giles, the architect.

Alexander pointed out his study across from the dining room. Which gave her an idea. That room would be her project and the first room to be put right. He had done so much for her, it was the least she could do for him.

Mr. O'Hara, wearing a sarcastic grin, came in through the back hall door with four men. "This is all I could round up. Most of them headed for the hills when they heard they'd be at Heddie and my wife Moira's mercy."

Alexander laughed. "I think we're equal to the task and the taskmasters." He clapped his hands together. "So let's get at this." Patience glanced up the stairs, torn. She wished he'd had the time to take her through the rest of the house yet she was relieved since all the rooms upstairs were bedrooms.

Patience was given the master bedroom at Alexander's insistence. He told Heddie to put his things in the smallest room, reserving the other two for possible guests. Patience had tried to protest that she should have the small room, but she lost the battle. She let herself be led upward by Moira O'Hara to change into one of Amber's old skirts and shirtwaists.

What ensued was several hours of hard work punctuated with the growth of genuine affection for Moira O'Hara, who'd followed her husband into the house only minutes after the men arrived to help with the unpacking. Between Heddie and Moira those rough cowboys hadn't stood a chance and were soon toting and carrying as willingly as the others. Each screech of a nail being pulled from a crate brought a new surprise all of them awaited with pleasure.

Alexander left for the barn with Michael O'Hara soon after the noon meal, leaving Patience free to dig around and find what she needed to complete the furnishing of his office. She closed the pocket doors just as

Heddie called a halt to the work for the day, announcing that Patience and Alexander were to wash up and sit down like civilized people to enjoy their first evening in their new home.

After bathing and dressing for dinner, Alex stood in the hall and knocked on the door that lead to the master suite. He felt like a fool. He hadn't even known the smallest room actually connected directly to the master bedroom. He supposed it was planned to be a nursery. Mothers in all but the most elite households in America tended to actually mother their children. In the West it was an even more prevalent practice. It was something he found refreshing and touching.

While the house was being built, Alex had been too busy on ranch improvements and learning from Michael O'Hara about running a cattle ranch to really care much about something as unimportant as the layout of the bedrooms. With the exception of listing the colors he didn't want used in the house, he'd left the interior to his architect. He'd found Alfred Giles in San Antonio on the advice of the owner of the lumber company there. Giles had configured the house and decided on the finishes, only checking with Alex on major decisions.

Then he'd had a letter from Jamie saying that as their son was a year old now, his family was leaving for Ireland and Adair. Wanting to say farewell, Alex had headed for New York. Armed with samples of the papers and woodwork color to be used inside in the house, Alex had enlisted Amber's aid on the selection of the furniture, carpets and draperies.

He started when the bedroom door opened and Patience stood before him wearing the dress she'd worn for their wedding. She was no longer disheveled from all the work. Perversely he regretted it. Which was foolish, as she looked so lovely. But her tousled hair, smudged nose and the apron tied around her middle had given him a glimpse of another side of her. The person he'd promised her she'd find again. He wanted to get to know that woman, too.

Just as he wanted to get to know the other side of himself. Except, of course, he wasn't sure if whomever that was still lived in there. He didn't have a clue who he was other than Oswald Reynolds's son and killer and Jamie's cousin and protector. He hadn't begun to know himself by his twelfth birthday when he'd started to live in shadows.

There was no hiding from the light with Patience around. She *was* light. And goodness. And she was his for now, though he couldn't claim her.

But he'd begun to hope he might prove to be worthy of her. Some day. Just as maybe someday she would be able to turn to him.

Knowing what a temptation she'd become, what an added invitation that damned connecting door would be, he took her hand and dropped the key to it in her palm. She looked down at the inside of her door. "I already have a key, Alexander."

He felt his jaws clench at the sound of that name. He was going to have to tell her about the way the sound of that name froze his blood. But it was their first day in the new house. He didn't want to ruin it with bad memories.

So rather than make the name an issue, he nodded stiffly. "I'm aware you have a key to the hall door. You'll remember I asked for the smallest room to leave the other two for guests, but I didn't know the small one was most probably planned as a nursery. Apparently, even though Heddie knows of our circumstance, she put me in there without mentioning that pertinent fact. That is the key to the door between our rooms."

First she paled then she looked down at the key and a blush stole over her creamy cheeks. "I heard murmurs but I didn't realize the door led to another room. To your room."

He raked a hand through his hair. He was going to have to warn Heddie against matchmaking somehow. Patience hadn't given him leave to discuss her history though he'd thought Heddie had a good idea of it. Clearly she didn't understand the hell this woman had lived in or how unsuitable he was as a husband.

"I didn't know until I heard Heddie exclaiming over how lovely you look." He took the key back, wanting to handle the problem himself, after all. Needing to show her he wasn't a threat, he skirted by her, over to the aforementioned door, put the key in the lock and snicked it into the locked position. Then, leaving the key in the lock, he turned back toward her and retraced his steps. She stood motionless, staring at the door to his room, as he passed her once again.

Now that he was safely back in the hall, he looked down at her and smiled, helpless not to. "You do, by the way. Look quite lovely, I mean," he said and offered his arm. "Shall we go and see how much more those busy bees have accomplished since you were banished?"

"We're to have drinks on the porch, Heddie says, as the parlors are still askew." She let him steer her to the stairs.

"I applaud you, you know," he said as they started

downward. "You managed to stay at it much longer than I."

"Yes, I did. And I believe you meant to say that I lasted past when you fled to check on a mare rather than help move the breakfront."

"Move it *again*. Donaldson came and—"

"And Mrs. O'Hara says you don't know a thing about a horse birthing."

Alex attempted to look affronted but he knew he'd failed when she laughed. She had such a beautiful laugh. "I repeat. Again. Move the breakfront *again*. That was the third wall Heddie wanted to see it placed against," he said as they turned into the hall toward his study. "It must weigh a ton. And the curious thing is that as I walked back through on my way to bathe and dress, I recall seeing it where *you* first suggested. This is *your* house, sweetheart. Put things where—"

He glanced in the study and the breath left his body. Dear God. How had he been so blind? He'd been in there to open windows. Of course, there hadn't been a desk. Or bookshelves. No tall high-back chairs before the fireplace. No brocade draperies on the window behind the desk. His heart felt as if it were about to pound out of his chest. Or explode in there. It thundered in his ears—a deafening rhythm.

It was the same. The damned dark desk. The ceiling-high bookcases on either side of the draped window, though these shelves weren't filled with his uncle's books.

Just that quickly, Alex was there, transported to that life-altering night. He heard that hateful name. This time his father saw him in the doorway. It was deepest night, then the silence burst wide-open with the report of a gun and blood blossomed on those rich beautiful draperies as his father smiled at him and said, "Congratulate me, boy. I've ascended. Now one day you'll be earl. Happy birthday."

"Alexander? Alexander, are you all right?" He heard Patience this time. Why was she there? Her words flowed through his brain, not understood or retained—perhaps it wasn't her, after all. Someone shook him. Hard. "Alex! Look at me," Patience ordered.

And that quickly he was back. Wrenched from hell. By an angel. The scene faded as if it had never happened. But, of course, it had. It was never, ever, far from the surface. Sometimes he feared his mind would stay there and not return to the here and now.

"Alex, talk to me," Patience demanded. She stood holding his arms, voluntarily standing close in front of him, her clear green eyes filled with concern.

Hearing her voice, feeling her touch, her face filling his mind…all of it brought him the rest of the way home. And he could focus on today. "You called me Alex."

"I'm sorry. You'd grown so pale. I was worried and—"

"No. No, don't apologize. I prefer it. I didn't know how to tell you how much I hate that name. No one calls me Alexander. Primarily my father did. Even my cousin and the countess avoid it these days."

A little frown dented her forehead right between those perfectly arched eyebrows. "Why didn't you tell me? I've told you so much more than I have anyone else."

"My past pales in comparison to what you went through. I'm a man, after all." Embarrassed, he looked away but that set his focus on the room. How had be *been* so blind? And when had he come past the doorway?

"Can you talk about it? About what just happened. Where did you go?"

He blinked and dragged his gaze to hers again. She had taken a step back but that was all. A scent, lilac he thought, surrounded him. "Go somewhere? I was standing right here."

"It happens to me. I know. After I returned to my father's house he kept complaining that I'd stare ahead and not listen to a thing he said. I began to realize things—ordinary things—were sending me back. Back to Edgar."

"When we played chess," he said, only now recognizing fully what he should have seen back then, "I teased you about your grin."

"You called it *a smug smile*. If I won at chess, he'd accuse me of looking smug but if he'd won too easily..." She shook her head. "I couldn't please him."

"Of course you couldn't. He didn't want you to. My mother was wonderful but she couldn't please my father. You're very brave to have played with me that day. And since. And you play to win—you even did that day. And now how am I to tell you of my demon?"

She gave him a wistful smile and the look in her eyes was tinged with sadness. Not pity, thank God. "Your demon is your father. You defeated him. You saved Lord Jamie and Amber and Meara and their staff when he set fire to their house in San Francisco. All I did was wait out Edgar. And run for my sanity when Father tried to send me back into hell with someone else. This isn't about me, though. What sent *you* there just now? What dragged you in here?"

Reluctantly he gestured to the room as the breath gushed out of him. "I've inadvertently let Giles create a library very much like my uncle James's. My only focus when building here was not to recreate Jamie's house in San Francisco."

She frowned. "Your wedding-cake comment," she said, her tone full of realization.

He nodded, feeling much less like a fool because she understood so well. But no more like a man someone as wonderful as her deserved.

"I thought you didn't want to copy him but…it has to do with what happened…what you had to do that night in San Francisco. Am I right?"

"Patricide isn't something I'd aspired to, ya see." He grinned and tried to sound flippant but he didn't quite get the tone right with her standing there *caring* about his damned feelings.

And she wouldn't let him get away with what the others did. As if having learned the gesture she raised an eyebrow and said sharply, "I wouldn't think you had." Then in her kind gentle voice she went on, "Am I right that you picked a style of house as far removed from their house in San Francisco as possible so the memories wouldn't surprise you?" She glanced down the hall that led to the small side porch. "It's a lovely evening. Suppose we go away from here and out to enjoy the back porch and the sunset."

He nodded. Cowardly though it seemed, he didn't want to be in there with his nightmare even a moment longer. As they stepped outside, the air, the setting sun and the rolling valley beyond seemed to release some of the pressure crushing his lungs.

Patience led him to a singularly perfect tableau. Two ladder-back rocking chairs sat waiting with a small table between them and a pitcher of lemonade. "I'm sure you wish this were something stronger," she said and sank gracefully into one of the chairs. He took the other as she filled the glasses then handed him one.

"It's fine," he told her and it was. The memory of his hangover the morning of the wedding ceremony was too close for him to make that mistake. "I'm fine," he added but that was a lie.

He was far from fine. Silence reigned because he had no idea what to say. He must have looked like a lunatic staring into an empty room as if a scene were going on before him. Leaning his head back, Alex let the breeze flow by.

The repeating *peew, peew, peew* call of a black-crested titmouse broke the silence. He counted seven *peews* before silence fell again. It was always between five and seven. He wondered why. Five, six, seven. Could a bird count?

"Alex." Hearing his name drew him out of his busy mind. His purposely busy mind. "Are you in there?" she asked. "I asked if you'd planned on coming here to heal."

He shrugged and nodded as a coyote howled in the distance.

"And now instead you're saddled with me and my problems. I'm so sorry I've added to your burden."

He leaned forward in his chair and glanced at her. She sat next to him, gripping the arms of the chair. The setting sun formed a nimbus about her hair, making it look as if it were afire. It matched the glow that radiated compassion from her eyes. Even with all the past haunting her and her fear of being followed, she sat there feeling concern for him. That inner light of hers warmed his soul and strengthened his spirit.

He didn't deserve a woman like her but oh, how he needed one. Needed her. In his life. Till death parted them. For that to happen he had to find a way to keep the memories from intruding. From defining him. Until then he was too damaged to offer anything but trouble.

"No," he told her. "Don't feel that way. You've lessened the weight on my shoulders. Helping you has helped me. It's made me begin to look outside myself. I tend to brood, you see. I'm sure the look of the study just caught me unaware," he said, but the boy cried out from behind the walls of his adult facade.

I'm still pretending. Pretending is what I do. Even to myself. It's happened before. I know where I go, I just don't know why or how.

"Suppose you let me help you," she said as if she'd heard his silent plea—as if she'd seen past the facade.

Could he let her see it all and have her not fear him more than she already did? No. He wasn't who she thought. He wasn't who anyone thought. Sometimes he even fooled himself but he didn't know *who* he was.

I don't know how to come out from behind the mask.

"There's no help for the past. Looking toward the future is the answer. I learned that at a very young age. It's called survival."

Chapter Nine

Patience woke to the sound of an animal in pain. She'd heard it several nights now. Each day she and the young boys living on the Rocking R had gone in search of it. But to no avail. There was no trace of an injured animal near the house.

Tonight the sound was louder. Closer. She sat up. Perhaps if she woke Alexander he could—

She winced. *Alex*—she really must remember to call and think of him exclusively as Alex. She'd mistakenly called him Alexander a few times since he'd told her his feelings. She'd done it that evening, in fact. She had to get that name he hated so much out of her mind. Whenever she made the mistake, she noticed the muscle in his jaw tighten. She didn't think his reaction was anger at her, but at the man who'd used it exclusively. His horrible father.

The sound came again. It was a person in pain. Terrible pain. She swiveled her head toward it. It came from within the house and it was Alex. She couldn't listen and not try to help him.

Tossing back the covers she stood. The walk to the door separating them seemed to take forever but another low cry pulled her toward him. She reached for the strength to unlock the door and another cry had her turning the key in the lock and all but running toward him in a heartbeat.

Sconces lit the room, revealing Alex lying on the bed atop the covers, fully dressed and writhing as if he were in pain. "No," he cried. "Don't. Please don't."

So much for survival, she thought. Before she had a chance to decide what to do for him, Alex bounded up. His tear-filled eyes were wide and tortured. He stared ahead, blankly, sweat glistening on his face, tears tracking down his cheeks.

"Alex, wake up," she whispered as calmly as she could manage.

He looked over at her, his expression clearly said he wasn't sure she was real, and then it changed to embarrassment. She hoped he accepted her help this time.

"Are you all right?" she asked.

He shook his head and looked away. Then he lied. "Of course. What brings you into the lion's den?"

She ignored his smart mouth and his lie, and sat in silence, watching him. He'd flopped back to his pillows and covered his eyes with his bent arm, as if denying her presence and the reason for it. "Go," he whispered. "Go back to your room where none of this can touch you. It's better that way."

"You said helping me has helped you. Was that true or have I done this to you?"

He sighed. "You haven't made this—whatever it is— worse. Helping you has at least given me some purpose beyond learning about the ranch. I know now it would never have been enough."

"Then perhaps helping you will likewise help me. Would you deny me that solace? Please, don't shut me out. Let me try. And please don't lie. I heard you shouting. Have heard for several nights."

She dragged a small chair next to the bed. "Tell me what you dream of. Tell me where you went when you first saw your study."

He swallowed as if trying to swallow the words she could see he longed to say.

"I need the words, Alex," she urged. "I need to help. Please."

It all seemed to pour out of him then. For her sake, not his. "I walked in on it," he said starkly. "I walked in and saw my father kill Uncle James."

She knew she didn't keep the shock from her expression or her voice. "Your father killed his own brother?"

He nodded. "Jamie never knew. I was too ashamed to tell him. I told myself all along that I'd explain it when he was old enough to keep it a secret and strong enough to protect himself. But by the time he was old enough, strong enough, we were estranged."

He thought having an abusive husband and a father she could no longer trust was worse than *this*? At least she'd been an adult when all that had come down on her head! He'd been a boy. "And you saw him kill his brother?" She blinked, as a revelation came to her. "It happened in your uncle's study?"

He raked a hand through his hair. "You are too intelligent by half. My office is arranged exactly as Uncle James's was at Adair."

"Have you told your cousin? Perhaps if you tell him you would be better able to deal with it."

"It came out that night. In San Francisco. No. Not all of it. I lied about some of it. I had to. I told him Uncle James never knew what was about to happen. Why make Jamie suffer more? But Uncle James *did* know. He'd fallen asleep at his desk. I arrived as my father woke him to tell him he was about to kill him and that Jamie would join him soon. Then my father pulled the trigger."

Alex swallowed, going pale as a sheet. "His head…" He closed his eyes then quickly opened them again and she saw fear and a hazy disconnect with her.

"Alex," she said, her voice as sharp as she could make it. She had to call him back from the precipice in his mind. She knew from experience memories could be frighteningly compelling. "Alex! Look at me," she demanded.

He did. And blinked, then looked toward the sconces as if afraid to see her expression or hear her reaction. "I know how this feels. I do understand."

"Really? What if I'd called out? Could Uncle James have saved himself?"

"That is nonsense. You were a child!"

"I loved it there at Adair. Did I simply let it happen? Am I as bad as he? As evil?"

She took a moment to modulate her tone. All he would hear in her voice was the respect she had for him. Because it was just a sliver of what she'd begun to feel. "Alex? You were how old?"

"Twelve. It was my twelfth birthday. I haven't celebrated another since."

"So you blame Billy Harken for what happened to his parents and sisters before the O'Haras took him in."

"No. Of course not! But I kept silent all those years. No, that isn't true. I told my mother a year later. On the day he tried to kill Jamie. He'd done something to Jamie's little skiff. It sank. I saved him but it was a near thing. I'd promised to keep him safe and almost failed. I confessed to her that night. I never thought she'd face him with it. But she did. He killed her and made it look like an accident."

If she'd have guessed at what drove him—haunted him—it would never have been this bad. "How did you put it together? When did you?" she asked.

He shook his head. "I must have been blind because I didn't. That night in San Francisco, the night of the fire, he admitted he'd killed her," Alex said, his voice raw, his emotions clearly stripped bear. "The mind is a mystery. It was all there but somehow I managed not to see. She was so graceful it never made sense that she'd fall down the stairs. I suppose I couldn't face the guilt. I caused her death, after all."

Patience felt as if her head would explode she was so angry. Her emotions must have shown because he looked away. How typical of him not to get angry in return. "You?" she asked. "You did nothing any child of that age wouldn't. You went to an adult. To your mother. You have no guilt in *any* of this."

Alex stared at her. "You don't understand. When he admitted it, I *still* didn't kill him. Why? Why wait until he'd set fire to Jamie's house endangering everyone there? Why wait until he'd shot at my cousin?"

"Your mother was dead and the man, however

odious, was still your father. You fired the gun when he gave you no choice if you were to save Lord Jamie."

"But why did I wait all those years with Jamie in danger? Maybe I didn't kill him before because I'm like—"

"Stop right there," she ordered. She'd been angry before. Now she was furious. He looked as if his spirit had been dragged backward through a keyhole. "Like him? You're afraid you're like him?"

She didn't wait for an answer. She already knew it. It was written on his dear face before he looked down. "You waited because you aren't a coldblooded killer. Had you fired in vengeance after learning about your mother, you *would* be like him. You waited because we love our parents. We just *do*. Even when they don't deserve it. When they hurt us. I don't think there's reason involved. We just *do*. *You* are who *you* are and *he*—God curse his soul—was who *he* was."

Alex's tired tortured eyes rose to meet her gaze. "I should let myself believe you, shouldn't I? Maybe if I did, I'd be able to move ahead. I'd be able to begin to believe I deserve to have someone so pure in my life. Maybe if guilt didn't haunt me, I could start to trust in who I am."

His gaze caressed her face then drifted downward, reminding her she wore only her flannel nightgown. Her every muscle tightened. She was so damaged. He'd said he didn't deserve her. No he didn't. He deserved someone better, someone whole. She told him so and left.

But she didn't lock the door. She wouldn't reinforce all those naysayers who'd judged him by the actions of his cursed father. *Spawn of Satan? I think not.*

Chapter Ten

Two weeks after they'd arrived in Tierra del Verde, Patience sat on a blanket near the stream behind the site of the schoolhouse. *Her* schoolhouse. Her back resting against a tall wide elm, she watched the men raise the first wall. She could hardly believe how quickly life had begun to fall into place.

"The walls should all be erected by the end of the day," Alex said as he returned to her side. "You're sure you're satisfied with the plans?"

She looked up and smiled. "Satisfied? I'm thrilled beyond measure. You altered the plans so easily after we talked to Abby Wheaton."

He shrugged, still unable to accept praise. She vowed to continue trying to make him see his value. She watched him sink to the blanket and prop his forearm on one upraised knee. "Jamie was interested in engineering, so over the years I've borrowed some of his books. The how and why of building is fascinating. This is a simple structure." He smiled that pulse-pounding smile of his. "I've decided I like simple."

She looked toward the town. Some would call it crude just because it wasn't in the middle of a bustling city. But it wasn't. It was just so much simpler here. Less oppressive and complicated. "I like it here, too. It's worked out well that Joshua and Abby Wheaton had begun to plan for a school and are willing to share the cost.

"I'm beginning to think your belief that Divine Providence sent you here applies to me, as well. I guess some would call it coincidence that I came here and met Helena Kane, the woman Amber was impersonating when she met your cousin. Then I find that Abby Wheaton is Amber's best friend from childhood."

"Your connections here aren't really a coincidence," Alex said. "Abby and Joshua Wheaton wanted to settle in the West partly to be near her brother, who is married to Helena. He also wanted to get away from mine engineering. Starting a bank with his inheritance was a good idea. Though their plan to be near her brother apparently worked out as badly as Helena's marriage to him."

"I suppose that does make sense but I like the idea that God has a hand in all of it. And I'm glad they came here. Amber told me so many wonderful stories about Abby and her family over the years, it makes me feel at home."

He nodded and glanced at the men building the school. The pounding of hammers had fallen silent. "Here comes the second wall," he said as several men raised it. "You'll be ringing the school bell before you know it. So tell me, how do you think you'll handle teaching that boy of theirs?" he asked his gaze suddenly intense.

"Daniel Wheaton?"

"I had pictured your students as small apple-cheeked children, not young men who tower over you."

She chuckled. "The towering part isn't that unusual. My brothers were already taller than me when they died. And don't worry about Daniel. Though he's up there trying to do the work of a man, he's still just a twelve-year-old boy. A tall boy, who according to Abby has shot up at an alarming rate since they came west, but he's a boy nonetheless."

"I suppose that's true. He seems like a nice lad and he's so excited about going back to school, he begged me to let him help out. I just didn't want you to be afraid, that's the only reason I mentioned him. Now, as one wall frame being nailed to the floor is pretty much like the next and the next, would you like to go for lunch at the hotel?" Alex stood and held his hand out to her. "I need to see to a few things in town."

Alex wouldn't leave her there alone, nor would she be comfortable if he did. He was kind not to point out what an utter coward she was. "Lunch sounds wonder- ful. It's such a beautiful day." She put her hand in his and allowed him to help her to her feet. That sort of contact had grown easier since the night she'd gone to wake him from his nightmare. "Could we walk, do you think? I used to love taking long walks."

They left the gig at the school and started out for the town center. Not five minutes later they rounded the corner of the first building in town. A loud bellow erupted from inside and Alex gripped her shoulders to stop her forward movement as a man came flying out of the swinging doors to land in the street at her feet.

The man stood up quickly, dust swirling off him into the air. He glared at her, his face beet-red with anger.

"Women!" he sneered and picked up his hat as Patience took a stumbling step backward. As she did Alex stepped in front of her, but the man whirled away and started toward the boardwalk as if he intended to return inside.

A woman stormed through the swinging doors of the establishment called the Golden Garter Saloon, her eyes wild with anger. Because Alex was trying to shield Patience from the altercation, she didn't have much time to see what the woman wore, but the impression was that her attire was bright and scandalously brief.

"You ever put your filthy hands on my baby again," the woman screamed, "they'll be calling you Stumpy. You got it? Now get on out of here. Go on. Find your drink and women over in Mountain Home."

"Baby?" he bellowed. "She's a full-grown woman. Near to it anyhow. And I ain't goin' nowhere. I rode to town with my boss, you harpy. I got the same rights as you. More. I'm a decent man."

"Decent? If I ain't decent, neither are you since you don't mind getting sweaty on my sheets with one of my girls. Stay out of the Garter. You're not welcome here." With that said, she turned and disappeared into a world Patience could only guess at.

The man radiated anger as he stepped close to Alex. "What are you looking at, Reynolds? And who you got hiding back there? Your woman too good to look on the likes of me?"

She could feel Alex fighting the urge to silence the man with his fists. He chose words instead but Patience got the idea it was a near thing. "I suggest you shut your filthy mouth before I put you back in the dirt. And I'd prefer to be left out of your problem with Sally Martin. Ah, good afternoon, Sheriff," he added, just after she heard the tread of boot heels on the boardwalk. She peeked around Alex's arm.

A tall rangy man in his mid-twenties with vibrant blue eyes, a gun at his hip and a star on his leather vest strode down the wooden steps. "Move along, Lynch," Sheriff Quinn ordered. "Reynolds wants no part of your arguments. You're welcome to sleep it off over in one of my cells if you feel the need to continue causing trouble."

"I checked my gun in there and the whore didn't give it back. I want my revolver."

Quinn punched the man square in the mouth. Lynch landed on his rear end in the street. "Learn to watch that mouth and you may reach thirty with your front teeth. There's a lady present, you sorry—" The sheriff seemed to have remembered she was present just in time to stifle her education in coarse male talk. She was supremely grateful to his mother, wherever the dear lady was. "Tell you what," Sheriff Quinn told Lynch, "I'll get your forty-five and keep it safe at the jail. You go sleep it off somewhere and come see me before you leave town."

"You expect me to go walking around with no firearm?"

"Don't worry, Lynch. I'll keep you safe," Quinn said in a sardonic tone.

Much grumbling ensued as Lynch got to his feet. "Fine, but she's the one havin' people tossed in the street and keeping their property. That's thievin' where I come from." Cursing, the man stomped off.

Sheriff Quinn and Alex shook hands then Alex stepped to the side to include Patience. "Thanks," he said. "I didn't want to have to plant a facer on him when I have my wife with me. Patience, this is Ryan Quinn, sheriff of Tierra del Verde."

"I gathered as much," she muttered.

Sheriff Quinn grinned and tipped his hat. "Pleased to meet you, ma'am. Sorry I missed your arrival in town. I was off handling a problem."

"Pleased to meet you, as well. Thank you for your timely arrival. Is your hand all right?" she asked. His knuckles were bleeding.

He looked at it in surprise. "It'll be fine," he said and pulled a handkerchief out of his back pocket to wrap it around his hand in a crude bandage. He seemed embarrassed that she'd noticed.

"How did that problem turn out?" Alex asked.

Sheriff Quinn shook his head. "Their tracks ended at the river. I couldn't find where they came out. I have my ideas but—" He flicked his gaze to her. "I'll get to the bottom of it."

Alex nodded, clearly understanding the meaning of the sheriff's abbreviated end of the conversation. "Let me know if there's any way I can help."

"So what's Lynch's problem with you?" Quinn asked.

"He still holds a grudge because O'Hara fired him for being disrespectful to Mrs. O'Hara. I wasn't even in the damned state at the time."

"Lucien Avery hired him again so I don't know what he's angry about."

"So Lynch said. He also said Avery's in town. I need to see him. O'Hara says our fence was down out at the canyon between his spread, mine and Shamrock. I wondered if he's had any similar trouble."

Quinn's eyes sharpened. Even the shadow cast by his wide-brimmed hat couldn't hide the interest in those startling blue eyes. "You missing cattle?"

Alex didn't seem to notice the sheriff's pointed interest. "Just the fence. It's pretty rugged up there for the cattle. There were tracks of several shod horses," he added casually. "It bothers O'Hara."

Their conversation was so oddly cryptic that she lost interest and transferred her attention to the town. This was where her students lived, or shopped and worshipped with their parents. She should get used to walking where they did. *You're free and you're safe here,* she told herself.

"Alex, would you mind if I went ahead to the general store? I wanted to check with Abby about the slates I need for the children."

Alex looked at her for a long moment then glanced toward the general store as if measuring the distance. She knew it wasn't to control her movements but to ensure her safety and comfort.

Her feelings for Alex had quickly become a puzzle whose key she had yet to discover. She no longer feared him. But there was that feeling that stole over her when they were alone. Or even if they weren't, when he touched her. Sometimes if he even smiled at her or looked at her as if he might admire her. Her stomach muscles would tighten just like the night she'd gone to him to stop his nightmare. Whenever it happened, she wanted to flee. It happened again right then.

"I'll be fine. Won't I, Sheriff?" she asked, sounding

a bit as if she'd run all the way to the store and back already.

Ryan Quinn nodded. "I haven't seen any strangers in town. You should be just fine."

"I'll be along in a few minutes, sweetheart," Alex said with a slightly mischievous grin.

He was always doing that these days. Using endearments in front of others. She nodded, feeling even more jittery now. As she fled she looked back. He was still smiling after her. Her stomach did a few quick somersaults and her heartbeat quickened. How she'd stand much more of this strange tension, she didn't know. If only she understood it.

As she reached for the door handle of the general store, Patience realized how horribly unladylike she must have looked all but running down the street. She glanced back, happy to find Alex engrossed in his conversation again.

Relieved, she straightened her shoulders, checked the fall of her skirt and pulled the screen door open. It squeaked then slapped shut behind her. Abby Wheaton, her head bent over some sort of bookkeeping journal, looked up and smiled.

"Patience. Good day to you. Still enjoying our town, I hope. Were you over at the school? Daniel said they were going to frame the walls today."

Patience walked up to the counter where Abby was working on a journal. "We watched the first two go up. It's exciting to see it move ahead so rapidly. But Alex said one wall is much the same as the next and he has errands." She shook her head. "Sometimes I think he works at being a cynic."

Abby grinned and shook her head. "It's a male thing. You get used to it."

"Your Daniel was in the thick of it and having the time of his life."

"Hasn't learned to keep his enthusiasm under wraps. I hope he never does. It's good to see him so eager for school."

Patience smiled remembering him zipping around helping wherever he could. "Well, he'll be able to tell his fellow students he helped quite a bit."

Abby sighed. "He seems to have inherited his talent for building from his uncles."

"Your brother Brendan?" Patience asked, still curious about Helena and her strange marriage.

"That one," Abby said, slapping her pencil onto the journal book, her eyes spitting fire for a moment. But then they softened all the way to sadness. "Yes. Himself…and my brother Michael, who we left back east to run the furniture company Josh owns with him. I miss them both but brothers go off and make lives for themselves, don't they?"

Patience felt the clutch of loss tighten around her heart, the grief made keener by the unexpectedness of it and by the guilt that always filled her. She still feared Edgar had had her mother and brothers killed. And, if he had, part of the blame was hers because she hadn't better hidden her misery from her mother. But then hadn't she told Alex just the other night that his mother's death wasn't his fault? Guilt was insidious, chipping away at the lives of those plagued by it till they had nothing but regret. Which meant Edgar was still winning.

"So tell me, where did Alex get to, then?" Abby

asked. "I don't believe I've ever seen you two lovebirds apart."

Lovebirds? Alex's pretense seemed to be working better than she'd have thought possible. "He's talking to Sheriff Quinn. Something about fences that fell down. I don't know a thing about ranching so I came ahead. I wanted to see if you were able to find those slates in your catalogues that we talked about."

Abby reached under the counter, beaming a smile, and handed her a slate. "Here's the one I got for Daniel last year. I counted the children I thought would attend and ordered extra." Her smile widened. "For the clumsy among them."

Just then the screen door behind her squeaked then slapped shut. Patience turned. Alex filled the doorway and off went her heart pounding again. What was the matter with her?

"Busy planning, are you?" he asked and even she could hear the indulgent tone in his voice.

And that made her all the more nervous. She cleared her throat and in her best schoolteacher voice—one she'd never had the chance to use—she said, "Abby has a slate like the ones she's ordered."

Alex walked across and gazed over her shoulder. "They don't change. Mine looked the same."

The screen slapped again. A young girl walked in and froze. She had gorgeous curling and waving blond hair that hung halfway down her back. She was dressed in a tired old dress that was a bit short. Her big brown eyes veered from Abby to Patience then to Alex then back to Abby.

Then her chin dropped to her chest. "I'm sorry, Mrs. Wheaton, I'll come back later."

Patience looked at Abby, who'd made an almost growling noise under her breath. Abby's eyes burned with anger before she blinked and there was only kindness written there. "Don't be foolish, child. You're always welcome here. What is it I could be gettin' for you today, Sierra?"

"Mam gave me a penny for candy again. But I want you to put it in my bank account. How much do I have in the bank now, ma'am?"

Abby made a big show of looking in the back of her journal. "With interest I'd say at least four-fifty thanks to last week's cleaning money. Keep saving. You'll have a nice nest egg soon enough."

Patience thought it a bit odd that this timid child of perhaps ten or eleven would be so focused on building a bank account. Most timid children wanted only to hang on to their mamas. But children were always a surprise in one way or another. "Sierra, my name is Mrs. Reynolds. I'm the new teacher."

She curtsied nicely but didn't look up. "Yes, ma'am. Everyone knows about you."

"Have you been over to the school?"

She looked up then. The sadness of her carriage was also written in eyes, which were so big and heartbroken it broke Patience's heart in return. "Yes, ma'am. I peeked," she admitted.

Peeked? What an odd thing to say. "Are you looking forward to school starting? Learning is so much fun. Reading alone can take you anywhere a book is set."

"I won't be coming, ma'am."

Perhaps her parents wouldn't allow it. "If your mother and father object, perhaps Mrs. Wheaton and I could talk to them and explain how important education will be for your future in the coming years."

The poor child's complexion went scarlet. She rushed ahead to the counter, handed the penny to Abby then ran back toward the door. On the threshold she pivoted. Tears had already streaked down her cheeks. "I don't have a father. Mam runs the Golden Garter. They won't let no dove's girl come to your fancy school," she cried. Then she was gone.

Patience turned stricken eyes on Alex and he stiffened. He didn't know whether to offer support and comfort or whether he was about to be disappointed in the reason for her expression. Not many women, women of society or of the working class for that matter, would look at the situation differently than little Sierra said, but he hoped Patience would. He waited anxiously.

What will she do?

At last Patience looked at Abby. "I'm so sorry. I didn't know who her mother is," she said, which was still no answer.

"So what is it you're really sayin'?" Abby Wheaton demanded.

"I wouldn't ever want to make a child cry. Does Sally Martin have other children?"

Alex looked at Abby, who stood still, something angry simmering behind her gaze. She shook her head leaving him to answer. "I don't believe so, no," he told Patience.

"Oh, Alex, that means she's the child that awful man tried to—" Her voice broke, unable or unwilling to express her words. She pivoted back to Abby then. "I'm sorry if this makes you angry, and if you and your husband remove your support from the school, then so be it. But…" She turned back at him then, fury and compassion fighting for dominance in her crystal-green gaze.

He wished he hadn't doubted her. He knew instantly what she wanted to say as she stood there giving him another glimpse of her sweet, kind soul. She wanted permission to say what she felt she needed to. But he didn't want her deferring to him. If he had to learn to let go of past guilt, as she'd told him, she had to learn to let go of her fear of offending him. Fear that they had been followed, he understood. He felt it, too. But she had to learn all men were not going to betray and abuse her. "It's your school," he told her. "Follow your instincts."

She nodded. Hesitated. Pursed her lips then after a deep breath said, "Okay. If you do withdraw your support, Alex and I will fund the school on our own. That child will be in a seat on the first day of school. As will Jerome Cabot. If he, Sierra and Billy Harken are the only ones in the desks, then that is who I'll teach."

He waited for the explosion from Abby Wheaton, but they got only a broad smile. "Remove my support? On the contrary. I'll see to it Sally knows Sierra is welcome. You won't find a more apt student than that girl. There may be trouble over it but I'll try to talk to the mothers. I'll make them see reason. How else do they expect her to avoid her mother's fate?" Abby shook her head sadly. "Small-minded witches. It's always the women who turn on their own, isn't it? The men won't care. I expected more trouble over Jerome and that went over just fine. Alex, you've married yourself quite a woman. Congratulations to you."

Patience's gaze flew to his and she blushed prettily but he knew she probably thought he'd gotten the short end of the stick with this marriage. How little she understood all he was coming to feel for her. He'd faced those growing feelings along with the truth she'd helped him face about his past. "I'll accept those congratulations and say Josh Wheaton is every bit as lucky," he told Abby. "Now, let me see that slate. By the way, were you able to find a shipping company to bring the blackboard from San Antonio?"

A few minutes later they left Abby's general store and headed toward the hotel for lunch. As they stepped inside the dining room, Alex felt a spurt of annoyance. He'd wanted Patience to himself but Helena Kane was there. Worse, she was with Lucien Avery, a man he was having trouble trusting. Perhaps because of his worry over their situation with Patience's father searching for her, he'd begun to doubt men he didn't know well. And with Helena being in the company of a man not her husband she could create a scandal. Not that Helena's absent husband inspired loyalty but Alex didn't want anything remarkable noticed about him and Patience. Especially nothing about Patience.

He was about to usher her back out when Helena looked up and saw them. "Alex. Patience," she called out and stood. "Come join us."

"There is nothing subtle about Helena. I suppose now we have no choice," he muttered, and began to lead Patience toward the table.

"It's all right. I'm not so craven that I cannot converse with Helena and her husband."

"That isn't Brendan Kane," he whispered, but then they arrived at the table so he continued his explanation aloud. "Darling," he said, putting his arm around Patience's waist, silently warning Avery off with word and action, "this is our neighbor, Lucien Avery. He shares our northern border. Up where our fence was cut," he added pointedly. "Avery, this is my wife, Patience."

He shook hands with the man but as usual, Avery's smooth hands and demeanor put off Alex. The two of them were of an age, but there was something about Avery that reminded Alex of his dead father. And perhaps that was all there was to it but he vowed to remain cautious. He couldn't imagine a happenstance where their fences being cut on Avery's border could be unimportant. Someone had done it, after all.

With an uncomfortable feeling of being trapped, Alex pulled out the chair next to Helena at the square table for four. He gestured for Patience to sit there, then he sat next to her.

Avery had clearly meant to sit there but Alex wouldn't chance Patience's comfort. "Sorry, old man, I still consider this our honeymoon," he added as he picked up Patience's hand and kissed it. Even though there were public constraints, he couldn't help being pleased that she didn't yank her hand away. He thanked God she was getting used to his touch and that he was getting used to the idea that he had a right to look for happiness with her. And so he went on holding her small hand in both of his.

"No wedding trip?" Avery asked, just a bit too inquisitively.

Was he merely being conversational or was he fishing for information? Alex wondered if he was imagining things.

"I had never been so far south, Mr. Avery," Patience said, surprising Alex. "There was nowhere else I wished to go but to our new home."

"And I make sure my lovely wife gets everything she wants," he added with a smile and a quick squeeze of her hand. She beamed a slightly wobbly smile at him.

And he went instantly hard, thanking God again… but this time for the snow-white tablecloth pooled in his lap.

"I assume that's the reason for this school idea," Avery grumbled. "Just because you want to keep your wife happy, I see no need for a public school here. This is a cattle town. What need of higher learning have these children? And I certainly won't have them taxing me for a school I see no need for."

"Don't be an old stuffed shirt, Lucien," Helena said. "You may marry someday and have children. They'll need educating."

"And they'll receive that education in my home where I can monitor what and how they're taught. Especially as you've allowed an ex-slave to enroll. What kind of education would they get waiting for him to learn?"

"Jerome is the *child* of ex-slaves," Patience all but growled. "Besides that, what has the color of his skin to do with his ability to learn? He's a very apt student already. I went to school to be a teacher of all children."

"I had tutors," Helena said in a way that said Avery had lost several points in her estimation. "It's a sad, lonely, solitary life for a child. The only thing I can imagine sadder would be not to be allowed to learn at all." Then she smiled. Falsely. As if by sheer will, Helena's eyes began to reflect the image she wanted to project. She was more like him than he'd thought.

Alex glanced at Patience. She'd clearly seen Helena's transformation, as well. And he was sure the sad little smile she gave him meant he'd always been as transparent to her. What a lowering thing. Perhaps not only would Helena be able to help Patience, perhaps Patience would help Helena as much as his wife had him.

"Speaking of the school," Helena said, calling them both back to the subject at hand, "how is it coming along?"

Patience blinked and looked back at Helena. "They'd raised the first two walls before we left a while ago. They're probably nearly ready to work on the roof. I'm so excited."

"Still, it doesn't do to have the lower orders too educated," Avery said, refusing to let everyone's feelings about his bombastic opinion silence him.

"Are there any children on your ranch, Helena?" Patience said, ignoring Avery.

"Three. The Mallory children. They're all going to attend," Helena said with a sharp glance at Avery. "Rest assured there *is* a need for the school."

"We also have Billy Harken coming. He works in our stable but only so he doesn't feel he's living on charity. Moira O'Hara told me about the death of his parents."

Avery's interest suddenly sharpened. "Is that where the boy got to?"

"He made it to the Rocking R that day? Poor kid remembers fishing that morning but nothing at all about the raid. Doc says it's a common happenstance after a terrible event combined with a head injury. He doesn't believe it will reverse," Alex lied smoothly.

"What a blessing he doesn't remember something so awful," Helena said.

"I had intended to buy out the mortgage. Now that his folks are gone the boy has little need of a farm," Avery said. "Joshua Wheaton refused to sell me the papers. Would you talk to the boy for me? If he doesn't sell soon, it'll go for taxes, anyway. Stupid idea…a farm around here with all the rock in the ground."

Alex tilted his head and pretended to consider it but he had no intention of doing anything like that. Back in March Billy had crawled under the house after being wounded during the raid that killed his parents and younger sisters. He'd shown up at the Rocking R in sad shape, according to O'Hara. When he'd survived thanks to Doctor Clemens and Moira O'Hara's nursing, Michael took the boy in and let him think he had a job. Young Billy swore, though dressed as Comanches, the attackers had been Anglos. Which fit with Quinn's theory, since he said the horses had been shod in both raids. Because the boy was his only witness, Quinn wanted to keep the evidence under wraps.

To both O'Hara and Sheriff Quinn and now Alex, too, it seemed too much of a coincidence that both the Harken and Ruiz farms had marched along Avery's border and were the only prime farmland in the area. It seemed odd, too, that both places had been raided by a supposed final defiant renegade band of the once fierce Comanche tribe. Rumor placed them down in the Three Canyons area—a little far afield for raids around Tierra del Verde. Also no one had ever seen the renegades.

Alex brought his attention back to Avery. "Buying the lad out won't be necessary. I'm keeping the place going for him. The Rocking R bought hay and vegetables from the Harkens' farm so we feel some loyalty to Billy. We've worked out an arrangement that will do nicely for him and our place for some time to come."

"I had thought to provide him with a nice nest egg for when he comes of age. I'm not even sure he can own property at his age," Avery added as if it was an afterthought.

Alex forced a smile. "Don't worry, Joshua Wheaton has looked into that. He's had the place put in trust for Billy. We're both his trustees."

Helena brought the subject back to the school smoothly. "How many students does Abby think will attend?"

Patience's face moved into a thoughtful frown. "I'm not sure. Do you think there would be much of an objection to Sierra Martin attending?"

"Sally Martin's girl?" Avery asked. "This brings me back to my point about these public schools. What on earth will that girl be teaching the others while you're teaching them? How to count the money she makes over at her mother's place?"

Alex didn't think anyone was more shocked than Patience when she stood. "Alex, I've changed my mind. I've lost my appetite. I'd rather go and watch the carpenters."

Quickly, as if he'd finally understood how far he'd overstepped, Avery said, "I apologize, Mrs. Reynolds. That was something I should never have said in the company of ladies."

Patience stayed standing but Alex could see the moment she realized she'd challenged a man. Inwardly, Alex had cheered but now he saw she'd frightened herself with her boldness. Alex stood, too. "No, you shouldn't have, Avery. But more to the point you shouldn't have thought it."

"She is a child still happily playing with dolls and wishing for a better life for herself. If Patience wants to give her the gift of an education, I say she may," Helena said.

"And I intend to see to it," Alex added.

"Your wife is a lady, Reynolds. She shouldn't be exposed to rabble like Sally Martin. I am quite remiss in even mentioning the woman's name."

Patience found her voice then and recited her new past. With growing relish. "Actually, Mr. Avery, I'm the daughter of a maid and a butler. Though I was given the very best education by my aunt, those are my roots."

"Patience's parents only run my home because they hate being idle. Her modest beginnings make my wife no less a lady than Helena."

"Of course it doesn't," Helena said.

Avery frowned but nodded, clearly uncomfortable to have misread the situation. "I stand corrected and concede your point, Mrs. Reynolds. You've obviously seen for yourself the advantage of an education. And I can see where one could save Sally's daughter from her mother's lowering fate. I'm terribly sorry to have upset you. Your husband and I have another matter to discuss, however." Avery stood as he said, "Sit back down with Helena and have a chat.

"Reynolds, let's go over to the men's dining room and discuss these cut fences you mentioned. After this latest raid on the Ruiz place, we all need to be careful."

Alex didn't like that Avery had issued Patience an order but he was reluctant to get in a pissing contest with the man just yet. Lucien Avery might be a viper or merely a horse's hind end. Until they were all sure which, Alex wanted to keep matters as "friendly" as possible.

"This won't take long," Alex told Patience and put a hand on her shoulder. Her muscles stiffened almost imperceptibly under his hand. "Would you like to order our meal as a picnic? Then we could go watch the building while we eat. How does that sound?"

"Fine," she said. "It sounds fine."

"In the meantime, we'll have tea then I'll be off for home," Helena said. "I can eat there."

Trying to keep it looking as if they were a love match, Alex bent and kissed Patience's cheek. As he straightened, he looked down at her. She now wore a hunted look in her eyes and he was sorry he'd pushed her.

How had he forgotten the abused woman who'd first pitched into his arms in Jamie's parlor? Or that it could be months, years—even longer—before she could return what he'd begun to feel for her. At that moment he felt utterly hopeless again.

Alex followed Avery across the lobby of Reiman House into a dark-paneled room. As soon as they were seated Avery asked, "Do you think she'll divorce him?"

Alex blinked. "Excuse me?"

"Helena. You've obviously given up on her."

It took Alex a moment to switch tracks. This was a far cry from the discussion he'd expected on cut fences. "I never considered Helena as a potential wife. She's a married woman."

Avery chuckled. "Oh, please. The British aristocracy diddles with married women all the time. Kind of foolish of you to let Helena get away considering the value of the Shamrock. That's a sizable piece of land she's got there. If you were attracted enough to bed her, why not—?"

"I've never been more than a friend to Helena. And she to me. It *is* possible, you know. You should leave off bandying the lady's name about. I hear Kane is a pretty fast gun. She steered me toward my foreman, Michael O'Hara. You also appear to have forgotten, but her husband is half owner of the Shamrock."

"That doesn't matter."

"Of course it does. If they divorce, he'd keep the ranch and as she used her inheritance to start up, she'd lose a good portion of her fortune."

Avery inspected his immaculate nails before raising his cold gaze to collide with Alex's. "I'm aware of that and more. But Kane signed ownership papers under protest, swearing he'd have nothing to do with anything her money bought. The man is a proud fool.

"As Helena is so unhappily married, I see no need to look farther for a wife. I plan to pluck her and the Shamrock up and luxuriate in both. Kane won't be a problem. He'll hand it all back. My only unknown is if she'll divorce him."

"I wouldn't know," Alex said and forced himself to look neutral. Avery had called Brendan Kane a prideful fool? That might be, but proud was actually the perfect description of Avery.

"I was a bit worried you'd come back and turn her head again," Avery went on, "but you've solved that problem by marrying your little maid."

Alex stiffened. "Actually, Patience was my niece's governess when I met her. You have an interesting plan for expanding your holdings but how will you gain Helena's cooperation? Sweep her off her feet?"

"I'm trying. Your arrival today put my plan off a bit."

Alex chuckled. "Helena being here put my own plans with my wife off a bit, too. Tell me, what will you do if you fail to storm Helena's emotions?"

Avery's eyes narrowed. "I'll think of a way to cut Kane out of her life, don't doubt it. I want her. I want the Shamrock. He clearly wants neither. And I get what I want."

Alex got a sick feeling in his belly. He'd better warn Helena to tread carefully. Ryan Quinn clearly wasn't far off the mark in his assessment of Avery. But he may have underestimated him. Alex grinned at the viper across the table. "Well, I have no love for Kane. My loyalty is to Helena alone." It was a statement but a veiled warning, as well, if Avery wasn't too full of himself to read between the lines.

It came as no surprise that he was. "We should toast to our alliance," Avery said.

Alex shook his head, still smiling. There was no way in hell he was toasting any alliance with Lucien Avery. "I'm sorry, I don't mean to insult you. I have no stomach for liquor before dinner. Tell me, assuming you can cut Kane out of the picture, how would you oversee such a large spread? I assume you know nothing of the cut fence?"

"No, I didn't know but I'm not surprised. It's damned isolated up there with that canyon between our spreads." Avery stroked his short beard thoughtfully. "I'll have to send some men up there more often. As for running an even larger place, I've hired enough men to handle anything I want done. I can hire more if need be. I'm curious. Did you talk to Quinn about the fence?"

"I mentioned it," Alex said. "Even though the kid is extremely popular with everyone, he seems to be in a little over his head."

And so he'd delivered his messages. He wasn't someone to cross but he'd stay out of Avery's business if Avery stayed out of Alex's. Also that the sheriff wasn't worth Avery's trouble but no one was likely to ignore his passing, either. Just then the clock in the corner chimed and Alex leapt on time as an excuse to leave. "Damn. I'm sorry to cut this short but Patience must be getting hungry. And as I said earlier, this is still our honeymoon."

Chapter Eleven

Patience walked to the gig Alex always used when he took her to the schoolhouse everyday. But today school was closed. With Christmas only days away and the children having grown increasingly inattentive she'd decided to close the school until after the season was over as her boarding school had. She now saw the wisdom in that.

Considering what she'd decided to do with her day, she almost wished she had her squirmy mischievous class to handle instead. Today she was going to Helena's. Because she was desperate. She had to talk to someone. Though it had been a difficult choice between Abby Wheaton and Helena, Patience had decided on Helena because Abby was still deliriously happy with Joshua after what had to be at least twelve years of marriage. Helena was more likely to understand that not all marriages were perfect and Patience needed some insight. Some advice. And if a miracle should happen, a solution to her problem.

It had been months since the school opened. She

loved her life. She'd stopped jumping at shadows and when the men on the ranch and on her trips into town came near. She'd told herself time and again that all men weren't like Edgar and Bedlow and it had begun to work. Except with Alex. For some odd and completely unfathomable reason he still made her incredibly nervous.

She trusted him. She was sure she did. But…

She huffed out a breath. Now she had something else to worry over. And another piece of guilt heaped on the rest.

While she'd been visiting with Abby in the back room of her store last week after an unexpectedly short day at school, Patience had overheard one woman telling another that she'd just seen Alex leaving the Golden Garter. And didn't she feel sorry for his new wife.

Alex hadn't been due in town until school usually let out. As he rarely drank and then only in the evening after dinner, she didn't think he'd come early to imbibe at scarcely noon. So now, every time he went to town, she pictured him with Sally Martin or some other painted woman.

She couldn't even blame Alex. In fact, it had occurred to her that the Golden Garter should be the solution to her inability to share his bed. Instead the idea tortured her.

A few days after that awful day, he'd given her the happy news that he'd secured Sierra's future. Sally Martin had given her daughter into the care of the kind widow woman who ran the boarding house. And because of that, Abby had added several girls to her class, the final objections to their attendance now removed.

Happy though she was about Sierra, Patience couldn't forget how obvious it was that Alex and Sally Martin must know each other very well if he'd been able to talk the protective mother into giving up her daughter. Patience hadn't known if she should thank Alex for arranging everything or take him to task for his relationship with the soiled dove.

She was also embarrassed to be an object of pity among the gossiping women of town, but worse, she felt as if jealousy and the guilt for feeling it was devouring her heart and soul.

"Hi, Mrs. Reynolds," Billy Harken called.

"Hey, Mrs. Reynolds," Jerome Cabot called out next as he hurried after his friend down the hill toward the barn. The barn sat near a winding, spring-fed stream and the original log ranch house. Also lying in the hollow were the corrals and a long, log bunkhouse. It was a lovely scene with big trees shading the buildings and the sun shimmering in the burbling creek making the clear water look like a luxurious spill of sparkling diamonds.

Patience forced herself to smile and wave. If a boy who'd lost everything and another who lived under the recent shadow of slavery could be cheerful, who was she to mope?

Instead of living in hell under her father's thumb and the ever-present threat of marriage to Howard Bedlow, she lived in this beautiful place in safety. Relative safety. It was sometimes easy to forget her father had hired the most notorious and effective detective agency in the country—if not the world—for the sole purpose of returning her to hell.

Alex never forgot, though.

He didn't overtly remind her and had made her security as unobtrusive as possible. He'd taken every precaution, though. He'd promised to keep her safe and was ever diligent about it. She was grateful because she wasn't sure Bedlow had stopped looking. She'd more than hurt his pride before New York City's society. That announcement of their betrothal would have held him up to ridicule at least in his eyes, if not in truth. He wouldn't easily forgive that.

Refusing to dwell on Bedlow, Patience forced her mind onto her surroundings. The temperature was warm enough for comfort but a hint of winter was finally in the air. Filling her lungs with clear crisp air, she watched Billy and Jerome troop happily back up the hill like bookends on either side of Alex, who led Big Boy behind him.

"Ready?" Alex asked when they drew even with the gig. He wore the coarse clothes of a cowboy today, his light blue eyes shaded by the broad brim of his black hat, a long tan duster swirling about his calves.

"All set," she answered.

"You're sure you don't want me to ride all the way with you?"

That was the last thing she wanted. "We'll be fine once we're on the Shamrock with the man you assigned as an escort. Dylan, right? His horse was restive so he went ahead to meet us at the head of Shamrock's road."

Alex nodded and smiled but she saw hurt in his eyes. Big Boy tossed his head, clearly having felt Alex's emotions. She knew Alex could see the other men on the Rocking R no longer frightened her but he did. *Spawn of Satan.* The epithet was beginning to haunt her as much as it did him. What was wrong with her that she would continue to hurt him? She knew she made him doubt his own goodness when it was she with the failing and when she had worked so hard to convince him of his own innate integrity.

"I'll only ride with you till we have to part ways at Helena's road, then," he said, nothing but empty false cheer in his eyes. "I have to ride into town to check on something, anyway."

Patience felt as if a knife had been shoved into her heart and she knew she deserved every modicum of pain. It was her betraying him and not the other way around. Had she forced him into another woman's arms?

All she could manage was a curt nod before she turned away, blinking back the tears that threatened to reveal her feelings. She quickly climbed into the gig without waiting for his help, which was no small feat with tears blinding her and the breeze setting her skirts flapping around. Then Billy and Jerome scrambled in on either side of her, chatting eagerly about seeing their friends, the children of Helena's foreman. She gained control of her waterworks and signaled to the horse as Alex had taught her. They were off.

It took about as long to get to Helena's ranch house after separating from Alex as it would for him to get into town. All she could see in her mind after they parted ways was Alex riding full out toward Tierra del Verde as if the hounds of hell were nipping at Big Boy's heels.

Patience held her tattered soul together long enough to wave the boys off and knocked on her new friend's door. She couldn't help wondering if Alex was walking into the arms of a woman in a scandalous red dress at that moment. By the time the door opened, tears blinded her.

"Oh, goodness, what is it?" Helena asked as her arm came around Patience's waist.

"I'm hopeless," Patience cried as she sank onto Helena's Spanish-style leather sofa a moment later. She didn't even remember walking into the parlor.

"What's hopeless?" Helena asked as she pressed a handkerchief into Patience's hand.

"Me! I'm a mouse! A craven coward. Now I'm sure he's gone to one of those soiled doves at the Golden Garter."

"You have to go backward for a moment, dear. Alex is insanely in love with you."

Fear and joy. How could she keep feeling such opposite emotions in the same moment? For the same reason!

All she could do was shake her head. If he had come to love her, it wouldn't last long when she couldn't be a real wife to him.

"Why would he do such a thing?" Helena demanded. "That doesn't sound like the man I know."

Patience felt her face crumple again. "Of course it doesn't. I drove him to it. He makes me so nervous. He smiles at me and my stomach turns over just the way it did when my nanny pushed me too high on the tree swing. If Alex touches me unexpectedly or gets close when I haven't readied myself…" She shook her head and knotted her fingers in her lap, unable to stem the flow of more tears. "I can't seem to fight the sudden tension that makes me stiffen up. And he sees. I hurt him all the time because he *knows*."

Helena stared for a long moment. "You don't share a bed."

"Not even a bedroom," Patience admitted, feeling a blush steal over her body. Then, in a blink, the old memories of a man who'd had free access to her washed away embarrassment leaving only fear. "He was so awful. I can't seem to forget."

"Alex?" Helena demanded. The incredulousness in her tone was to be expected had she been talking about Alex. Everyone became enamored of him, even on short acquaintance. Look at her. Though she was nervous of him, she loved him deeply.

Shocked by the unconscious revelation she repeated silently, *I love him.* It wasn't an accidental aberration of a stray thought. It felt right. She loved him. She really did.

Yet she was still afraid, though not of his integrity. Or his control. She'd never relocked the door between their rooms because she was sure he wouldn't use it. But she was just as sure he waited every night, hoping for the sound of the handle snicking open.

Every night she must disappoint him.

It *was* hopeless.

Helena's hand covered hers, calling her back. "Patience? What on earth did he do? Sometimes men try things we aren't ready for but they don't mean to scare—"

"Nothing," Patience cried. "*Alex* didn't do anything. Alex is *wonderful.* He knows how afraid I am so he took the nursery as his room. It was Edgar, my first husband. He was horrible. A monster." All it took was Helena taking her hand to loosen her tongue. She told it all from start to end.

"After Edgar died, my father almost immediately betrothed me to another monstrous man. My father is

Lionel Wexler. He's very powerful. And he's probably still looking for me."

"My father did business with yours," Helena said. "He could afford to turn the country upside down looking for you if he wanted to."

Patience nodded. "I climbed out my window and down a tree to escape. I arrived at Amber's hoping for help but she'd left for Ireland. Alex stepped in. He rescued me with the Winstons' help and brought me along. Then we learned Pinkerton agents were on the train looking for me, so Alex married me to keep me safe."

"Now I know why Alex told me you needed a friend." Helena's gaze collided with Patience's. "I don't know what to say."

"I don't want sympathy. I need you to tell me what to do. About Alex. Women in town are saying Alex is going to the Golden Garter. And I can't…I can't—"

"I won't believe that of Alex. He's too honorable."

Patience stared down at her twisted fingers and agreed with another stupid nod. "But men have needs," she said.

When Helena's silence stretched out, Patience looked up and was shocked to see tears in her new friend's eyes. "I'm so sorry," Helena said and swallowed hard. "You should never have been given into the care of a man like your first husband. No woman should. But Alex is too honorable to treat a woman as anything but a precious gift. You especially. When I see him look at you… You need to trust him."

"I do but he still makes me so jittery."

Helena's eyes widened. "Are you sure what you feel is fear and not tension?"

Patience felt so defeated and disappointed. "I so hoped you could help me. Helena, tension *is* fear."

Helena grinned—a very mischievous one. "It's also anticipation. All brides feel it to one degree or another if only for a moment. In your mind, you know Alex can be trusted. You've trusted him with your life in coming here with him, in marrying him. Surely you can trust him with your body. You've seen the worst of a man. Let Alex show you the best. Let him change your life and abolish the bad memories. You say when he touches you unexpectedly, you freeze."

Patience nodded.

"But not when you brace yourself? Then you aren't afraid of him but the feelings he makes you feel. The sexual feelings. Have you told Alex specifics of what your first husband did?"

"Only enough so he'd help me and so he knows I fear men. But that's changed. I've been thinking about this a lot. Not all men can be like Edgar or there wouldn't be any happily married women like Heddie Winston, Moira O'Hara or Abby Wheaton. I'm not afraid of the cowboys at the Rocking R but that's made things worse between Alex and me. I'm hurting him by still being so tense around him."

"What he makes you feel aside, you need to tell him what that man did. He's riding blind here. He doesn't *know* what you fear so how can he show you the gentle, wonderfully passionate side of marriage? There is one. Your body knows that even if your mind doesn't."

Patience stared blindly out of the windows. Helena was right. She had to have a serious talk with Alex, embarrassing though it would be. When she looked back at Helena her own problems seemed to take wing and fly away. Because there sat Helena with a sad, wistful look on her face. And big tears clinging to her lashes. Then they each fell. "What?" Patience asked

"I'd do anything to have Brendan look at me the way Alex does you."

"You still love Brendan, don't you?" she asked Helena.

Helena blinked and opened her mouth to talk, but more tears sprang to her eyes and followed the first two. She nodded. "I can't dynamite that man out of my heart."

"Then what were you doing having a meal with that Lucien Avery person? Helena, I know things with your husband aren't good but you're still a married woman. Standards here are different to be sure but not that different. Look at the uproar over one illegitimate child attending school. Look at the gossip Alex caused by spending time at the Golden Garter. You could set tongues wagging."

"I'm hoping it'll get back to Brendan through Abby even though it's completely innocent."

"But Lucien Avery? Alex already warned you. Avery has designs on you and on the Shamrock. You need to be careful."

Helena bit her lip. "Lucien is a friend just as Alex is. I'll see Lucien knows it." She went on to recount a dizzying set of circumstances and mistakes that had separated the couple. The last of which was that after a brief affair, Helena had forced Brendan to marry her at the point of a gun.

Seeing Helena so sad and not in control of her own happiness broke Patience's heart, but it also made her determined to wrestle the last of her life from Edgar's cold dead hands. Brendan Kane's anger might be out of Helena's hands but Alex's hurt wasn't out of Patience's.

Only she had the power to change things.

Patience arrived home and asked Heddie to serve an early dinner on the porch outside her bedroom before the night chill set in. She and Alex needed to talk and they needed privacy. If she didn't turn coward, she'd offer to share herself that night. If Helena had it right about how he felt about her, he'd accept. And their marriage would be real before morning.

After a quick wash before dinner, Alex came down to find the dining room deserted, the table not set.

"There you are, Mr. Alex," Heddie huffed from behind him. He turned toward where she stood in the doorway to the dining room. "It's such a lovely night Patience thought we should set up your meal on the upper side porch."

The upper porch was outside her bedroom. Though he found the double-decker porches lining the entire back of the house charming, he'd yet to set foot on it. He was having enough trouble sleeping for both of them so why risk upsetting her? He was used to losing sleep over nightmares but since the night he'd told Patience about his father and the murders he'd committed, that one had never returned.

But she'd come into his room that night and now he couldn't fall asleep for remembering her there. He'd taken to submerging himself in the icy stream around midnight every night then he'd stumble shivering into the old log house to sleep.

Not only did she haunt his room, but she also haunted his sleep with sensual dreams. She came to him in them and once he was aroused beyond thinking, in the odd way of dreams, it would turn into a nightmare. Patience would melt into mist and Iris would have taken her place. He'd awaken with a jerk and that would end any chance he had of more sleep.

Earlier that day O'Hara had told him the men had begun to feel they'd never measure up to his expectations because he worked so hard himself. Alex wasn't trying to make anyone feel inadequate or even to lead by example. He'd simply been trying to exhaust himself so that spending time with Patience through the evening wouldn't mean dreaming when the night ended so differently than he wished.

So far his plan was an utter failure.

Now, Alex took the stairs two at a time, sure this wasn't about an invitation to do anything other than eat an evening meal on this unexpectedly lovely evening in a perfect setting. After that morning's set-down when she'd refused his accompaniment to Helena's home, he was sure she'd have eaten alone if she wasn't too embarrassed to demand it.

Still he was eager to see her any way she'd allow.

His gaze fell first on the table. It was set formally with fine china, silver and crystal but the fare was a cold picnic meal. The juxtaposition was utterly charming—just like Patience.

She stood silhouetted against the cloudless sky, so lost in thought she appeared not to have heard him thundering eagerly up the stairs. She looked like a goddess surveying all she held under her power. He wondered if she knew that included him.

Then he noticed what she wore and went instantly hard. Her pale blue satin nightgown and the flowing lacy wrapper over it nearly matched that big sky all around. What the hell was she playing at? From frightened virgin to siren in one short day?

Then the truth hit him. He'd feared she might hear the rumor about him and Sally Martin. She must have then gone to Helena for advice. And the result stood before him prepared to grit her teeth and bear his attentions.

Dammit!

Patience turned. There was so much in her eyes, but mostly there was determination.

Damn, damn, damn!

He wanted her but not like this. Their first time shouldn't be about gratitude for his help. He wanted it to be about attraction and caring and need. Commitment.

And them.

Seeing her like this had him more aroused than he'd ever been in his life. Considering these last weeks that really said something. "I don't want a virgin sacrifice, Patience. I'm not that desperate," he growled.

"That's good, as I'm not quite certain I am one."

Her pithy retort and the myriad circumstances it could point to stopped him from slamming back down the stairs. Instead his heart broke in two. "Oh, God." He took a step forward. "I'm sorry. Even though I meant what I said, I should have said it more kindly." He squeezed the tense muscles at the back of his neck. "I'm under a lot of strain right now—"

"Caused by your mouse of a wife."

"Don't call yourself names."

"Why not? I notice you didn't deny the strain is my fault. Or that I'm a mouse." She laughed, a sound wrenched from her soul.

It nearly broke his tentative control. He managed to stand still.

"I've let Edgar use me from the grave. And it's hurting you. You don't deserve that. Or to have to go to town...."

"Please don't believe those rumors," he begged, hoping to dispel at least a portion of her anguish. "I had a good reason to go to the Golden Garter."

He'd been hurt that she'd seemed to prefer her bodyguard Dylan Varga's escort to his. And the hurt had bubbled into a pool of anger in his gut, knowing she didn't trust him after constantly telling him he was worthy of trust. May as well be hung for a sheep as a lamb, he'd thought.

So he'd ridden toward the temptation of the Golden Garter and a woman there who looked a bit like Patience—though her hair was a garish version of his wife's rich auburn. He'd nearly got there, when he'd glanced sideways and seen the neat little schoolhouse they'd planned together. And he'd come to his senses.

At least now he could truthfully tell her the only reason he'd ever set foot in the Garter was to secure Sierra Martin a promising future. "I should have spoken to you when I first heard about the rumor. Joshua warned me over a week ago.

"The truth is I went to see Sally Martin for her daughter's sake. You said how bright and kind the girl is and what a shame it was that she was going to miss out on an education because she lives in the saloon. Mrs. Hampton agreed to finish raising Sierra. She'll have the chance she's been wanting and a nice lonely widow will have a wonderful girl to keep her company."

Hope blossomed in those clear green eyes of hers. "So you didn't—"

He shook his head and tried to ignore the sting of her mistrust. "Absolutely not."

"I'm so sorry. It isn't that I doubted you as much as I did me. And if you had I'd have driven you to it."

He shrugged. "You can't help not trusting me. I'm the spawn of Satan, after all," he said shamefully aware how defeated his voice sounded.

"Alex," she cried and closed the distance between them. In a shocking move, she took his hand in both of hers and pulled him down to sit next to her in the wicker settee. She didn't let go.

"That woman who first called you that and all the people who copied her cruel sobriquet were *wrong*," she said, full of righteous indignation. "You must believe me. You're as far from being the spawn of Satan as the East is from the West. In my eyes you are all that is goodness. And kindness. You had more honor as a twelve-year-old boy than most men have as adults."

Until I give in to some temptation and disappoint you, he thought.

"I only considered the rumor because I cannot imagine you would wait for *me*. Or want a real marriage with me. I am not afraid of you. At least I don't think I am. Helena says what I feel is attraction."

"I don't think she under—"

She silenced his lips with the press of her fingers for a beautiful moment. "Actually, she does understand because I've told her. Now that she's explained it all so much better than my mother did, I am beginning to believe she is right. If I'm afraid, it's of the unknown and…of the memories. Helena says I need to tell you more about my marriage."

She let go of his hand then characteristically knotted her fingers around each other in a way it was painful to watch. She stared down at them and Alex put lingering doubts about himself out of his head so he could focus on her. Help her. He reached out and took her hands, parting them to hold one in each of his. He moved to kneel at her feet so he could look up into her lovely face. "Nothing that bastard did to you matters to me. Nothing he did can diminish all you are to me. It only diminished him. Do you understand? I don't need confessions about your marriage bed."

"Yes," she cried and took a deep breath that ended on a shuddering sob. "You do. I do. I understand it all now. He was ashamed. Not of me. Of himself. Helena is very wise for one so young. And fierce. She wants to go north, dig up Edgar and kill him again. Painfully."

He chuckled. Patience was right. "Helena is wise. She can also be quite fierce but she would need to stand in line behind me. And I'm not sure there would be anything left of Gorham when I got done."

She laughed but tears flooded her eyes. "I wish I could get back some of my own before you and Helena get started but I don't think I could stand to see his face again."

"Ah. After me, then. He wouldn't be recognizable after I got done with him."

She laughed but it quickly sputtered to an end. "I hate him. I hate him so much."

"Shh. I'm so sorry he hurt you. Some men like to abuse those who are smaller and weaker than them because they are not men at all—only bullies."

She shook her head, silent tears tracking down her flushed cheeks. He took his handkerchief and dried her tears as gently as he could. She allowed it, not shying from his touch. But he could feel no joy in her acceptance of him when she was in such anguish.

"It wasn't only that he hit me," she whispered. "That wouldn't have been so bad. He struck me all the time in front of the help. It was when we were in private that he was at his most degrading and vicious."

"What the hell did that bastard do?"

Her voice was raw, her gaze anguished as she said, "He'd come to my room. I'd wake up and see him standing over me. Then it would start. He wouldn't stop until I was black and blue under my clothes. He tortured me, Alex." Her sob rent the air.

She was killing him. He couldn't stand watching her suffer without offering comfort so he slid back onto the settee and pulled her into his arms.

She came, unresisting, and sank against him as she began talking again. Slowly. Quietly. Terribly. "He had been unable to consummate our marriage and blamed me. After my mother's death, he went to his doctor and came home in a fury. He'd learned his heart was the reason he couldn't consummate our marriage. That it wouldn't get better. He was going to lose his strength and eventually die. And so, before he grew weaker than me, he held me down, cursing and screaming that he would have no man laughing at him after I took my next husband."

Alex tucked her head under his chin, instinctively knowing what was to come, but he found himself praying he was wrong. He wasn't. His blood chilled as she explained the abject perverted cruelty that was the reason he wouldn't find her a virgin when she'd never experienced intimacy.

"He hurt me so badly," she whispered finally. "What did I ever do to deserve being treated that way?"

"Nothing, love. Not a thing," he said, his throat aching. "The man was a monster." Thank God he'd felt the need to hold her close. This way she hadn't seen the expression he knew he wore. He'd never want her to think it was caused by distaste for her.

Why did you stay? his mind screamed.

She nodded against his chest and sniffled. Almost as if she'd heard his silent plea, she sat up and looked him right in the eyes. "I had the jewelry from my mother. I was going to run away once I'd recovered enough. But I couldn't get away. He'd already effectively made me a prisoner but after that night any pretense of freedom was gone. He had me watched by guards during the day and locked in my room during the night. If he deemed it necessary to entertain, he wouldn't let me out of his sight."

She shook her head as if trying to shake loose the nightmare that had been her life. "Then one night approaching our third year of marriage, I heard a great uproar after he'd gone back to his room after beating me. He'd overexerted and had a heart attack. It left him so weak he could scarcely walk or hurt me afterward. The most he could do was swipe at me with his cane. I was free but I stayed. He couldn't hurt me physically anymore, and foolishly I thought I'd have his money when he was gone to do as I wished with the rest of my life. God help me, I rejoiced when I heard he'd died."

"I'm sure you did. His hell will last an eternity. Rest assured, angel, your hell is at an end." He would die to keep that promise. He'd called her angel and realized how well it fit.

"There is one other thing he did," she said, then shuddered.

He caressed her back, hoping to calm her, support her. "What is it you want to tell me?"

"Do you remember when I told you Edgar had purposely run through his money to leave me penniless?"

"I remember."

"Sometimes I think Edgar was too mean to die. He lived so much longer than expected. Finally, he found himself destitute with no funds even to remain in the house, though I didn't know it at the time or I'd have run away somehow. He—" Her voice failed and tears welled up in her eyes. She looked away at the hills beyond the terrace. "He…sold me to Howard Bedlow for the night." She blinked and her tears tracked downward again. "My maid, Mitzy, saved me when she heard me screaming. She hit Mr. Bedlow over the head and knocked him out."

"Thank God for her."

"I think perhaps Mitzy stole some of the money Howard had paid Edgar because she gathered me up and had the funds to take me to my father's home. We left before anyone knew Edgar was dead. I wish we had kept going. I hadn't realized my father's anger over my mother's death had turned into such hatred of me. I thought he would listen when I told him all Edgar had done. Instead he acted as if I were insane. I feared he'd have me locked away. But he planned to give me to Howard, who promised to keep me in the country where I couldn't embarrass Father."

"Honestly, if I ever meet your father, I may have to

flatten him." Alex wished he'd known this all along. He felt so damned selfish and guilty for getting aroused around her and for feeling put upon and discontented about their chaste marriage. He'd known what he was getting into, he thought as he stroked her hair. She'd told him she feared men because of how she'd been treated in bed and out. He'd also offered her an annulment.

But he hadn't understood what an absolute nightmare her life had been. How could any sane person envisage such treatment of another? Though, thinking of how courageous she was, he should have realized only abject terror could have pushed her to where she'd prefer death to a marriage to Bedlow. If only he knew what to do now to ease the hurt and fear she must live with every day.

He wanted a life with her. But he couldn't tell her how he thought he felt. If he did, she'd make herself that virgin sacrifice he didn't want. She deserved so much more than that. She deserved the freedom she so deeply craved. He wished he knew how to give her what she needed from him.

Chapter Twelve

"Will you make love to me?" Patience asked, unable to keep the quaver out of her voice. It had been so hard to relay all the awful secrets from her marriage. She felt emotionally drained. So drained she couldn't even feel the now familiar tension his nearness usually caused in her.

Alex looked completely shocked, as if toads had fallen from her mouth instead of words. "I'm going to strangle Helena," he muttered and gave his head a slight shake. "Or hug her. I'm not yet quite certain which. What about your freedom? It would put an end to that."

"I am free with you. Aren't I?"

"Yes. I wasn't sure if you understood that. I've never even kissed you, angel. Don't you think you'd like to get your feet wet with a bit of a courtship, before leaping into the raging river of emotional intimacy involved in lovemaking."

She could feel a blush heat her cheeks. "Is that what it's like? I thought it was something more deliberate, cold and emotionless the way my mother described it. But Helena seemed to think—"

He put a finger to her lips. "Shh. It wouldn't be unemotional or cold. Not between us. Never that between us."

He moved closer and hesitated. She could see his demons were involved in this, too. Fear that she'd put too much pressure on him seeped into her thoughts. But then he replaced his finger with his lips. They were warm and firm and mobile, moving over not just her lips but her cheeks, eyelids and forehead, then back to her mouth. His arms came around her slowly, gently. And he sighed. Then his mouth pressed harder and his tongue traced the seam of her lips. She gasped when he nipped at her bottom lip and her stomach fluttered nervously.

But no. Not nervous. Not scary. *Exciting!*

Helena was right. This felt good. So, so good. Then his tongue swept inside her mouth. No, not just good. This felt wonderful. *He* felt wonderful as he cradled her against him and stroked her tongue with his.

Then he broke contact with her lips, stepped back and put his hands on her shoulders, cupping them gently. She felt so bereft of his nearness, his warmth, even though he still touched her. Somehow she found courage enough to look up into his pale blue eyes. His eyes looked troubled at first but then in an instant she was sure she saw desire. Then he smiled.

Not his irreverent smile. Or his teasing one. Or even his happy amused one. This smile was gentle and sensual at once. Filled with peace but arousal, too. This smile was full of paradoxes. This smile was just for her. At that realization, her stomach did that somersault thing his smiles always caused. But now she understood.

"Tell me, do you still think lovemaking between us could ever be cold?"

She shook her head then found her voice. "Helena says it can be wonderful and warm with the right man. I think you're my right man, Alex Reynolds."

"And I think between us it will be earthshaking and hot. Because of that maybe we should take things more slowly. It would kill me if I did something to frighten you, angel."

"You won't. Helena says you can heal my bad memories by making good new ones." He looked worried but she forced herself to continue. "I trust you. And I'm proud to be your wife. But I'm *not* your wife. Not really. Not yet. I feel like a burden."

"No—"

"I must be. You've done so much for me and I've done nothing for you."

"Not true." He shook his head. "I've begun to believe in myself and in my worth as a person because you believe in me. And I enjoyed planning the school and the way you arranged the house." He grinned. "You play a mean game of chess. You're a joy to behold sitting across the dining table from me at meals. I rush to get to the breakfast table in the morning and cannot wait to see you when the day is done. The men tease me for making excuses to return to the house for luncheon even though Willow has already prepared a saddlebag meal for me. After years of solitary dining, having you here is like giving sustenance to a starving man."

She tilted her head, looking for the right answer. Then it came to her. "Have you thought that I'm starving, as well, Alex? I've been *so* lonely. Not because I'm far from all I've known but because no one has held me when I've cried since my mother died. No one until you did a little while ago. I've been as alone with all these terrible memories as you've been with yours.

"Show me there's another way to live. And perhaps you will finally understand why it is I…" She hesitated. She couldn't confess her love. It was too new. "You… you make me happy. It's been so long since I could say that."

"You're killin' me, angel," he said on a sigh, a hint of Irish having snuck in to betray his upheaval. "All right. You win. A desperate man can resist temptation only so long. We'll take it a step at a time, though. If anythin' alarms you, I want you to tell me. Honesty between us is our most important weapon against the darkness that bastard created in you. Is that clear?"

She nodded, unable to look away from the strength and integrity in his gaze. Or from the need she finally understood. If she could assuage even some of the need she saw in him, they would be on a more even footing. And perhaps then, when she was indeed an equal in their partnership, she would have the right to his love and could confess hers in return.

"Patience, I meant what I said when I first got to the top of the stairs. I want no sacrificial virgin. And before you say you're not, yes, you *are*."

She felt her cheeks redden. She'd hoped they'd gone past such talk, but that was foolish. What they were about to do was more intimate than any chess game. Than any confession of the past. "I promise to tell you if anything makes me at all uncomfortable. As long as you promise to tell me what I can do to make you happy tonight."

He smiled and took her hand. "I promise but you should know that you just being here is enough."

She thought he'd lead her to the bedroom and tried to ready herself but instead he drew her over to the table. She frowned. Did he not want to do this? He'd kissed her. He'd said their lovemaking would be full of emotion but he hadn't said she was any more than a temptation to him.

She hadn't thought this through. Fool. She was such a dolt where men were concerned. He probably didn't want to consummate their marriage at all, but he was too honorable to go to another woman. If he did this, he couldn't have their marriage annulled.

Where had her sense gone?

"What *are* you thinking?" he demanded gently. "You've all but turned into a pillar of salt, angel mine."

She discounted the sweet nickname. "That you don't want to do this. That I've pushed you and tempted you but you'd rather keep annulment as a possibility."

He chuckled. "Make no mistake. I have been ready for this since the moment I first laid eyes on you. You're simply a gorgeous woman. And since getting to know you, I've come to admire your courage, your integrity and I've come to cherish you. I don't *want* any other woman."

"But what if you meet someone you feel deeply for? What if Helena were to become free?"

"Then I'd be sad for her because she loves that idiot who put his pride before her. She will always be like the sister I never had. She simply isn't you. I really did fall under your spell that first night."

"Then why…"

"Why the meal?"

She nodded and he sent her one of those incredibly sensual smiles. "Because seduction can start anywhere. Why should we rush this? This is the wedding night we didn't have. Come." He gestured to the picnic fare on the table.

He held out a chair then grabbed the one across from her and placed it close to her side but facing her. "Now what would you like? Ah. How about one of these strawberries?" He chose a big ripe berry and she nodded. Her lips suddenly dry, she licked them and his gaze all but devoured them. Something zinged through her at the intensity in his eyes.

Then he looked back to the berry he'd chosen. "And how about a dollop of clotted cream?" he asked, his voice rougher. He dipped the strawberry in the bowl of cream and held it out to her.

She leaned forward with her lips parted but he shook his head and grinned. It was devilish and sexy and she felt the folds of her femininity tighten and grow moist. He took her chin between his crooked index finger and the pad of his thumb and painted her lips with the cream. She didn't know what she was supposed to do but the sweetness of the cream tempted her so she ran her tongue over her lips and gathered the cream. Alex sucked in a quick short breath and surprisingly dropped the fruit. It hit the top of her breast then bounced onto the plate.

"Sorry, angel. I guess I'm a bit nervous, myself. Taking a woman on this journey is a man's greatest responsibility. And his greatest pleasure. Let me mop you up a bit."

But he didn't pick up one of the snowy napkins Heddie had set out. Instead he went down on his knees before her then leaned forward and dipped his head. His lips and tongue on her skin left a fiery trail. He didn't stop at the accidental streak of cream but continued downward.

She couldn't hold back a groan and tunneled her fingers in his thick white-blond hair to hold him to her. She dropped her head back and closed her eyes when he untied her wrapper and peeled down the front of her gown, exposing her breasts to his gaze.

Embarrassed, she tried to cover herself.

But Alex took her hands and looked up. His expression was intense and needy. It was clear the sight of her pleased him, which eased some of her embarrassment. Then he banished the rest. "There is no shame between us. Only pleasure and passion."

She nodded.

He smiled crookedly, his eyes sparkling in the fading light. "Now where was I?" He took her face in his hands and nipped at her bottom lip, then laved the same spot before sucking on it. "No. Tasty though your lips are, that isn't what I was about, is it?" He looked down at her exposed breasts and grinned, teasing and sexy at once. "Ah. Here we are. How could I have forgotten such a scrumptious berry? And it's all mine."

She knew she should be mortified to be nearly naked from the waist up, but found she wasn't. Couldn't be. Because the look in his eyes was nothing short of worshipful.

She did please him.

It was everything.

Then he closed his eyes and pulled her close. He

nuzzled her neck and nipped and laved her there, too, before he trailed his tongue downward to her nipple. He latched onto her, teasing her nipple into a tight knot of need. When he suckled her, Patience was shocked to feel her womb tighten and her whole being quake with a need so fierce she let out a little squeal.

Perhaps pleasing him wasn't everything.

Perhaps there was more.

Next, he lifted his head and captured her gaze with his, blindly seeking the strawberry where it had fallen. He found it and lifted it to her lips again. "Take a bite, angel mine. I've had part of my meal. You should have a bit, too."

His huskily spoken words had her heart thundering. Willing to just do about anything he asked now, she took a bite and the flavor exploded on her tongue. He traced the juicy berry from her chin to the tip of her breast, and then proceeded to lick and sip and even nip his way downward until he had her in his mouth and drew on the already hardened nipple.

She felt herself tremble as he finally put his hands on her there, massaging her to a swollen orb of need. "Please," she muttered as his lips hovered over hers again.

"Please what, my lovely?" he whispered against her mouth.

"I don't know. More. Make me feel more. It's glorious. *You're* glorious."

He chuckled, the deep tone winding her muscles up even tighter. "I would say the same of you. We can't have my passionate mate not knowing what she wants."

That was when she realized his clever hands had found the hem of her gown. And her ankles. With his lips devouring hers, his beautifully tapered fingers began to create a path of fire that spread upward as he trailed them from her ankle to her thigh, causing a flow of liquid from her core to moisten her folds.

She forced herself to open her limbs to his exploration when he pressed them apart. She expected pain. But all he did was tease and rub her, his fingers slick with her fluid. She was unprepared when one of his strong thick fingers moved inside her, then it withdrew and a second joined it when he thrust his hand forward again.

Patience was about to protest. To tell him she'd grown worried when his thumb found that surprisingly sensitive nub whose purpose she'd always wondered at.

She wondered no longer.

Her body was his to command as the slick pad of his thumb circled her there, building what felt like a storm inside her. She heard herself mewing as his fingers massaged her within and his thumb wound her nerves tighter and tighter until she was moving helplessly against his hand. He pushed her relentlessly toward an abyss she didn't completely understand.

She didn't want it to end, yet she sought an unknown end with desperation. Then the storm crested and wave after wave crashed over her. At last she lay against his shoulder, utterly spent and depleted of all sensation, content to breathe in his musky scent.

It was a shock to hear him whisper in a broken voice, "So, angel mine, are you ready to see how much better it can be?"

Then he started to move that clever, oh, so talented thumb again and she understood there was more. She wanted more. And more. And still more.

She wanted to know how much better this thing called lovemaking could get.

"Yes. Show me more," she begged shamelessly, and then realized he'd been right. There was no shame between them. There was only glory. And beauty.

Alex nodded but pulled his hand away from her. "Oh, no. Don't stop," she protested, her voice breathless and pleading.

He grinned. "This is just a brief interruption," he promised, his voice rough and silky at once. He stood, pulling her up and into his arms. "I'll give you every bit of the pleasure I promised," he whispered against her lips, as he pressed his fingers into the small of her back, nestling his alarmingly large erection against her belly.

She sucked in a shocked breath, unable to ignore how large he was. She almost asked how all that would fit where his fingers barely had. Worry nipped at the outer reaches of her thoughts. And expanded. Would this hurt as badly as what Edgar had—?

She silenced the worry. Alex wouldn't hurt her. Hadn't he already played her body like a familiar instrument? He clearly knew what he was doing.

Without warning the world spun as he scooped her up in his arms and whirled toward the door to the bedroom where she slept. He stopped and bent to catch the handle with one of his fingers and cracked it enough to get his foot to flip it open.

He stopped just inside the bedroom and lowered his lips to hers. The kiss was fierce but gentle. When he lifted his head, the look in his eyes held both of those conflicting emotions as well as a bit of trepidation. "I promise I'll try not to hurt you. You're small but we were made for each other. Please trust me in this."

She cupped his cheek in her trembling hand. "I trust you in everything."

He stared at her as if trying to discern the truth of her statement. Then he moved to the bed. Putting his knee in the middle of the mattress, he laid her on the cool sheets. The bed had felt so welcoming when they'd first arrived, but it had grown lonely. She hadn't known why but when he followed her down to lie beside her, she understood at last. "The Bible says man wasn't made to be alone. Apparently neither is woman."

He chuckled then framed her upper torso with his bent arms and powerful chest. "All turned down and ready for us. Pretty confident, weren't you?" His smile faded. "It isn't too late to stop."

Staring into his serious gaze, she thought about what he'd already made her feel. In spite of a bit of worry, she was greedy for more. He'd take care of her in this as he had every moment since she'd collapsed in his cousin's parlor. "I'm as ready as you are," she told him.

"Oh, I doubt that, angel mine. But you will be. Very soon you will be." His lips were on hers, giving promise to his words. His hands roamed her body, kneaded her breasts and ramped up the excitement, the yearning and the desperate need. It was all back. Fourfold. And wondrous.

As he stroked and caressed her naked skin, she remembered she wanted to be his partner in this, too. Which meant she should touch him as he did her. So she grabbed handfuls of the shirting tucked into the waist of his trousers and yanked it free, finding the smooth skin of his lower back and sides. She touched her fill, letting her hands roam, lost in his feel and texture, wallowing in his ministrations. Wild with need, knowing the fulfillment he'd already shown her awaited and wanting more, she moved her hands to his chest. She ran her hand through the crisp hair there.

When she grazed his pebbled nipples, he jerked back a bit and gasped, pleasure sweeping over his features. She hadn't known that would pleasure a man. Smiling at the discovery, she pushed up on her elbows and laved first one nipple then the other. Alex started to quake, his already heavy breath grew more labored.

He pulled back and knelt at her side, his hands dragging her loose gown and wrapper down over her arms and hips. His blue eyes looked like twin flames as he stared down at her, his chest heaving. She felt a surge of pride when she realized the look on his face could only be described as enraptured.

His fingers, nimble, clever and gentle with her clothing suddenly turned clumsy as they went to work on his own. His hands actually shook. Patience felt astonishingly powerful as she watched him struggle. And that steadied her as nothing else could have. She had turned this strong capable man into a mass of need.

Moving to her knees, wanting to see him without the coverings of civilization, to touch him again, too, she unbuttoned his shirtfront and cuffs, then pushed the garment up over his head, skimming her hands over his powerful body as she did. He was magnificent, his muscles rippling with every movement.

Once free of his shirt, Alex tossed it to the floor, where he'd thrown her things. Then he reached for her, pulling her to him. Crisp hair abraded her nipples. His kiss when their lips met was nearly uncontrolled. He broke the kiss, panting for air.

Patience smiled up at him and traced the hair that fanned out from his areolas then trailed downward toward his navel. Emboldened by the hiss as he sucked in air between gritted teeth, she followed that path with her own fingers to his belt, unfastening it.

But when she went to work on the buttons of the front placket of his trousers, he stilled her hands. He looked as if he was in pain. "I'd better take it from here. A man can handle only so much," he explained.

Rather than be insulted by what she thought was a clumsily phrased compliment, Patience smiled. To witness his silver tongue so undone drove her onto more discoveries. Not only was everything suddenly new and exciting, but she also recognized in herself a newer, braver woman. "In that case, I'll lie back and enjoy," she told him.

He choked. "I believe I've created a monster," he said as he slid to the side of the bed, and went to work on his boots.

Rolling to her side, she reached out and ran her hand over his back. A shudder ran through him.

Then she encountered several deep depressions and other raised welts that marred the perfect expanse of skin. In the rapidly dimming light she could see numerous scars crisscrossing his back. He jumped to his feet and turned toward her. His jaw had gone rock-hard and shame now lived in his gaze.

Patience crawled to the edge of the bed and reached up to stroke his taut jaw. "Are you forgetting? There's no shame between us." He looked down, lost in thought, so she moved closer, hoping to force him to look at her.

"I must warn you, though," she told him. "When you go off hunting down Edgar's grave to kill him again, I shall go hieing off to California to find your father's."

Alex's gaze finally met hers and he chuckled. "Helena isn't the only woman in town the West has turned fierce."

"The West gets none of the credit. My new husband gets it all." She walked backward on her knees and pulled him with her. He had no choice but to sink back to the mattress. But he sat with one long limb bent on the bed and the other on the floor, his scarred back facing the headboard. "Now strip off the boots and the rest. And let us get back to all those promises."

He sighed, having no choice but to turn his back on her to get his boots off. Patience refused to let some ugly-hearted dead man spoil the beauty between them. She asked if they were earned by circumventing his father's attempts to see Jamie dead. He admitted they were. And so she kissed each mark, telling him that to her each scar was a badge of courage.

To get them back on the path she'd set them on, she did as he had and nipped at his exposed neck then sucked the spot when he shivered. He cried out then and stood. Turning to face her, he stripped off his trousers and small clothes. As she'd guessed, there was nothing small beneath.

He was magnificent. She swallowed. And large. All her bravery suddenly evaporated. "Are you sure that's going to—"

"Going to fit?" He grinned then chuckled. "Trust me on this. You'll fit me like a glove."

She frowned. "I've had some of those that were rather

uncomfortably tight. Until now I never stopped to think how the glove might feel."

This time he laughed outright and moved onto the mattress. Feeling a bit intimidated, she lay back as he moved forward. Perhaps to give herself a bit of space. Perhaps in invitation. She was honestly unsure which as he aligned his body next to hers. With one finger he traced her profile, stopped to outline her lips then and moved on, straight downward to her core. Each muscle on the gentle journey tightened in anticipation of a repeat of the joy he'd brought her on the balcony.

When he found her still slick center and that hidden nub, she arched and dragged in a breath that felt as if it might be her last. If it were, she'd die a happy woman. She wanted this. She wanted him.

But it wasn't death that awaited her. It was a fiery new life. She burned yet felt herself expanding as he stroked and teased.

Then he moved over her, keeping most of his weight on his arms. She felt protected, not imprisoned. "Pick up your knees, angel mine. Let me into your…body."

She could feel him there, hot and hard, and did as he asked. She pondered for a moment the hesitation in his words. But it proved unimportant when, supporting his weight on one arm, he slid his hand between them and used the pad of his thumb to toy with that one spot that nearly drove her out of her mind each time he touched it. At the same time he massaged her curl-covered mound with the rest of his hand.

Her hips started to rock with no conscious effort or control on her part and Alex pushed his hips forward, groaning as he moved into her. She gasped at his entry, feeling only a little uncomfortably full. But complete. And transported the rest of the way into her new life.

She was a complete partner now. A wife. A lover.

No longer an escaped prisoner or the promised toy of a wealthy fiend.

Then what he was saying as he kissed her face tenderly sank in. "I'm sorry. So sorry," he said over and over. Then he started to pull away.

Desperate to keep him with her, in her, she hooked her limbs around his waist, locking him in place. "Don't go. Oh, please. I'm not hurt. Just surprised by all these feelings. This is what was missing and I didn't even know it."

As if in answer, he thrust forward. "Still all right?" he whispered, nipping at her ear and neck.

"Better than," she said on a sigh.

"Better than what?" he asked, a smile in his voice as he sucked and nipped at her neck, making it even better somehow.

"Anything. It's better than anything," she told him.

But then he showed her how much better it could be when he started to move in her. She didn't tell him she'd been wrong. She didn't tell him the most beautiful piece of poetry she'd ever heard had nothing on him. She didn't tell him she knew how the birds of the air must feel as they took wing.

Because her powers of speech deserted her along with control over every other part of her body.

What had felt like a storm building when he'd touched and stroked her as he'd knelt at her feet on the balcony now raged in her like a hurricane. From all sides wave after wave of a pleasure so deep and dark yet light and bright washed over her until she finally went under in what felt like death. Then rebirth as she was tossed back to the surface. Gasping for air, she arched and cried out. He swallowed the sound with his mouth then he reared up, fighting for air himself, his face changed by the same transporting pleasure she'd felt.

Then he collapsed to the bed, rolling to pull her over him, their bodies still united. Feeling as boneless as her childhood rag doll, Patience could only lie on him, her head on his chest as she listened to his heart beat as one with hers.

He stroked her back, ran his fingers through her hair, as she fought the kind of tears only the most moving painting, or passage of a book, or scene in a play had ever caused in her. She felt overwhelmed with beauty, emotion and joy.

Her last thought before sleep claimed her was: *So this is love.*

Alex lay awake, still hard within the heat of her body. He would wake her again but she needed rest and he needed to think and relive every moment of the past hour.

It had never been like that. Not even with Iris, whom he'd thought he loved. With her it had been dark and forbidden. Intense and soul-enslaving.

With Patience lovemaking was a benediction. It was a thousand rays of sunshine warming him. It was so beautiful that tears gathered in his eyes and he let them fall because there was no one to see.

She'd kissed his scars.

He'd never before let anyone see them. Whenever he'd felt the need of a partner, he'd always put himself in situations where the pretext fit that it was too chilly or that it was too dangerous to disrobe. But Patience had made him forget his shame until she'd gasped at the sight of his back.

Jamie was the only one who knew of the scars and only because he'd heard Oswald Reynolds beating Alex and had tried to stop him. Jamie had even demanded equal punishment. His father had cuffed Jamie and split his lip, punched and slapped him, but he'd been no fool. He'd known scars on his nephew would have come to light if one of his attempts on Jamie's life were successful, making him a suspect. So he'd made Jamie watch Alex beaten as punishment for daring to still be alive and for trying to interfere. And he'd doubled the number of lashes Alex was given. Jamie'd never interfered again, poor kid. He'd cried inconsolably all night, his guilt all-consuming. Alex had tried to make light of the beating but Jamie hadn't been fooled.

Now, for the first time, Alex actually felt healed. Because Patience had cried over him. And kissed the ugly scars. God, he loved her. But he didn't think he could tell her. Not yet. He needed to be sure. He'd been wrong before. What, after all, did he know of love?

Thank goodness Patience hadn't seemed to need the words. That left him free to wait, to make sure before possibly straining their newly found closeness. Just in case he was wrong again.

But in the meantime, he'd show her how he felt every time he touched her. And he intended to do a lot of touching. Then, when he did tell her, she'd look back on his lovemaking and understand what he'd been saying with his body all along.

He pressed his hips upward so she took more of him

in and grew harder though he hadn't thought he could yet. He rocked upward again and smiled when she began to respond though still sound asleep. He kept up the gentle penetrations, anticipating her surprise when her mind finally realized this wasn't a dream. Finally when the first flutters of her climax began, she gasped and picked up her head.

"What?" she puffed out, her breathing labored already. She stared at him and he pulled her hips into his, going even deeper and her slumberous eyes widened. "Oh. Oh. Oh."

Alex remembered then that her husband—her first husband, may he rot in hell—used to wake her from sleep with his unholy treatment. He nearly panicked. What if he'd frightened her? Shocked her, even?

Then she smiled and tried to sit up. That would mean she'd be riding him! He hadn't dared hope she'd be ready for adventure. He should have known better.

So he gladly helped her straddle him and pulled her knees forward, wanting to reward her for her bravery and trust. He pressed upward and seated himself as deeply inside her as he could go, and at the same time he caressed her nipples. Then curled his back forward so he could bring his mouth to first one breast then the other.

Extremely sensitive because of their earlier loving, her shuddering response was immediate and profound. She caught onto his rhythm and drew him tighter to her, driving him inside, wonderfully deep. Then her inner contractions started rippling around him again. Her breathing changed, her movements grew uncontrolled and he grasped her hips, showing her how to find a rhythm to pleasure them both.

She was a quick study, his angel was. Soon shaking and gasping, it was his turn to lose control. He thrust upward, praying his ferocious movements didn't scare her.

Just as he was about to force himself to fall still, though he was nearly sure it would kill him, she threw her head back and rocked harder, drawing him more deeply still. And just as the setting sun blasted into the room, lighting her hair like a flame, her cry and his mingled and drove every coherent thought from his head.

He was about to sink into sleep when his thoughts cleared a bit. He smiled because in his arms was his goddess, his angel, his wife.

His.

Chapter Thirteen

Alex rode toward the school, eager to see how Patience's day had gone. He loved hearing stories of the children and their antics. Oh, who was he fooling? He was simply eager to see her. He'd finally trusted his feelings for her.

He was in love with her.

And he was finally going to tell her.

Today! St. Valentines Day.

His hand moved to the inside pocket of his vest, where his mother's ring lay nestled in tissue. He'd almost given it to her for Christmas. But he hadn't been ready. And today was a better day for it than any other.

His marriage proposal had been nothing more than part of a strategic battle plan to free Patience from the threat of her father's schemes for her. And so they'd married under dubious circumstances. The only emotions involved were fear and anger on her part and sympathy and resolve on his.

Partners. Then finally lovers. But being lovers was different than being in love.

That fledgling bond had changed. Grown. Blossomed. Into a love so all-encompassing she had become his life. The Rocking R was no longer a retreat from his old life but a stage for his future. His future with Patience.

He'd saved the ring, hoping for a time like this. A special time. One she would want a memento of. He was sure his admission of love would make this that special time for her.

Because he was sure she loved him as much as he did her.

It was in her every smile. It was there in her every action and reaction when they made love, which they'd done with increasing ardor ever since that first desperate night two months earlier. If he spent all those magical moments in adoration of her body, she spent them worshiping his.

He was quite sure she held back telling him to keep him from feeling pressured to reciprocate. He didn't blame her. He wouldn't want a false statement of love from her any more than he'd want to hear a confession that his feelings weren't returned.

Which made him just a bit nervous because, before he told her how he felt, he should probably tell her about Meara. Patience was his wife and she had a right to know his child was in the care of his cousin.

He'd tell her when they got to the falls.

Or maybe after they'd made love one more time.

Or maybe he should wait until after he told her of his love for her. That way she'd know she was first in his heart but that she shared it with his daughter.

Secretly.

Alex turned onto the short trail to the schoolhouse,

and his mind emptied of everything but knowing he'd see her soon. He waved to Dylan Varga, who watched both the front and side doors from the woods. Dylan waved back and stood to ready his mount for the ride home.

Though both Alex and Patience were relatively confident her father no longer had an interest in her after all these months, she still worried about Howard Bedlow. She believed Bedlow would want revenge so Alex took no chances with her safety.

The sound of erasers clapping made him smile. Daniel Wheaton stood out in front banging them together, creating a dust storm, as usual. Daniel had shadowed Patience at the schoolhouse ever since accidentally overhearing she might be in danger.

Alex appreciated a second set of eyes and ears but he'd told the kid to run for the sheriff and not try to be a hero if trouble did make a showing.

Pulling the gig to a stop next to the school, he nodded his thanks to the boy. "Afternoon, Daniel. Everything quiet?"

"Hi, Mr. Reynolds. Just a regular day," Daniel said and tossed the erasers into a small pail. The kid wore his usual wide happy smile. "Mrs. Reynolds is stacking the books. I already swept the room so you can leave right away. I'll get her."

Patience stuck her head out the door and smiled brightly when she saw him. "I did hear my name, then."

"You certainly did!" Alex vaulted from the gig to the boardwalk. "I came to fetch my lovely wife."

"I'm all set," she said as he reached her. She stood on her tiptoes and planted a kiss on his cheek. "I'll be right with you. Let's get our lunch pails, Daniel," she said and rushed back through the door.

Alex watched her go, soaking in the sound of her laughter and the wondrous feeling of knowing he made the woman he loved happy. His mind wandered to the picnic he'd planned for the two of them. The weather in Hill Country was a constant pleasant surprise. The temperature had begun to grow warm during the days again, though it was still quite chilly at night.

Their picnic dinner was tucked under the gig's seat with the patchwork quilt Willow had made and given them for Christmas. He planned to make love to Patience on it until the stars came out in the perfect secluded setting he'd found. He could see them in his mind's eye wrapped up together in that soft quilt, studying the stars, secure in each other's love.

She and Daniel stepped out of the door and he took the key to lock up for the weekend. "All ready to go," she said then turned to Daniel. "Thank you for your help again today, Daniel. You *do* know you don't need to stay behind every day, don't you?"

Daniel glanced at Alex, his eyes older than his years, then he shrugged nonchalantly. "Except sweeping out the store for Ma after she closes, I got nothing else to do."

"I *have* nothing else to do," Patience corrected.

Daniel grimaced, making Alex laugh. "School is out, teacher," Alex reminded her.

"Practicing good grammar is never out," she said primly.

This time Daniel rolled his eyes. "Yes, Mrs. Reynolds," he said with a rather disgusted attitude.

Alex held back not knowing if he should laugh or

correct the boy. Since he was neither Daniel's teacher nor his parent, Alex remained neutral.

"Are you headed home, Daniel?" Alex asked. "I could give you a lift into town."

"Nah. I'm going down to the creek to practice rock skipping. I'm up to four skips but Billy can get five now."

It was Alex's turn to grimace. "Sorry. I suppose that would be my fault. I can see I need to give you the same pointers I gave Billy."

"That's okay. You can teach Billy. His da died. I have a da now and he showed me some tricks last night. I'm gonna go *practice*. To make it perfect, Da says. How come *everything* is about *practicing* when you're a kid? It ain't fair."

"Isn't," Patience piped up.

Disgruntled Daniel looked at Alex. "See?"

"That's just how it is. My job is to oversee the ranch, your father's is running the bank and Mrs. Reynolds's job is being your teacher. Your job is to learn. And skip rocks."

Daniel nodded and sighed. "I just hope four skips isn't the best I'll get or Billy isn't *ever* going to let me forget."

Somehow she waited until Daniel was out of earshot before letting out a quiet snort of laughter, her shoulders shaking. He tried valiantly to keep his amusement hidden, but when he looked at her he lost all restraint and let out a laugh.

"Daniel keeps my day interesting," Patience said when she got hold of herself and wiped tears of mirth from her eyes.

"I would imagine he does," Alex responded, fighting the laughter that wanted to bubble up again.

"What do you suppose he meant by saying he has a da *now.*"

Alex shrugged but he knew. Perhaps that could be his lead-in to tell her about Meara. He sighed. Or perhaps not. He had to stop planning and just let the conversation flow. If she decided to ring a peal over his head for keeping Meara's parentage secret until now, he really didn't want to be driving.

At the deer trail he'd found several days ago halfway between town and the house, Alex stopped the gig and jumped to the ground.

"Why are we stopping?" she asked.

"I found a great spot a bit up this trail. But we can't take the gig. It's such a delightful day. I thought we'd go for a bit of a tramp through the woods. Are you up for it?"

Patience thought of what Doc Clemens had said that morning after confirming her pregnancy. The newest theory said women should remain relatively active as long as possible. She was glad because being confined until mid-September would be awfully hard on her after all the years of living as Edgar's prisoner.

"Of course I'm up to the walk," she told him. "I want to enjoy this warm spell. I love the out-of-doors and all the beautiful weather here. Back east you can't go for walks in February without wearing layers of heavy clothing." A walk in the woods couldn't have come at a better time. She'd tell him their news when they got to the special place he wanted to show her.

Alex lifted her to the ground but held on to her

waist when she would have moved toward the path. She looked up and found his gaze studying her intently. Then he cradled her face in his strong hands, touching her with such gentleness it nearly brought her to tears. His lips took hers in a kiss that was arousing and tender at once. He had the most uncanny ability to make her feel cherished with just a touch.

Alex lifted his head then, and smiled. "Wait till you see what's up ahead."

"If it has you this excited it must be something. I can hardly wait," she told him, marveling at the wide range of feelings he could engender with just one of his sensual smiles. He softly traced her cheek with his fingertips, then let go of her before turning away to walk around to the back of the gig.

She thought of what was ahead for them. Parents. They'd be parents by the end of the summer. He'd be so much better a father than either of them had experienced themselves that it was dizzying. She hoped this was a good time to tell him. Mostly she hoped he'd be happy about the baby.

Her heart pounded with excitement. And perhaps a small bit of worry. They'd never talked about children but Alex certainly must know that making love more than once a night nearly every night increased the possibility. She smiled as she thought of his lovemaking.

She followed him to the back of the gig where he pulled a picnic basket and their quilt from under the seat. "You didn't say we were having a picnic."

"I wanted this afternoon to be a surprise for as long as possible. I told Heddie we'd stay in town for dinner but then I bought a picnic lunch from Reiman House." He reached under the seat and tossed the bright quilt

Willow had given them over one arm, picked up the basket and reached for her hand. "Ready?"

She nodded and let his hand swallow hers, secure in his care. *He'll be happy. He'll be so happy.*

If only he loved her as much as she loved him. If only she felt free to say it aloud. If only he'd admit to what she saw in his eyes each time he looked at her.

The trail climbed steadily and after a while she could hear a roaring sound ahead. It wasn't an animal noise, though. But a more constant noise that was unlike anything she'd ever heard.

Then the deer path widened a bit and turned. She gasped when an incredible scene came into view across a wide clearing. It had to be the most beautiful place on earth. "It's a waterfall. Two of them! Oh, Alex! What a wonderful place!"

Water came tumbling over a rock cliff high above them, falling into a deep pool that overflowed over a second smaller cliff into falls that formed another pool that lay below where they stood. Then it burbled gently away, flowing downward along a leafy, rocky creek bed. "Is this Johnson Creek?"

He nodded. "That's how I found this place. I got curious one day after I dropped you off. So I followed the creek up here. The deer track is a much easier climb than the creek bed, believe me." He dropped the basket and a sensual look moved into his eyes. It was one she'd seen so often in the last two months it was easy to interpret.

"Here, Alex? Out in the open? What if someone stumbles across us?"

He flipped the quilt in the air, letting it float to the ground so it settled on a thick bed of leaves, neatly spread and waiting for them. "I have a powerful need to see you bathed in sunshine," he told her and sat in the middle of the quilt. Then he held out his hand. It was no casual invitation.

When she took hold of his hand, he pulled her down next to him, catching her about the ribs and letting her fall gently onto his chest as he lay back. She started to protest. "But—"

He cupped the back of her head and pulled her down so their lips met. The tender kiss brought a flood of tears to her eyes. He pulled back and smiled. Then he frowned. "What is it?"

She shook her head. "I told you women cry when they're happy sometimes. Today just feels so perfect. What if this is our only *perfect* day?"

A small smile replaced his worried frown. "I can see Daniel Wheaton is having a grave effect on you. Have I a rival for your affections?"

"I think you're safe for ten or fifteen years," she teased. "Unless you get me involved in a terribly embarrassing scandal this afternoon."

She felt his laughter echo through his body. "Relax. I don't think anyone has been here since the Comanche abandoned the area. O'Hara didn't even know we had a waterfall on the spread so I'm relatively sure we'll be undisturbed."

Patience arched an eyebrow and traced his nose with her index finger before giving it a playful tap. "Just how many picnics of this sort have you planned, sir?"

He tilted his head, pretending to think, and pursed his lips as he continued to consider the question. "The strangest thing has happened to my memory. I can remember no women in my life save my sainted mother.

And you, my angel. You've supplanted them all. *If* there were any, I've forg—" He stopped abruptly and lost the teasing light in his eyes. His whole demeanor turned serious.

"Alex? What is it?" She levered herself backward to kneel next to him.

He sat up, looking troubled. "I was about to say I'd forgotten all the other women I've known. But there is one I cannot forget. Not because I have any lingering feelings for her. Indeed any I have are not good ones after learning the truth about her. Iris, Jamie's first wife was mine first, you see. She gave me a gift I can never claim. She was the cause of a rift between Jamie and me that lasted many years. Because he married her when he knew I loved her—or I thought I did. She was already expecting Meara. *My* daughter. Months after her birth when Iris was killed, Jamie refused to grieve. I didn't understand it then. I later came to understand it all too well. It was nearly too late."

She remembered him showing her the miniature in his watch and thinking Meara looked like Alex. She was instantly angry on his behalf. "The most important question is, would you have wanted to be Meara's father?"

He stared at her for a long moment, clearly surprised. "I would. Very much. What are you angry about?" he asked cautiously.

"That he did this to you. Why, after all you did for him, would Lord Jamie do this to you? And why would she?"

He took her hand and gave it a little squeeze. "It's not on Jamie's head. It was the damned title. She wanted to be a countess. She used me to get to Jamie. I was only her tutor so she could learn how to attract him. But Jamie was too loyal to me. As she was expecting Meara and unable to attract his attentions, Iris made sure they were found by my father and hers in what looked like a compromising situation. I didn't find out the truth for a long time. Not until the night I killed my father. It was yet another revelation of that infernal night."

Her heart ached for him, remembering that look in his eyes when he'd gazed at the miniature. "Does Lord Jamie know you're Meara's father?"

Alex nodded. "Jamie—being Jamie—says he loves her all the more because she is part of me. Now that I'm settled here with you, he has suggested they visit each year. Legally she is his and has a better future as his legitimate daughter than as my illegitimate one. So we've decided to let things remain as they are. Meara adores Jamie and he loves her as his own. She knows no other father and I would never want to take that away from either of them."

"That was very wise and good of you. You are you know. Wise and good."

He didn't argue but gave her a gentle smile. Then he started to toy with a random curl that had escaped her bun before moving on to run the tip of his finger around the shell of her ear. He stroked her cheek. "You understand, don't you?"

At her nod, he smiled. "I knew you would. I needed to tell you but wasn't sure how. I couldn't put it off any longer because I set up a trust for her. If something happens to me you need to understand why. And so that when they visit, you wouldn't say how much we look alike. I worry that enough of those remarks might lead her to questions that would alter her life, if not break her heart.

"And speaking of questions, the same could be said of Daniel's little slip earlier. I went to the bank to set up the trust for Meara. Not because I think she'll need it but because she deserves it as my child. I could tell Josh felt it was a poor reflection on Jamie, as if he couldn't properly care for his own daughter.

"I had to set him straight about Meara's birth. I expected Josh's poor attitude to transfer to me. Instead he confessed that he and Abby have only been married a short time. That's why they moved west. So Daniel would have a life free of the harassment and ridicule he suffered back in Pennsylvania. Apparently Josh's father kept them apart for ten years because she was the daughter of one of his miners, even though he knew about Daniel."

Patience huffed out a breath. "I cannot understand some fathers. His, yours, mine. I could go on. Thank you for trusting me with the truth about Meara. And Daniel."

She had never felt so discouraged and angry. How could he ever trust in love when that woman had done such awful things while claiming to love him? He might not be ready to love again but he was clearly ready to be a father. So why let her dissatisfaction with their relationship color the news of their child or her feelings for him? It would do until he was ready to trust her completely. Knowing she'd made him happy would be enough. For now. But she could no longer hold back all she felt for him. She had to tell him or burst with her feelings.

"I have something to tell you," she said as brightly as

she could and reclined on her hip, propping her upper body on one elbow. He mirrored her pose, and kissed her.

"Too much talking," he whispered against her lips.

"Please. Perhaps I can make up for all you've lost."

"Done. And done." He kissed her again, pulling the pins from her hair with his free hand, then tunneled his long fingers through it. "See how much better this is than talking," he whispered in her ear then nipped at her earlobe before drawing it into his mouth and laving it.

She shivered. "You have to be the most stubborn man in the world." He nipped her neck and she giggled.

He sighed deeply. "If you're going to get insulting. Giggling at my lovemaking," he said in pretended offense with a smile he couldn't hide. "Honestly. You've cut me to the quick, angel mine. I suppose you may as well bore me with facts, but make it fast before we lose the light. There is still the sight of seeing the sunshine glow on your skin, which I refuse to wait much longer to see."

"Well, Abby came and watched the class for me at lunch hour today."

"Be still my racing heart," he quipped.

"Will you please be serious! This is serious. She helped with the class so I could see Doc Clemens."

His eyes widened. "You're ill? And I have you out here in the chilly air—"

"Stop! I'm not doing this very well." And because of that she rushed through her great announcement. "I am expecting your baby in mid-September. And unlike the mother of your first child, I love you more than life itself."

His face transformed from a look of abject terror to something so wonderful it defied description. She supposed the only word was worshipful. He looked at her as if she truly were an angel, and raised his hand to her hair, smiling that wonderful smile of his. "Oh, angel mine—"

He paused then rooted for his vest pocket. "I have something for you. I wanted you to have this because I—" He looked down at his pocket.

And a shot rang out

Alex's head snapped back. He fell to the quilt, his blood flowing. Spreading. She screamed his name and reached for him. But someone dragged her backward by her hair, gripped her arm and cruelly spun her around. He latched onto her other arm almost before she even thought to struggle.

She looked up and screamed again.

Howard Bedlow's florid face hovered over her.

"Whore!" he screamed. "I offered you everything and you ran off with that Irish-born scum." He slapped her hard. Her ears rang as her head snapped to the side, giving her a momentary view of Alex's prostrate form, blood pooled around his head.

She looked away, unable to face the loss of him. The destruction of their dreams. She stared up at Bedlow, her hands balling of their own accord into fists. He had taken her love from her. Destroyed all they could have had.

"You killed him," she shouted. Then, without thinking of the consequences, she broke his hold on her wrists and flew at his face with her fists. Striking wildly, she felt the crunch of his nose and gloried in the blood that spurted from it.

But she didn't count the damage as nearly enough. She landed a blow to his mouth, then she raked her nails downward over one of his eyes, laying open his cheek. He tried to fend off her unrestrained attack but he finally shouted to someone for help. The coward.

He grabbed her by her upper arms, trying to control her again. But she remembered a lesson Alex had taught her to keep her safe from other men. She jammed her knee into Bedlow's groin with all the strength and all the fury that was clawing to break free of her anguished heart. The blow landed true and he let go. Howling, he doubled over.

She was about to bring her knee up again to his face when a blow from behind exploded stars and even brighter lights inside her head.

Her last thought was that Alex had been going to tell her he loved her. She was sure of it.

And then mercifully before that thought disappeared, blackness fell.

Chapter Fourteen

Patience woke to enveloping cold. Throbbing pain pulsed in her head and jaw and dizziness rolled over her, stealing her breath. Awareness of her surroundings came next. Lying on the ground, she cautiously opened her eyes and found herself staring at pitch darkness.

And then the horror flooded back.

Alex was gone.

They'd taken him from her. From their child. From all those who loved him.

Fury and grief warring in her heart, Patience looked toward the sound of voices. Her ease of movement made her realize they hadn't tied her. Probably because she'd been unconscious and presented no threat of an escape attempt. She'd learned something over those terror-filled years with Edgar and later her imprisonment by her father. Careful planning translated into better success than simply reacting. Look at where her fury had gotten her. Now she had an atrocious headache and she was still a captive of Howard Bedlow. She narrowed her eyes, trying to see the faces of her captors, but otherwise she lay perfectly still, not wanting to alert them that she was conscious.

There was a campfire burning about ten yards away. Three men sat around it. "I thought she was a real timid mouse," the man sitting on the other side of the fire said. It was a voice she'd heard before. Then he continued and she knew why. "She hid behind Reynolds the first time I saw her. Acted like I was the devil himself. Pissed me off good and proper."

Lynch, the man Sally Martin had ordered thrown out of the Golden Garter.

"Well, she don't have Reynolds to hide behind no more," another man said, then cackled.

Patience pressed her lips together to keep from crying out when a picture of Alex's still form flashed in her mind. He was gone. Her kind, brave, irreverent Alex was gone. She honestly couldn't imagine life without him. But she had to live on for his child. She would protect Alex's baby no matter what she had to do. But she would also see his death avenged if it took the rest of her life.

"He turned her into a real hellcat," Howard said after a protracted silence. "I should have thanked Reynolds before I put that bullet in his head. Taming her again should prove amusing."

"When you recover," the cackling man said and laughed again.

"Watch your mouth. I don't pay you to be disrespectful."

"No offense. I had it happen to me once. Some little Injun squaw caught me that way. Couldn't use it for a week. But I had my fun with her anyhow. Carved her up real good. Slowly, too. Played with her till she begged me to end it. I could have at yours. A little payback for the damage she did you. If you're real careful they last a long time."

Patience fought her burgeoning fear. Fear made you weak. She'd learned that, too. It made you a victim of its power. They had to pay and the only way that would happen was if she kept her head. By God she'd do both.

"I'm not interested in your sadistic hobbies," Bedlow growled. "I want her unblemished. I'll put my *own* stamp on her. In my own way. If she lives. Did you have to hit her so hard? She's been out for hours. I only asked for a bit of assistance in controlling her. I didn't expect you to use the butt of your rifle on her head. If she's turned simple, I swear I'll kill you. I'm sick of missing my opportunities with her."

Patience nearly vomited at the thought of his plans for her. But then the memory of Alex's final moment flooded back.

He'd died because of her. She would deal with the guilt of that later—and for the rest of her life. But right now, if she became the weakling she'd been when she'd met him, Alex's life would have been lost for nothing. She would never be cowed by a man again.

She had to be strong. But maybe if she *pretended* to be cowed, they'd leave her untied. Then she could look for her chance to escape, even if it took a while. She lay still, listening. Planning.

"Hurry up with that meal, Thompson," Lynch snapped. "We have to get the fire out."

"If you hadn't gobbled down that dinner Reynolds had for them, we wouldn't need to cook nothin'," the man named Thompson fired back.

"It wasn't enough for all of us anyways and my

stomach was shakin' hands with my backbone," Lynch argued. "I hid in that damned bush near the school all day. Meanwhile you two were back here at camp and could eat and take a piss whenever you wanted."

"You still ate their chow on the way here. 'Sides, ain't no one lookin' fer us yet and in this here bowl with hills all around they won't see the flames. Why should we eat cold chow and sit here gettin' chilled 'fore we need ta?"

"I certainly don't intend to freeze because you can't find that line shack you said we could use tonight," Bedlow said.

"I was there in summer. Everything looks different with the leaves off the trees. I'll scout around for it in the morning and come back for you three. If you hadn't been in such an all-fired rush to grab her, I'd have had time to find it first."

"You hid their horse and gig. No one's even missed them yet. I won't do without a fire. Sleeping out here is bad enough," she heard Howard grouse.

"Look, dammit!" Lynch snapped. "I'm trying to keep your neck out of a noose. You're the one who killed Reynolds. You didn't say anything about killing him when you hired me."

"I doubt it'll be a problem," Howard said, his tone careless and dismissive. "They'll hardly come looking for his murderer in New York. And if you're right about what scavenger animals will do to the body tonight, no one will ever find enough of him to identify, anyway."

The thought of Alex's body torn asunder by ravening animals made her gasp. If she got hold of a gun they were dead men.

And just that quickly Howard Bedlow was there

dragging her up next to him. Fury made her forget her plan and she nearly went after him again but remembered it in time. She started to sob. Tears were easy to manage with her memory full of Alex's still form. She curled her shoulders inward and looked at her feet.

Bedlow let out a booming laugh. "Back to being Edgar's little shadow that quickly, eh?" Then he slapped her so hard across the face she was on her knees before she could draw another breath. She had her hands full of dirt to throw in his eyes before she remembered her plan. She dropped the dirt as he dragged her back up with a punishing grip on her upper arm.

"Get over to the fire and eat. I won't have a weakling holding us back once I can ride for any length of time."

Then he kicked her, making her stumble. She nearly fell into the fire.

"Think twice before kicking me again, bitch. Now we have to hide in the area before riding to Dallas. It's going to give me a lot of time to whip you into shape before we get to the train. By that time you won't have the nerve to ask anyone for help."

When she tried to get to her feet her legs were so shaky she nearly fell back down but Lynch caught her. Then his hands started roaming her body. She let out a whimper that this time, shamefully, was a reflex.

"Hands off what's mine," Bedlow growled. "I didn't make her a widow so you could enjoy the fruits of my labor."

Lynch let her go and she scampered to the other side of the fire. She sank to a log, shaking like a leaf in a windstorm, praying for the strength to survive.

And for revenge.

"Not like you can do her right now anyhow," the man

called Thompson said then he let out another bone-chilling, cackling laugh.

"Your friend is starting to annoy me, as are you, Lynch. I gave you both the parameters of this position when I hired you in Mountain Home."

"What'd he say?" Thompson asked Lynch, who shrugged.

"Rules for the job, you imbeciles," Howard snapped. "And I expect the tasks I outlined done and done right. We have the woman. There is still more to do."

"The first part went real good. You even got in some target practice," Thompson said, then cackled again. Patience cursed him to hell in her mind. Alex. Target practice. She'd never thought a broken heart would actually physically hurt. But it did.

Bedlow ignored Thompson, then stalked to the fire and said, "You have still to get us to the train line and onto the car I've rented. You'll get paid then. And, Lynch, you don't get any part of that payment from time with my future bride. The woman is mine. I want to know any child planted in her belongs to me."

As that terrifying thought exploded in her mind, he stared at her from across the fire. Her heart pounded as his beady eyes bored into hers. "Then she'll have no other choice. She'll marry me in front of all of New York society and she'll look happy about it. My honor will be restored. Or her father will die in an accident the way I managed her mother and brothers' little accident."

She sucked in a shocked breath. Bedlow had done it? Not Edgar? That made no sense. What had Bedlow to gain? He'd still been married and so had she.

A supercilious smile twisted his overly full lips.

"Surprised I was involved? Or are you so stupid you still thought their deaths were an accident?"

She stared at the dirt at her feet. Thinking. Planning. He'd be surprised by how intelligent she actually was. Did he think Vassar graduated just anyone off the street? She looked up in pretended confusion still trying to puzzle out his involvement.

"Do you really think a man as weak as Edgar could spend all that money without leaving his house? Or that he could make *that* many bad investments? He asked me to arrange their deaths before they could talk to Lionel about you. He couldn't have your father finding out the kind of man he really was. Edgar was wealthy and powerful in Troy but your father wields real power in New York City and Albany.

"I had to help my *friend.*" Sarcasm was rife in his tone. Then the tone changed to a dark and deadly one. "So I ran your family off that cliff. But I did it close to Edgar's home. Ingenious. It truly was. I threatened to expose him. And you were all the proof the authorities would have needed to hang him. So I started to collect.

"Look at me!" he shouted because she'd continued to stare at her feet.

She, no doubt, had robbed him of the chance to gloat over her surprise. And her horror. But she knew better than to openly challenge him so she obeyed and shivered at the look—the less-than-sane look—in his gaze.

"At first it was the money. Then I realized my triumph would only be complete if I had you as well as the rest of the things he owned," he went on. "I had to win, you see. I've waited a long time to claim the rest of my prize. Once I'd drained his finances, I knew he'd hand you over. And he did, didn't he? It was glorious knowing he was up there on his death bed thinking I was off somewhere in the house making you mine."

"I don't understand, Howard. Why? I thought Edgar was your friend."

"Edgar Gorham was my *father*. He had an affair with my mother and when she turned up pregnant her father married her off to Jeremiah Bedlow because Edgar was already married to his first wife. My legal father had the same *problem* Edgar did, and he wanted an heir. But as I grew up under his roof, he made our lives a living hell. Finally Mother's husband and Gorham's wife were dead. She'd waited for him all those miserable years thinking he'd marry her and make me his heir. But instead, he refused her and married you. It killed her. She told me the truth on her death bed."

The striking similarity of Alex's and Bedlow's upbringings was shocking—but only because of the stark difference in the character of the men. Good and evil embodied in two men.

But this time evil had won. Alex was dead.

"I got my revenge on both of them," Bedlow continued. "Mr. Bedlow's fortune came to me. Then I bankrupted Gorham and now I'll have his last prize. You. I'd have already had you but that maid of yours got in my way. If I ever get my hands on her, she'll be sorry for her interference. Is she here in Texas?"

"I don't know what became of her," she told him, keeping her voice meek and just above a whisper...the way she'd spoken around him while Edgar was alive.

"I found *you* didn't I? I'll find *her*, too. It's been years since I took the time to choke the life out of a woman then strung her up so everyone would think it was suicide."

Thompson cackled again. "You may be a highfalutin son of a gun but you're a clever man, I'll give you that much. Think I'll try that a time or two."

She looked away when Bedlow glanced at Thompson. So Bedlow's first wife hadn't hanged herself. Patience turned cold. She knew then with certainty that she would die if she didn't get away.

If only Alex were there to save her. Grief swamped her and tears blurred her vision. He'd never be there for her again. She tried to take comfort in the fact that he hadn't known what danger she'd soon be in.

She shivered from cold and fright and grief. She didn't think she'd ever be warm again. Wrapping her arms around herself, she closed her eyes and sought the comfort of a good memory. The last one she'd ever have of her time with Alex rolled across her mind. It was a vision of the look in his eyes when she'd told him about the baby. And when she'd confessed her love.

For one beautiful shining moment they'd been so perfectly happy.

"Up ahead. I see the quilt," someone shouted. "Here. Up here. It's Alex."

The voice blasted into Alex's hard-fought-for slumber. More shouts followed, echoing from all directions. Why the hell was everyone shouting?

Confused, Alex hugged the quilt to him and shivered. He'd awakened before, his head pounding from yet another beating. In the black-as-pitch darkness, he'd gathered the blanket around himself and wondered what room his father had locked him in this time. Then he'd smiled, knowing he must have kept Jamie safe again.

Then he'd forced himself to escape in sleep, to let his body heal.

"Lord be praised, you ain't dead!" Virgil whispered, pressing something to the side of his head. Alex yelped at the intense burning pain in his scalp. Now he understood the torturous pounding in his head.

Actually, no, he didn't.

"Just you lay still, now. We come to help," Virgil said.

Virgil?

He'd met Virgil on the train west. Which meant his father was dead. So what the hell was wrong with him? Alex forced his eyes open. There was a torch stuck in the crook of a small tree. He was out of doors?

How could he be outside and locked in a room at the same time? He looked down at the cloth wrapped around him. Not a blanket, then. He recognized the quilt but couldn't think why.

Then Dylan Varga knelt at his side, turning Alex's head toward the light of a torch. He'd never heard Varga curse before. "He's been shot," Varga called out. "The bullet grazed his head."

Moments later, as man after man arrived with torches and the place began to grow ever brighter, his surroundings became more familiar. The roaring in the background had to be the waterfall he'd found.

"We'd better get Doc and the sheriff out here." That was Michael O'Hara talking. Alex watched him bend and picked up something. "Her reticule," O'Hara said. "Women don't just leave them behind willy-nilly."

"Someone must have her. She wouldn't have left him unless she went for help and we didn't pass her on the road," Dylan said, handing his torch to Virgil.

Dylan...Dylan had a younger sister...he always worried about her...which made him protective of Patience.

Patience?

Patience was missing?

"Patience," Alex croaked.

"We'll find her," O'Hara promised then he turned away to hold his torch high and look around. "There was a struggle here." He hunkered down. "Three men. One left carrying her." He pursed his lip. "We should get you home, Alex. Do you think you can ride? We can't find the gig."

"If someone took her it had to be Bedlow. She's out there with a man who attacked her back east," Alex said, his voice weak and thready. He struggled into a sitting position. He tried to kick his way out of the cocoon he'd made of the quilt. "Help me up. We have to find her. It had to be Bedlow. Her father is a ruthless businessman. He may wield power like a club but he wouldn't break the law."

"I may be splitting hairs here, boss," Dylan said, "but a sixteenth of an inch to the right and you'd be dead right now. I don't think someone shot *at* you so much as tried to kill you. I'll head for town for Doc." He finished tying a bandage around Alex's head. "That needs stitches and we need Ryan Quinn."

"They can catch up to us. Doc needs to see to—"

In a blinding moment of clarity it all came back. That beautiful moment. The baby. Patience's declaration of love. He'd been rooting for the ring to have it ready when he told her he loved her, too. He'd never gotten the chance. He'd looked down at his right vest pocket. If he hadn't, he'd be dead. His love for her had saved his life. He reached for his pocket. It was still there.

Oh, God. He really hadn't told her.

Did she know?

She had to know. She had to.

Oh, hell. She must be terrified. For herself. For the baby. And for him.

"Doc needs to see to Patience. She's expecting," Alex told them as he struggled up with Virgil's help. "We have to find her before he hurts them." Once on his feet the world seemed to tip to the side. Dylan and Virgil flanked him, wrapping their arms around his middle as he looped his arms over their shoulders. Alex felt as if his head was about to explode.

Dammit. He was as weak as a kitten.

And Patience needed him.

"You've lost a lot of blood," O'Hara said. "You aren't going anywhere right now, Alex. We have a few hours till dawn. We need supplies and no one can start after Patience till we can pick up the trail. It's a miracle we found you tonight. It's a new moon. If you hadn't asked me about the falls, I wouldn't have had a clue where to find you. The men who took her aren't riding anywhere in this darkness, either."

"But they had a good two hours till complete darkness fell," he protested.

"Alex, you have to listen to me. You pay me to make smart decisions about the animals. Getting Big Boy's leg broken won't get Patience back. You have to wait till first light. That's the time to ride after them. If you can't ride by morning, staying behind will be the best thing you could do for her."

He knew O'Hara was right. But he didn't have to like it. "I'll be ready," he vowed.

Several hours later Alex sat on the porch staring

eastward, waiting for the sky to lighten enough so they could get moving. Heddie and Willow were rushing around the kitchen serving up a quickly readied pot of oatmeal and packing saddle bags with sandwiches for the trail.

He couldn't even think about food.

Both women were fretting so much he'd had to come outside or go insane. But watching dawn's slow approach wasn't much better. He needed to be out there. Looking. Waiting was agony.

At least his headache had settled down to a dull roar. Doc said his skull wasn't split so he could safely ride. And he would. Nothing would stop him.

At the sound of horses in the yard, Alex got up and went to meet the new arrivals. Ryan Quinn, Josh Wheaton and a dark-haired man, who was about the same height and age as Josh, were handing their reins to Billy Harken. They turned to approach him.

"How are you?" Josh asked.

"About how you'd be if it were Abby. O'Hara insisted we wait for dawn so we should be okay to move any minute. He's staying here on the off chance this is something other than the past catching up to us. Like Raiders." His voice sounded odd even to his own ears. Hollow. Grief-stricken. It was too early for that. He had to believe that or lose his mind.

"I brought along some help," Josh said. "This is Abby's older brother. We thought a Texas Ranger would come in handy." He gestured to the dark-haired man. "Brendan Kane. Alex Reynolds."

Alex had heard too much of Kane's reputation with a gun not to be grateful for his presence even though he took issue with Kane's neglect of Helena. Beside he didn't have any right to criticize. He'd promised to keep Patience safe and he'd failed. He swallowed back the tears burning in his throat. He'd get her back. "Thank you for volunteering," he said and held out a hand.

"'Tis my pleasure," he replied and shook the proffered hand. "I'm told you've been a friend to my Helena. I'm obliged."

Ryan Quinn approached, drawing Alex's attention. Behind him walked Dylan Varga and the other men from the Rocking R who were coming along, but in the dimness Alex had trouble making them out.

"Alex," the young sheriff said, nodding his greeting. "I've deputized everyone. That gives all of you protection under the law in case this turns into a fight. It also says you do as we say." He looked around. "We have to try not to get into a shoot-out with these men. It wouldn't be good for Patience. She's our main concern. They probably think Alex here is dead. That makes her the only one who can identify the culprits. We'll try to surround them. If there's even a chance to sneak in and rescue her before any shooting starts, we have to do it that way."

"What chance do you think we have of finding them?" Alex asked.

"We'll pick up their trail. And we've got more than enough firepower."

Billy and Jerome came out of the morning fog leading a very restive Big Boy; Virgil walked next to them.

"The horses are saddled and packed, Mr. Alex," Virgil said.

"Then let's get a move on," Kane said, and all the Rocking R men standing around waiting turned as one and stalked back down the hill toward the corral.

Tears in his eyes, Billy held out Big Boy's reins. "Please find her, Mr. Alex," the boy said. "Please." Jerome just cried, unashamedly, his tears tracking down his cheeks. Alex was tempted to join him.

O'Hara came up behind Billy and put a hand on the boy's shoulder as Virgil pulled his son into his arms.

"That's the idea," Alex told the boys. "I won't come back without her." And he wouldn't even if the trail led all the way back to New York, he vowed as he mounted up.

"Have faith in the Good Lord, boys. In this life, you got to have faith," Virgil said.

Then Virgil put his hand on Alex's knee and looked up, his dark eyes solemn. "You remember that. Have faith. You got to have faith."

Alex clung to faith. And to hope. But he sure as hell knew he didn't have a drop of charity in his heart for whoever had her. And neither did any of the men who thundered down the main ranch road with one goal only.

To bring Patience home.

Chapter Fifteen

Patience sat up and looked around the camp in the gathering light of the gloomy morning. The men had fallen asleep only a few hours ago. She'd spent the night thinking and planning. All the while she'd watched Lynch and Thompson, who'd been told to take turns standing guard. Instead they'd drunk furtively so Bedlow wouldn't see.

He slept on the other side of the fire ring, taking up all the space near the warmth. She'd settled against a rock that had retained the warmth of the day and the heat of the fire. One fact besides Alex's death dominated her thoughts. If Bedlow had any warning of a rescue party, he was vindictive enough to kill her to keep her from being taken from him. Which meant she was safest if they stayed out in the open.

She had no choice. She had to try to stop them from taking her to that line shack they talked of. Any rescue party would certainly have an easier time surprising Bedlow and his cohorts if they weren't hidden behind walls.

She looked behind her and felt a little thrill. She could finally see the horses. There were six in all. They were tied to a line stretching between two of the Mexican pinyon trees that covered the slope behind their camp. It was what she'd hoped to see as the blackness of the night gave way to dawn. Getting rid of the horses was her only chance of staying out in the open.

She'd try to mount one and escape but, though she couldn't see her exact surroundings, Thompson had described the uphill climb on all sides of the camp. That made flight nearly impossible even without the danger to the baby if she fell off while riding bareback.

Silently rising to her feet, Patience lifted her skirts and crept over to the horses. She untied the line at one side so it would look as if the knot had come loose. Then slowly, quietly she slid all but the last horse's lead off the line, leaving that one nearly at the end. The horses milled around once free but thankfully stayed silent.

Picking up a handful of small rocks, she dropped her skirts, hoping to wipe out her footprints, and snuck back to where she'd been lying in feigned sleep. Once back on the ground, she covered herself with the thin blanket they'd given her then hunkered down into her previous position. After waiting to make sure none of the others were stirring, she sat up and tossed the rocks toward the horses with all her might.

Dropping back into a lying position, she let out a breath as the thoroughly spooked horses screamed and reared then trotted toward freedom.

Lynch bellowed, "The hosses!" as he tried to kick his way out of his bedroll. Then, once on his feet, he tripped across the clearing in a clumsy, drunken attempt at giving chase.

In the meantime, Thompson got to his feet. Cursing a blue streak he kicked over the cook pot and coffee-pot, making a wonderfully loud racket. Even better, he dropped the remains of his bottle of liquor. It hit the stone circle and flared the embers of the fire to life in a loud whoosh.

The din was more than she'd hoped for. All the noise spurred the horses into a flat-out thundering gallop. "What's happening?" Patience screamed in pretended panic as she bolted to sit gleefully in the middle of all the commotion. She put a hand to her heart in pre-tended fright and cried loudly, "Is it the Comanche?" She watched the fleeing animals with satisfaction as the six of them disappeared quickly over the steep rise.

"Thompson, you idiot," Lynch shouted. "Didn't I tell you to make sure that line was tied tight?"

"It were! I swear it were." Thompson pointed at her. "She did it. She untied them. Had to be her."

Uh-oh. She'd underestimated Thompson. Desperate to deflect suspicion off her, Patience jumped to her feet. "I was asleep. Besides, I'm terrified of horses. Why do you think Alex used the gig to fetch me at the school every day? And why would they run away like that? What scared them?"

Then she screamed again and jumped over her blanket, scampering closer to the now enlivened fire. She pointed to a stick lying in the shadow of a clump of bear grass near the rocky rim of the basin floor. "Heavens! Is that a snake over there?"

"If it's a snake it's a dead one. It isn't moving," Bedlow said and stared at her, a predatory gleam in his cold gray eyes. He waved his hand at the two men. "You two get after the horses. Find them," he ordered.

"I don't care how far you have to walk. That should give me some alone time with my little betrothed. I find myself restored by a good night's sleep but don't need an audience for *this*. How convenient that you'll both be gone."

Terror invaded her entire being. *Lord, help me. What have I done?*

Thompson cackled and walked away. Lynch followed him. Then Bedlow stalked toward her. Patience backed away. She couldn't let him touch her. She couldn't. She turned and ran but got only a few steps when Bedlow grabbed her by her hair. He whipped her around and pulled her against him.

Oh, Alex, help me! Help our baby! Baby! That's it!
"You can't do this," she shouted. "If you do, you'll never know."

He stilled and grabbed her face again, forcing her to look in his cold eyes. She shivered. "Know what?" he demanded.

There was so much violence in his gaze she nearly panicked again. But she had to try to thwart him. And she had only one chance. Only one weapon. His pride. Wasn't that why he'd come all this way?

He clenched his hand on her jaw. Forcing her to look into his wintry gaze. *"Know what?"* he demanded again.

"You told Lynch and Thompson you want to be sure any child I have is yours. I am Alex's widow. We've been sharing a bed for months. I could have gotten pregnant any day in the last month. You'd never know if it was yours or not. You want an heir. But not Alex's heir."

His eyes widened with fury. "You were supposed to

be mine! Only mine! Whore. You're just like her. Just like *her!*"

His face was so contorted with rage he looked like an unholy demon. She'd miscalculated again. And now she was going to die at his hands. It was nearly a relief that she'd be joining Alex, but there was the baby to fight for. Their child had a right to live the kind of rich, full life Alex would have wanted to give him.

Even though she was halfway prepared, his punch to her face knocked her head back and stunned her mind. She went numb. Limp. She started to sink to the ground.

"No! Fight me, damn you." He grabbed her shoulders and shook her. "Beg for your life!"

For the baby's sake she wanted to beg, but she couldn't make herself move. Or even speak. He let go and she dropped to the ground. All she could manage was to curl up and pray he didn't do anything to make her lose the baby. Because, if she lost that last part of Alex, she didn't know how she'd go on. Or if she'd even want to.

Thwarted, Bedlow went wild with rage, screaming and shouting obscenities and oaths and threats. But he must have feared he'd kill her if he touched her again because he just stalked around, raving like a wild man.

She felt a tingling move up her arms then her neck and blessed oblivion descended.

After finding the gig and picking up the trail, they knew they were hunting three men. Alex and Josh followed closely behind Quinn and Kane. Dylan Varga and the men from the Rocking R rode about fifty yards behind.

Two hours later they all waited for the sheriff to

remount and settle into the saddle after he'd examined the ground. "It's still their trail. From the depth of the hoof prints, I'd say they rode as fast as they could for as long as they could but the light had failed by this point."

Nodding, Alex looked ahead, his mind tortured by all the things that could be happening to her. "Where the hell are they heading? This is the opposite direction of San Antonio."

"Well, now," the Texas Ranger said, "I'm thinkin' they're headin' northeast to Dallas or Fort Worth instead of due east to San Antonio. Probably thinkin' to outsmart Quinn. If we weren't on their trail now, it would've worked. There's some mighty rough terrain between here and there."

"Hopefully we can pay them a surprise visit when the sun's in their eyes. Let's ride," Quinn said.

And ride they did—with either Quinn or Kane checking for tracks every mile or so to make sure they were still on the trail of the same men. At one such stop, anxious to be on the way, Alex fidgeted and looked ahead as he waited for the sheriff and Kane to remount. He squinted against the glare of the morning sun but after a moment, he decided it wasn't glare clouding the horizon. "Does that look like a dust cloud to you three?" he asked and pointed.

Kane shot him a cheeky grin. "Could be a wild bunch of mustangs," he said as he remounted. Then he clapped Alex on the shoulder. "Or it could be something wild of the two-legged variety. No time like the present to find out which." He kicked his horse into a canter. Alex followed suit, taking the lead with Brendan Kane for the first time, his nerves strung tighter than he could ever remember them being. His sense of urgency had increased tenfold.

They hadn't ridden long when a team of six riderless horses thundered over the rise and right by them. They wore bridles and their reins dangled dangerously. A few men gave chase after the runaway animals before they hurt themselves in their flight.

Alex followed Kane and Quinn, dismounting to watch as they examined the prints. It was knowledge he was determined to master. This was his new world and one hoof print still looked like any other to him. Josh walked up, watching the men confer.

Brendan Kane looked over as Alex tried to puzzle what it was the two were looking at. "See that nick there?" he asked. "The missing nail there? The diamond shape on the side of the shoe print here?"

Alex frowned and nodded. "Right."

He looked at Josh to see if he understood but Josh shrugged. "I'm an engineer and a banker," Josh said as he gestured to the shoe prints and asked, "And it means?"

"Three of that six are the same horses we've been followin'. Sans riders. That's the good news. The bad is that now we don't know if those others were spare horses or if we're going to face six kidnappers instead of three."

Alex cursed.

"Don't get downhearted, boyo. It also means they're all on foot."

"Mighty careless of them to lose their mounts," Quinn said, as the Rocking R men returned with the runaway horses.

"However many there are," the Ranger said, "we just

got our break, gents. We can be pretty damned certain they can't go far as we now have their transportation."

"But this also means Patience is on foot, too," Alex said, his worry making his tone sharp. He didn't care. She was his priority. Patience and the baby.

The sheriff looked at him and nodded, then hurried to the horses, checking them over. "By the look of them, I'd say we're no more than half an hour from their camp. The less dust we kick up the better. String up a temporary corral in that grove of post oak over there. The bastards can walk here after we get them rounded up."

"Bedlow isn't going to be able to walk after I get done with him," Alex growled.

"Don't do something stupid. Your wife is going to need you at home, not at the end of a rope or in prison. Save that for them. Killing them to save your wife is one thing but if we take them alive, I have to take them in, much as I'd like to enforce a little frontier justice myself, we aren't going to turn into vigilantes."

Alex gripped Big Boy's reins. "I just want her back and them where they can't ever hurt her or anyone again."

"Getting her back is why Quinn wanted me along," Kane said, and looked around at all of them. "I have experience with this kind of thing. You all saw how far off we could see those horses. From here on, no matter how much we want to get to her, we ride real easy. Like the sheriff said, we want to kick up as little dust as possible. We also have to keep a careful watch for at least one of the men on foot looking for those horses. He'll be harder to spot."

Alex wanted to get there as quickly as he could and snatch her back.

It must have showed. Kane mounted and pinned him with a hard look. "We'll get there, boyo. Then we'll plan according to the lay of the land. No one fires a shot until we know *where* she is, *how* she is and how vulnerable she is to them. She is our number-one priority. Our second is us. If a life is sacrificed, it's one or all of them. They started this. We finish it and ride home with all of us alive."

"And with that in mind, Alex," Sheriff Quinn added, "you need to keep your head down. If it is this Bedlow fellow who your wife was running from and there's a chance in Hades he can take you out, I'm thinking he will. He clearly already gave it a good try."

"If any of you have any more questions," Ranger Kane said, "ask now, then pipe down. Voices carry out here."

When no one spoke up, Quinn and Josh nodded and climbed back into the saddle. Alex followed suit with his blood pounding. As they waited for Dylan and the others to secure the runaway horses, Big Boy, no doubt feeling Alex's nervous energy, grew restive. He side-stepped into Josh's mount.

"You doing okay?" Josh asked.

"What if we make a mistake?" Alex winced at the slight quaver in his voice. "The way Patience described Bedlow, he's a crazy son of a bitch. If he has her…"

Josh nodded toward Brendan Kane. "He's trained for this. He doesn't make mistakes."

"Why is he here? In town I mean. It's an incredible coincidence."

There was a satisfied little twinkle in Josh's eyes

when he said, "Word of the raids reached Bren. He's worried about Helena. So he got assigned to her to solve our problem."

"And *he* can hear you both. Button it," Kane growled.

Josh looked ahead and said no more. Which left Alex alone with his own tortured thoughts. He'd had weeks to tell Patience he loved her. Months. But he'd been so wary of his own feelings, of making another mistake, he'd held back words that would have meant the world to her. Had he hurt her with his reticence? He must have.

Then when he'd been so bursting with the feelings that he couldn't think about anything else, he'd let down his guard. And now while the last of his men mounted up, all he could do was sit there and pray he got the chance to make it all up to her. *Please, God. Let me get them back.*

They started off again but moved carefully ahead for about a quarter of an hour. Alex had just detected the sound of a man shouting when Kane raised his hand then dismounted. He was gone for another quarter hour on foot. He came back and made a hooking motion toward a shadowed rise a short distance away. They'd mentioned the advantage of getting the sun at their backs earlier so Alex assumed this was the reason for their northwesterly direction.

Following Kane, they walked their mounts to the base of a pinyon-covered hill. A tall, majestic bald cypress, a tree that usually grew along streams and creeks, speared upward from somewhere on the other side of the hill. The smallish evergreen trees would provide excellent cover on their way to the top.

Kane signaled for them to move in close to the line of trees and tie their horses. Then his pistol was suddenly in his hand and he moved into the pinyon with Quinn. Alex looked at Josh, more than a little shocked at how quickly that gun had cleared the leather of the holster.

"I know," Josh whispered. "And he's faster than that when he has to be. Was back in Pennsylvania." Alex started to follow but Josh stopped him and tugged him back. "Let them scout ahead," Josh whispered. "Don't waste your strength."

The five minutes the two men were gone were the longest of Alex's life. He'd probably paced a mile or two by the time the two men finally returned. Quinn walked to the Rocking R cowboys and Kane toward him and Josh. "It's them. I'm thinkin' the blowhard screamin' is this Bedlow you thought took her," he whispered. "Alex, Varga told me you're deadly with that Winchester you have strapped to your saddle. How's your vision now? I know you were a bit on the blurry side when we left the ranch."

"Better. My balance still isn't good, though," he admitted. He wanted to run to her rescue but he couldn't jeopardize Patience in a stupid attempt at playing hero.

Kane nodded. "Doesn't matter. I want you up on that rise. Josh, Varga—both of you, too. Lay down ground fire and keep them pinned. Alex, if you see one of them making a move toward Patience, take him."

Alex nodded. So did Josh and Varga.

"They're on the floor of a steep canyon. Steep hills in all directions. They're near a stream bed. Patience is off to the left. She's under a smaller cypress with a cluster of pinyon a bit farther to her left. Between us and them the terrain is nearly naked, save a few big rocks here and some clumps of mountain laurel. It's not a good camp, thank goodness. Only a greenhorn or a fool would have thought it was. Hopefully we've a combination of both down there with your wife. If it were up to me, I'd have all of us stand up top and shoot them like fish in a barrel but she's down there, too."

"So the rest of you are going to…?" Alex asked.

"The stream cuts in there through a passage too small for a grown man to squeeze through. So we'll have to slide down and run from rock to rock. That's our primary plan. But it's one I don't think is going to work. That's where you three come in. You're our backup. If any of them makes a move toward Patience, take him out or pin him down. Doesn't matter which to me. Or if they see us on the way down, you're going to keep us alive. No pressure." Kane shot him a cocky grin.

Alex narrowed his eyes. "You remind me of someone."

Kane raised an eyebrow in inquiry.

"Me," Alex said and turned away to get his rifle and ammunition, hungering for his first glimpse of Patience.

Chapter Sixteen

Before she'd passed out, Patience had been sure Bedlow would kill her. Regaining consciousness was a shock. And then she heard him screaming at Lynch and Thompson for coming back without the horses. She was alive but still in hell.

"It ain't like we're not going back out after them again," Lynch shouted. "Now get out of our way."

"I won't stand for this insolence!"

"Will you listen, you damn fool, tinhorn, dandified city slicker," Thompson shouted back. "All you talk about is what you want. You been caterwaulin' at us since we come over the rise! We needed our canteens and bedrolls. This could take all day and into the night."

"Yeah, if you won't help, then get the hell out of the way!" Lynch shouted and shoved Bedlow to the side.

"Don't you put your hands on me. You said they'd settle down if we weren't chasing them," Bedlow shouted again.

"They was too spooked to settle real fast! I ain't a gypsy mind reader, 'specially not a horse's mind. The girl could be right. They might've been scared by a snake. They're probably jest a ways away," Thompson explained. "Maybe…uh…along this here stream. Let me fill up and we'll be off after them."

She heard the truth in Thompson's hesitation. They'd talked it over. They weren't coming back. She was afraid and triumphant at once. Then she heard something else. A rifle lever being cocked. A bullet injecting into its chamber. "Leave now! Take nothing with you but your sidearms."

"Look, Bedlow. You don't go traipsing around in the hills without a rifle and water," Lynch said.

"Yeah," Thompson added, "you come up 'gainst a nervous mama bear and you'll find out real quick like the difference 'tween here and New York."

"We'll get after them again. We'll leave the saddles behind if us taking them makes you nervous. And while we're gone," Lynch said, "think about how stupid it was to risk this to get that woman back if all you wanted to do was beat her to death. You could'a done that up there where you plugged her man."

"*I'm* her man. Get that straight!"

Lynch turned away and joined Thompson at the stream to fill their canteens. Bedlow started for her and she closed her eyes. His footsteps came closer then he pivoted and stomped back toward the stream. "Before you leave, tie her up. If your partner is correct that she untied the horses, she can't be trusted."

Lynch dropped his full canteen and walked toward her. He was nearly at her side when she saw just a sliver of compassion in his eyes. Then a shot rang out, driving into the dirt between them. Cursing, Lynch dove for cover behind the rock she'd slept near.

More shots exploded from all around and she rolled to the trunk of a small oak and pushed herself to a sitting position. Leaning against the trunk, she prayed the shots meant rescue. She had no idea where this canyon was. This could be that Three Canyons area where talk placed the band of Comanche who were raiding around Tierra del Verde. Or they could be under attack from the Comancheros, a group of mixed-blood traders who dealt with the Comanche as well as white settlers. It was rumored they could swing to either side of the law when the mood struck, especially when dealing in slaves taken in raids.

She sighed. Would life as a slave really be worse than life with Howard Bedlow? Unsure of the answer, Patience dropped her head back against the trunk of the tree, her hand covering Alex's child as she awaited their fate. She'd done all she could to even the odds. The rest was up to Sheriff Quinn and the men from the Rocking R. She was out of ideas.

Then she heard Bedlow shouting for Thompson to find his revolver. Patience looked around and noticed a revolver lying on the ground near where Bedlow had attacked her. Lynch tried to move out from behind the boulder toward it, but a shot had him diving for cover again.

Lynch couldn't see her from where he was but, if she reached that revolver, she'd be out in the open. If he looked her way, he'd see her and could easily kill her. And then there was the identity of the shooters on the canyon rim to question. She hesitated.

But there was that gun lying in the clearing, calling to her. She could use it to defend herself. Her mind made up, Patience rolled to her hands and knees and crawled forward from behind the tree. As she made her way toward the gun, no one fired at her. Not only that, but they also seemed to fire at Lynch in a way that kept his attention off her. For the first time she dared hope help had arrived from Tierra del Verde or the Rocking R.

But she couldn't count on them. She grabbed the gun and backed away from the clearing toward the cover of the tree trunk, planning how best to use the weapon. The truth was she'd never fired a gun like it. Alex had insisted she learn but she'd used a rifle. She'd watched Alex and the men practice, however.

She made it to the tree again and leaned back against it, her heart pounding. Remembering the need to cock the gun, and knowing how awkward that would be with her small hands, she pulled the hammer back, flinching at the four loud clicks it made in the lull of gunfire. But soon the sound of shots echoed in the little canyon again. She arranged her skirt over the hand that held the gun, then she just sat there, praying she wouldn't need to pull the trigger. Wouldn't need to fire at anyone. But she was ready to defend herself. And her child.

Because one of the things she'd learned in the last day was that Bedlow would stand for no one having what he wanted. He'd killed Alex for that very reason. He'd also destroy the object of his desire if he couldn't have it.

This whole ordeal had very little to do with her as a woman. She was merely the object of his insatiable quest for revenge. Marrying her was the last piece of vengeance against a father who'd rejected him.

Alex fired again at Lynch and cocked the Winchester's lever to chamber another round. When he'd seen Lynch moving toward Patience with that rope, he'd opened fire without a thought. Seeing him there had been a surprise. The troublesome cowboy had been working for Avery the last time their paths had crossed. Apparently he'd either gotten fired or been offered a better deal by Bedlow.

"Let me cover Lynch, Alex," Josh said. "I can keep his head down but there's movement off to the right creeping toward Patience. I'd rather you take him in case the shot has to be accurate."

"Good idea," Varga said. "The boss can take Bedlow out from here if need be. I still can't keep the guy firing by the stream busy." Dylan rose to his knees to fire again. "He's got that big ol' bald cypress to hide behind and he has Quinn and the rest of our men pinned down."

"Reload," Alex said and swung the Winchester toward the bald cypress. He took a shot at what looked like a foot. Then took two more in rapid succession about five or six feet above the ground. A howl and loud curse rent the air. "There, he has something else to think about now. That ought to keep him busy for long enough to free up the men," he muttered, getting more and more desperate. He was so close to her yet so far away.

"Nice shooting, boss," said Varga as he finished reloading, then went back to peppering the tree as the men on the slope moved forward again.

Alex quickly shoved ten more rounds into the Winchester '73, cocked the rifle and turned back to searching out Bedlow.

"You see him?" Josh asked, firing again to keep Lynch pinned down. "He disappeared into the pinyon on the other slope."

Alex narrowed his eyes, straining to see. "Not yet. What's he wearing?"

"A green frock coat. Buff pants. Real shiny boots."

Heart pounding, Alex scanned the area behind the clearing. There! There was movement in the brush near her. "Where are our men?"

"Moving down, except Kane. When you freed him up he really moved. He's almost to my guy at the cypress," Varga said and fired at the one behind the big tree again.

"You see them all? You're sure it couldn't be any of them in the pinyon?" Alex demanded.

"Fire away," Josh said and drove Lynch behind the rock again with a well-placed shot. His next shot hit the top of the rock and blew shards everywhere. It was Lynch's turn to howl out in pain.

Counting on the sun to keep him from being too easily silhouetted against the sky, Alex stood and sighted on the form moving furtively toward Patience. He could see her clearly, leaning against a tree, but not whether she'd been hurt.

Just after he'd driven Lynch to cover, she'd crawled forward but must have decided she was safer behind the tree. It had been heartening to see her moving around but she hadn't so much as turned her head since. His arms ached but not from the strain of firing one shot after another into the canyon. No, they ached from the need to hold her—protect her.

Patience heard a scuffing noise off to her right. Then a twig snapped. She looked that way in time to see Bedlow standing just inside the cover of the pinyon grove. Tightening her hand on the weapon she prayed for the strength to pull the trigger. He killed Alex, she reminded herself.

"I had a feeling I'd find you right about where I left you. Too bruised to run to your friends?" he taunted. "Waiting for them to rescue you? Let me tell you something, bitch, if I can't have you, no one will." He stepped a bit closer, out of the cover of the pinyon, and lifted his rifle to his shoulder.

With Alex's baby to protect, Patience had no choice. A look of utter shock came onto his face when she raised the pistol. Then a rifle report thundered across the canyon before she could pull the trigger. Blood blossomed in the center of Bedlow's chest and he fell backward like a toppled tree.

But a tree had more of a soul than he had, she thought and an out-of-control bubble gushed forth from deep inside. Close to hysterical, she left the revolver cocked and leaned back against the tree trunk. His death was a sight she'd never forget but she wasn't sorry about that. He'd killed Alex. He'd paid the price for his actions but death had come too fast for him. She'd rather have witnessed him being hanged by a bad executioner. He'd deserved nothing better than slowly choking to death while struggling for air.

She heard Sheriff Quinn shout, "It isn't worth your lives now. Bedlow's dead so there's no more money coming your way. Toss out your guns. Huntsville's better than hell, boys."

"What you gonna do, Lynch?"

"That's it. I'm done," Lynch shouted. "None of this is worth dying for."

"They don't call Huntsville 'Walls' for nothin'. I ain't goin' back there," said Thompson.

A volley of gunfire echoed again and then silence reigned.

She looked over at Lynch. He stood and pitched his revolver into the clearing, then put his hands up. He had no intention of coming after her. She breathed a sigh of relief, her first in days, then set the pistol on the ground. A flood of grief followed quickly on the heels of her relief. She hugged her knees and huddled into herself. She ached more in the heart than anywhere in her abused body.

All for nothing. Alex was gone. And he'd died for no reason but to appease Bedlow's need of revenge on a man who'd died before she'd ever met Alex.

For the first time since seeing Alex die, she was free to really feel it all. Sobs she could no longer control welled up. She wept, wondering how she was going to go on.

How she'd raise his child?

Run his ranch?

She didn't have the slightest idea. But what she did know was that somehow she'd do it all.

For him. For their child.

But she'd have to do it alone.

Alone.

She hugged her knees tighter. She was so horribly alone knowing he was gone. She wished she could have said goodbye. Could have heard his voice just once more. She could almost believe she heard him calling. Maybe now that he'd been avenged he was free and had been allowed to say goodbye. She shook her head. How desperate she'd become.

"It'll be okay, Mrs. Reynolds," a stranger said. His Irish accent sliced a new wound in Patience's heart.

Alex had occasionally lapsed into that same lyrical pattern of speech, when he was emotionally off balance. "It'll all fade," the man went on, hunkering down next to her. "You'll see. You'll have to be decidin' not to give them the power over you they tried to take. Never let a bastard get you down, lovey."

She looked up into kind, luminescent, green eyes. "They killed him," she managed to say.

He looked over at Bedlow's body. "Him? Oh, deader than a doornail, he is. I could go give him a good kick but I promise you he's on his way straight to hell. He'll never hurt you again."

Patience shook her head. A mistake as the world tilted in three directions at once. Her stomach would have rebelled but she hadn't eaten since a smidgen of dinner last night. What kind of fool was he to think she'd care about Bedlow when her heart was bleeding in her chest? "No, Alex!"

The stranger looked a bit puzzled.

And then she heard it again. "Patience! Angel!" But this time, smiling broadly, the man glanced toward the rocky cliff across the canyon. Three men were scrambling and sliding from rock to rock down the steep face of the canyon wall. "He'll be a bit of an annoyance for a while I expect. He was a pain in the tail all the way here. That's for sure."

She blinked. Alex? She looked back at the green-eyed stranger. "Alex is alive?" she asked, hesitant to even say the words lest the miracle before her prove a trick of her mind.

"Oh, no! Good Heavens! I'm an idiot. Of course you'd think... Yes. Didn't you hear him callin' just now?"

Patience struggled to her feet. Dizziness assailed her but her eyes fastened onto the sight of Alex with Josh and Dylan, charging down the steep slope. She picked up her skirt and ran toward him. He reached the floor of the canyon when she was halfway across the space between them and started to run toward her. She jumped into his arms and wrapped hers around his neck.

She closed her eyes and inhaled the scent of him. She gloried in the feel of his hard chest against hers. In the wonder of him alive and holding her as if his very life depended on her. She gasped in pain but having him hold her tight was worth it.

"Did I hurt you?" Alex asked and set her back on her feet. And that fast her world suddenly tilted then seemed to spin away from her. Her vision went black. And her eyes wouldn't cooperate by opening again. But then again, there didn't seem to be any pain in the darkness so just maybe her body knew best.

Chapter Seventeen

Alex scooped Patience up at the same time Kane reached them. "Do you need help?" he asked. "You've about done all a man can do with a crease in his scalp and fifteen stitches closin' it."

"No. I've got her," Alex told him. He needed so desperately to hold her. There was no way he'd hand her off.

Kane shook his head. "She's in a bad way. Thought all this time that you were dead, poor lamb."

Alex looked over to where she'd been sitting against the tree. "I want to get her out of the sun but he's there. And the other's at the creek. Can you…?"

"She could probably benefit from some cool water. I'll go make sure they got that one out of the creek," Kane said and stalked that way.

Alex glanced down. She looked like a broken doll. The bastard Bedlow had battered her beautiful face. Any remorse he might have felt over taking another life fled. He was glad he'd sent the bastard to hell.

Once in the shade of the mammoth cypress, he sank

to the ground with the tree at his back and cradled her against his chest, wishing he'd been able to shield her from all the pain and fear this last day had brought her. One question haunted him. Had the bastard raped her? It wouldn't change her a bit in Alex's eyes but it might change her in her own.

He kissed her forehead and muttered nonsense words, hoping the sound of his voice would rouse her or at the very least soothe her. Then someone put a pot of cold water next to him and Josh handed him a clean handkerchief. Alex wasted no time soaking it with water and bathing her face. He'd thought she'd open her eyes then, but she lay perfectly still.

"Bruises heal, Alex," Josh whispered. But they all knew what could have bruised her spirit beyond healing.

"How close do you think Doc is with his buggy?" Alex asked them.

"Varga, suppose you go make sure Doc was able to follow our trail," Kane suggested. "And make that bastard Lynch show you an easier path out of here."

"Come on, angel mine. Wake up," Alex urged as he bathed her face. Her continued unconsciousness terrified him. There was quiet conversation going on around them but it all seemed ridiculously superfluous. All he cared about was that even though he had Patience in his arms again she still wasn't out of danger.

They got her to the buggy about ten minutes later and Doc looked her over quickly. "She hasn't lost the baby," Doc Clemens said, "but I can't promise she still won't."

Alex nodded. Would this nightmare never end! "Why is she still unconscious?" he asked Doc.

"She's been manhandled pretty badly. She has an

egg on the back of her head the size of Texas. Whatever caused it gave her a concussion. No doubt about that. Her being unconscious this long isn't good. I can't foresee the outcome, son. The next twenty-four hours will tell the tale. If she doesn't wake up by then, she may never."

"But she ran to me before she collapsed."

"Happens that way sometimes. It's all up to the Man upstairs now. Let's get her on home. That's the best place for her."

So they started for home with Doc driving. Alex cradled her, trying his best to keep her from being jostled too much on the bumpy ride to the Rocking R. He cherished every breath she took, grateful for each.

As soon as he laid her on their bed, Doc ushered him to the door. "You've done all you can. It's my turn now. Go on and rest."

"I'd rather stay. I can help."

"You're wasting time." Doc glanced out the doorway, his chin mulish with determination. "Would you gentlemen see to it he follows his doctor's orders?"

Josh put an arm around his shoulders. "Come on, Alex. Let Doc get to work. You need rest, too."

For a banker Josh turned out to be surprisingly strong. Alex found himself in the hall, the door slamming behind him. Then a bit of hope sparked in his heart when the door opened only to have it extinguished when Doc yelled, "Heddie. Willow. I need your help."

They rushed out of Heddie's room and shut the door in his face when he went to follow them back inside.

"Come on, boyo," Kane said. "No doctor wants a worried husband nattering over his patient."

About to protest that he didn't natter, he held his

tongue. He probably would and he didn't want to be a distraction. He wanted Patience to have the very best care available. So he nodded and followed Josh down the stairs, with Kane bringing up the rear.

He walked into his study and froze. Patience was everywhere he looked. She'd created a haven out of his nightmare of Adair. It wasn't the same room that had sent him tumbling back there into the past that first night they'd arrived. She'd brought him back from the brink and had shown him a future full of possibility every day since.

She'd banished the nightmare memories of his childhood with love.

With her lying unconscious, in danger of losing her life or that of their child, the nightmares of the past felt petty and childish. *This* was a nightmare. A nightmare of the worst sort because there was no way to wake from it. He could still lose her.

He sat behind his desk all but numb. Brendan Kane walked over to his desk and put two fingers of whiskey in front of him. "Drink," he ordered then raised his glass in a salute. "Nice shot taking out Bedlow, by the way," he said quietly and sat in the chair next to his desk.

Alex sat back in his chair and nodded absently.

"It isn't going to bother you, is it?" the Ranger asked. "I know you're new to the West. Not every town even has a sheriff. Citizens sometimes have to take care of these things themselves."

His mind was upstairs with his unconscious wife. Not on the brute who'd put her there. "I'm not going to spare him a thought other than that I'd do anything to have gotten to him sooner. Like before he took her."

He heard Josh say, "Bren, did Patience really almost get her own shot off?"

"If Alex hadn't killed him, she'd have put a hole right through his black heart herself," Kane said.

That perked Alex's ears up even more. "She got hold of a gun?"

"And raised it to fire. She must have come up with one of theirs," the Ranger added. "Lynch swears she let the horses loose. That's one hell of a woman to endure what she did then nearly take out her kidnapper. I hope she recovers."

"I'm more than grateful for all your help," Alex said.

"You did all right for yourself," Brendan said. "You aren't exactly the greenhorn I'd pegged you for when you insisted on coming along."

"If there's ever anything you need, anything, let me know."

"Keep bein' a friend to Helena."

"Maybe it's time you think about being a *husband* to her."

Kane stared at him and pursed his lips. "It's complicated," he said, then turned and walked out.

Josh stood and put his glass on the desk. "I should get home. Abby must be ready to burst by now. And Daniel won't be much better. At least I can tell them we got Patience back home. Let us know how she's doing, all right?"

Alex nodded.

There was a knock on the study door. Winston entered at Alex's command. "Is it Patience? Did Doc call for me?"

Winston frowned and shook his head. "No, sir. I hate

to bother you with all you've been through but there's a gentleman here." Winston looked completely undone.

"Who is it? What has you so upset?"

"I'd gotten used to having a daughter, sir." Winston sighed. "I'm afraid I'm about to be supplanted. Lionel Wexler is here."

Alex's head started to throb. He feared he might lose control and fought his growing rage for Patience's sake alone.

"Now *this* could get ugly," Josh quipped.

Alex couldn't agree more. He set his jaw. "Show him in."

Josh stood and put out his hand. "Remember to send word on Patience."

Alex shook his hand then watched his friend leave. He'd barely had a moment to breathe before Patience's father rushed in. Wexler wasn't a particularly large man and for someone who wielded so much power, he looked rather tentative.

Good.

"I came to warn Patience about Howard Bedlow," Wexler said. "He bribed one of Alan Pinkerton's agents for information that would have led him here. Am I to understand I'm too late to protect her?"

Alex glared. "Protect her? You? Is that why you locked her in her room with no food for days? Then had her hunted like an escaped lunatic? All that *loving* behavior to protect her?"

"She'd been acting erratically since her return to my home. I even took her to Poughkeepsie so she could rest. But then she risked life and limb climbing down a tree to escape. It was an insane chance she took!"

"Because she'd rather have died than be handed over

to Bedlow! And now, after all you put her through, he got hold of her, anyway," Alex shouted. "You have no idea who she is. What she feels. What she thinks. If you did—"

"I knew her once!" Wexler yelled. "She was my little girl."

Alex's anger spilled over again. "So you married her off to a sadistic monster, then betrothed her to another when she was finally free of the first?" he yelled.

Wexler's eyes widened. Perhaps he'd come to understand how precarious Alex's control was at that moment. His tone conciliatory, he said, "I knew none of that. I judged those men by their business ethic. I have since learned the truth from her maid. I should have had more faith in the daughter we raised. At the very least, I should have listened to her after Gorham died. She tried to tell me—" He shook his head. "I was a fool and filled with anger and resentment in my grief over losing Penelope and our sons. I will go to my grave regretting my mistake."

"Is that what you call it? A mistake? Let me tell you something, Wexler. If she doesn't wake up, you *will* go to your grave regretting the way you treated her because you'll follow her as soon as I can find you. Were I you, I'd get myself safely back east. Then I'd pray her husband doesn't come looking for you."

"Mr. Alex," Virgil said, having opened the study door, "Doctor Clemens says you can come sit with Miz Patience. She's not awake but he wants you to talk to her, hopin' she'll follow your voice back."

Alex pushed off the desktop and looked down at Lionel Wexler with a cold direct stare. "I'm not interested in anything you have to say. You're too late to do

Patience any good. Had you sent a wire, I'd have been prepared for Bedlow's arrival here. I cannot help but think this visit was about *you*, not *her*. I refuse to soothe your guilty conscience."

Wexler tugged his vest into place. "I'll be waiting at the hotel for word. You'd be a fool to kill me, young man, and you don't appear to be a fool. You'd hang. I won't let you keep my daughter from me. I need to see her."

"Again, it's about what *you* need. About what *you* want. If she awak— *When* she awakens it will be up to her if she wishes to see you. I would never make a decision for her. I respect her too much to treat her as if she were my property. It's a shame the same couldn't be said of her father. If she doesn't awaken, I'm not sure I'd want to live so don't count on the threat of a hangman's noose to keep you alive. It won't bother me a bit to dispatch the man who cost me the lives of my wife and child."

Chapter Eighteen

Alex stepped into their bedroom. Patience lay still on the bed, a compress on her forehead. She wore her pretty white nightgown. Her hair had been arranged perfectly by either Willow or Heddie. Fear sat in his stomach like concrete. Had they so beautifully prepared her for death?

He stood staring at her, able to breathe again only when he saw the covers over her chest move. But the fear lived on. He went to the bed to kiss her hair, and then he moved toward Doc Clemens. The elderly doctor stood looking out of the doors to the terrace, the sun reflecting off his bald head.

When Doc didn't turn to face him, Alex touched him on the shoulder. "Doctor? Winston said you wanted to see me."

Pulled from his thoughts, Doc started, blinking. "Oh, Alex. I'm sorry. I didn't hear you come in." He took off his glasses and began to polish them. "Let's…uh…let's step in there," Doc said, pointing to the adjoining room where Alex had stayed in those first torturous months of their marriage.

"Sit," Doc said as he sat in the chair and gestured to the bed after putting his glasses back on.

"Is it bad news?" Alex asked as he sank gratefully to the mattress, his legs now rubbery with fear.

Doc put a hand on Alex's knee. "You have to calm down, son. Patience isn't the only one who's been concussed during this whole terrible incident."

"But I'm conscious. Why isn't she?"

"You weren't at first but I think that was partly the blood loss. Truth is, Patience may have sustained more than one concussion within the last day. I'm hopeful because you said she did run to you. And she'd talked to Kane. He also said she had been conscious during the whole shoot-out in that canyon. Being alert that long after a blow is a good sign. The brain is a mystery to us. I'm afraid all we can do is wait and be thankful her breathing is good and her heart is strong. She may just need a good long rest and this is her body's way of getting it." Doc gave him a penetrating stare.

"Now about that other worry," he said.

"No, I don't need—" Alex stopped himself from telling Doc to keep the knowledge of whether or not she'd been raped to himself. Much as he didn't need to know for himself, he did need to know so he could help her through any bad memories.

"You can calm down about it," Doc went on. "For whatever reason, she wasn't raped. But…son, she suffered some very rough treatment for a little gal. So far she's holding on to the baby." The older man smiled gently. "Your baby seems to be as stubborn as its mother.

"I wish I could stay longer but I'm needed back in town. There is really no more I can do right now but sit with her. I'm sure you'd rather handle that duty. I've given Mrs. Winston instructions on when to call on me again. Right now, the best thing you can do is talk to Patience. And wait. That's the hardest duty of all. Stay by her side as much as you can. She may need you when she wakes up to the memories."

Alex nodded.

"But be mindful of your own health, young man," he added, shaking his finger at Alex in warning. "I'm going to get very cranky if you don't. You won't do her any good if you put yourself in this bed the way she is in that one."

Again Alex nodded. He had no intention of leaving her side until she awakened. And he had to believe she would or he'd lose what was left of his mind.

"Now that we understand each other, I'll be on my way. You go spend time with your wife."

Alex didn't need to be told twice. He returned through the connecting door and pulled the low chair from her vanity over to the bed and sat, taking hold of her hand.

"I wish you'd open those lovely green eyes of yours. I miss seeing them sparkle when I'm being absurd. I miss our long talks, too. We never seem to run out of things to say, do we?"

Alex talked for hours about their future. He told her he loved her, terrified she'd never open her eyes to hear him say it. He talked about how they'd met and confessed that he'd fallen in love with her at first sight and stupidly called it lust. He told her she had to awaken if for no other reason than to keep him from being stupid again. Then he said since he'd fallen in love first it was okay he'd been the last to say it.

After that, he told her he loved her about every five minutes. He would never tire of saying those three words to her if they were married for fifty, or sixty, or seventy years.

Winston and Virgil came in and switched the chair he was sitting in for an upholstered one from the informal sitting room. Which gave him a new subject to natter on about. He told her about the furniture he planned to order for their child's room, then realized he'd described the nursery at Adair that had been Jamie's. It had been a happy room for a happy child. He wanted their child to have a happy room, too. A happy life, he told her. So she had to wake up.

But she didn't.

She just breathed.

As darkness fell, he began to be satisfied with just her breathing. He began to rejoice at each one, terrified there wouldn't be a next.

Someone—he wasn't sure who—came in. Lit a lamp. Brought him a tray of food that he was too worried to eat.

Finally someone said he was to rest and put the lamp out. In the darkness, when he couldn't see her chest move anymore, he found he needed to feel it. So he lay next to her, still holding her hand. He kissed her forehead, her eyes, her nose, her bruised lips…then begged God for another chance at the life they'd planned. Not long after that he fell headlong into exhausted sleep.

Patience felt a breath puff against her neck and smiled recognizing the scent.

Alex.

She opened her eyes and looked his way, enjoying

the perfection of his dear profile. Dawn's light seeped in through the doors to the terrace, illuminating their room. He was so handsome and he was all hers. She sighed happily and his eyes popped open as if he'd been caught sleeping in class. Then a spasm of pain came swirling through her head.

And that quickly the nightmare came flooding back.

"Alex!" she cried and reached out to touch him, sure he'd disappear—an apparition of desperate, wishful thinking.

But the vision took her hand and slid off the bed to kneel at her side. Tears welled up in his eyes and fell to her hand as he bent to kiss it. "It's going to be fine, angel," he said, looking back up into her eyes. "Everything's going to be fine, now."

She nodded. "You're alive. You're really alive. I thought you'd died at the falls. I thought—" A sob burst from her chest. "I though he'd killed you. He said he had. They all said he had. And he meant to kill me, too. I don't know what stopped him. I was going to kill him. But someone else shot him first."

"Me. I was up on the bluff tracking him through the pinyon grove. I was put up there to be a sniper in case it was needed. When Bedlow stepped out and raised that rifle, my heart about stopped. I pulled the trigger without thinking. I had to save you. I'm sorry you had to see it."

"Don't be. He'd meant to kill you. For that, I wished he'd suffered longer. Otherwise I didn't care. He didn't deserve care. He didn't deserve life."

"My life would have been over without you."

She smiled a bit even though it hurt. He looked so desperate for her to feel better than she did. "No. You're too brave not to go on. I wanted to give up but I had the baby to think of—" She broke off, almost afraid to ask the question she most needed answered. But she had to ask. "The baby! I didn't lose it, did I? Surely, I'd know, I'd feel it if— Oh, God, please tell me he didn't take that from us."

"Doc says the baby's as stubborn as his mother and he'll lead us a merry chase one day soon."

Now tears of relief flooded her eyes. "Oh. Thank you. I never prayed so hard for anything. When I thought you were dead, the baby was my only link to you. So I kept fighting. But if I'd lost him, thinking I'd lost you, I'm not sure I'd have fought back."

"Then we're going to have to be extra careful to name this child something fitting."

"I'd thought Alexander. Or Alexandra. But now I think if it's a girl I'd like to find out what Edgar and Howard's first wives were called. They killed their wives. But they didn't kill me. Or her. If it's a girl I think—" Tears welled up in her eyes again. "I guess my mother's name needs to be in there, too. Edgar got Howard to cause the accident that killed them. So much pain and anguish. And oh, Alex, I know why now."

She went on to tell him about all she'd learned. He looked very serious as she related the tale of the trail of destruction Edgar Gorham had left in his wake. "I could almost feel sorry for Howard because of his bad childhood, but your life was actually worse and you didn't go around doing the kinds of things he has. You were misjudged by all of society but no one else knew of his personal struggles. Men like my father actually respected him."

"Speaking of your father, he's here," Alex said, his

tone so deliberately flat she could tell they'd met and it hadn't gone well.

Fear flooded her. It started to become difficult to breathe. She grabbed hold of his hand needing to feel his strength. "Here? In Tierra del Verde…? Or here on the ranch?" She couldn't shake the irrational fear that he could destroy all they had. She gripped his hand even tighter. "He can't take me away, can he? We're so close to having a wonderful life. Please don't let him find a way to take me back."

"Never. He isn't taking you anywhere. You're mine. I'm yours. Till death at a very advanced age do us part. Did I tell you both my grandfathers lived into their eighties?"

She smiled at that, picturing him still handsome with snowy-white hair, a few character lines and a wicked grin.

"Your father came here, but he's in town now. I'm afraid I wasn't very polite. He does want to see you, however. He says he came to warn you about Bedlow. He'd learned that Bedlow had bribed a Pinkerton agent for information on your whereabouts. Your father has known for a few weeks you were here and married. He also knows he's on thin ice with me already for the way you were treated."

That made her smile again but something still felt wrong. It was her father's intent. "He came all this way to warn me? Why didn't he send a wire?"

"I posed the same question but got no answer." Alex's jaw hardened and he looked down, no longer meeting her eyes. "Had he warned us, none of what happened would have come about. I suppose you should know I threatened to kill him if you didn't live."

She tipped his chin up so they were looking directly into each other's eyes. She gave him a small smile. "So fierce. Never has a girl had a stronger, braver knight defending her. Thank you."

Patience thought for a long moment and Alex patiently waited. He was so excellent at being still. At giving her time. He'd been giving her the gift of time since the moment they'd met. "I don't think I want to see him. I need more time, Alex. He *is* my father, but there's so much I'm angry about. Tell him to go home. I'll write when I'm ready but I'm not sure I'll ever want to see him again. He turned his back on me. He believed lies without ever hearing my side. He blamed me, but the truth is my mother and brothers would be alive today had he accompanied them to Troy. Now he almost cost you your life and the life of our child. No. I'm not sure I'll ever want to see him again."

"Then you never need to," Alex promised, tracing her profile with a gentle finger. "Winston will be so relieved. He was quite concerned about you and about being replaced as your adoring father. I believe I'm going to have to get another hall rug. I'm sure he's worn a path in the one out there with his pacing. Did you know there is a squeak in the hall floor precisely halfway between the back terrace door and the stairs. Very annoying. But what could I do? I had to let him wait for you to awaken in his own way."

She laughed at his absurd sense of humor then winced. "Only you could help me laugh at a time like this, I love you. I love you so very much."

"And I—" He reached for his vest and his eyes widened. "Dammit. I took it out of my pocket. He's not spoiling this again! I'll be right back." And then he rushed across the room, out the door, thundered down the stairs. He was racing back less than a minute later and kneeling next to her again.

"I love you more than life itself," he said, his eyes luminous in the light of the new day. "I wanted you to have this as a memento of our love. Happy St. Valentine's Day, belatedly unfortunately." He took her hand. In his fingers he held a beautiful, silver-colored ring with a round rose-cut diamond surrounded by a multitude of smaller diamonds.

"Oh, Alex," she said as he slid the ring on her finger to join her wedding ring. "It's so, so lovely."

"It was my mother's," he went on. "It had been her mother's betrothal ring." He smiled. "My grandparents' was a great love and they would have loved you."

As if he were afraid to touch her, he ran his index finger through the fringe of hair near her face. "Would you marry me again, Mrs. Reynolds. With Reverend Turner blessing our union? No quick and dirty ceremony but a celebration with all our new friends rejoicing with us?"

Her heart expanded. She remembered this feeling! "This is perfect happiness," she told him, not caring that her split lip hurt when she smiled.

His smile widened too and she saw the truth dawn in his eyes. "It must be. How could we be any happier?"

* * * * *

HISTORICAL

Where Love is Timeless™

HARLEQUIN® HISTORICAL

COMING NEXT MONTH
AVAILABLE MAY 22, 2012

WEDDINGS UNDER A WESTERN SKY
Elizabeth Lane, Kate Welsh and Lisa Plumley
(Western)

MARRIAGE OF MERCY
Carla Kelly
(Regency)

UNBUTTONING MISS HARDWICK
Deb Marlowe
(Regency)

MY FAIR CONCUBINE
Jeannie Lin
(Tang Dynasty)

You can find more information on upcoming Harlequin®
titles, free excerpts and more at www.Harlequin.com.

HHCNM0512

REQUEST YOUR FREE BOOKS!

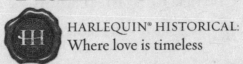

HARLEQUIN® HISTORICAL:
Where love is timeless

2 FREE NOVELS PLUS 2 **FREE GIFTS!**

YES! Please send me 2 FREE Harlequin® Historical novels and my 2 FREE gifts (gifts are worth about $10). After receiving them, if I don't wish to receive any more books, I can return the shipping statement marked "cancel." If I don't cancel, I will receive 6 brand-new novels every month and be billed just $5.19 per book in the U.S. or $5.74 per book in Canada. That's a savings of at least 17% off the cover price! It's quite a bargain! Shipping and handling is just 50¢ per book in the U.S. and 75¢ per book in Canada.* I understand that accepting the 2 free books and gifts places me under no obligation to buy anything. I can always return a shipment and cancel at any time. Even if I never buy another book, the two free books and gifts are mine to keep forever.

246/349 HDN FEQQ

Name	(PLEASE PRINT)	
Address		Apt. #
City	State/Prov.	Zip/Postal Code

Signature (if under 18, a parent or guardian must sign)

Mail to the **Reader Service:**
IN U.S.A.: P.O. Box 1867, Buffalo, NY 14240-1867
IN CANADA: P.O. Box 609, Fort Erie, Ontario L2A 5X3

Not valid for current subscribers to Harlequin Historical books.

Want to try two free books from another line?
Call 1-800-873-8635 or visit www.ReaderService.com.

* Terms and prices subject to change without notice. Prices do not include applicable taxes. Sales tax applicable in N.Y. Canadian residents will be charged applicable taxes. Offer not valid in Quebec. This offer is limited to one order per household. All orders subject to credit approval. Credit or debit balances in a customer's account(s) may be offset by any other outstanding balance owed by or to the customer. Please allow 4 to 6 weeks for delivery. Offer available while quantities last.

Your Privacy—The Reader Service is committed to protecting your privacy. Our Privacy Policy is available online at www.ReaderService.com or upon request from the Reader Service.

We make a portion of our mailing list available to reputable third parties that offer products we believe may interest you. If you prefer that we not exchange your name with third parties, or if you wish to clarify or modify your communication preferences, please visit us at www.ReaderService.com/consumerschoice or write to us at Reader Service Preference Service, P.O. Box 9062, Buffalo, NY 14269. Include your complete name and address.

HHI1B

HARLEQUIN® HISTORICAL:
Where love is timeless

FAN-FAVORITE AUTHORS
ELIZABETH LANE, KATE WELSH AND LISA PLUMLEY
BRING YOU A TRIO OF HISTORICAL WESTERN TALES FILLED WITH RUGGED COWBOYS AND DARING WOMEN.

Weddings Under a Western Sky

The Hand-Me-Down Bride
Arabella Spencer's trip out West was supposed to end in marriage to her longtime sweetheart. Instead she finds her heart racing at the sight of neighboring rancher Stewart McIntyre.

The Bride Wore Britches
Just for one night, rancher Rhiannon Oliver longs to feel like a lady, so she ditches her britches for a ball gown...and finds herself in the arms of cowboy Dylan Varga.

Something Borrowed, Something True
When Everett Bannon's ranch hands order him a mail-order bride, he plans to send her back home...until he sees beautiful Nellie Trent step off the train.

Available June 2012 wherever books are sold.

www.Harlequin.com

HH29691

*Explore the luxurious, dangerous world of the
Chinese Tang Dynasty with Jeannie Lin's fantastic
third book from Harlequin® Historical,
MY FAIR CONCUBINE.*

A twist on My Fair Lady, *Yan Ling, a common tea girl,
is trained to pass as a princess. Unfortunately Fei Long,
the hero, begins to desperately desire this girl
who he's grooming for another man....*

Fei Long waited for the door to shut and separate him
from the rest of the world. From Yan Ling. He continued
to wait long enough for her to walk the short length of the
corridor. She'd go back to the gardens or retire to her room.
Wherever she went, it would never be far enough. He would
still think of her and seek her out to the farthest reaches of
his senses.

The grasslands of Khitai were not far enough.

If he'd had his sword, he would have killed that fool
Bai Shen. Seeing Yan Ling in another man's arms had been
the most vicious of taunts, because Fei Long knew what
was inevitable. In less than two months, she would be taken
from him to be delivered as a peace offering.

Fei Long sat on his bed at the far end of the room and
sank his head onto his hands. He'd been in Yan Ling's
chamber not two weeks ago. He knew how her skin glowed
beneath the moonlight. Knew where she slept only a short
distance away from his chamber.

He dug his fingers into his scalp until there was edifying
pain. All those afternoons they'd spent together. Alone. He
had always remained respectful toward her as their stations
demanded. He would never take such liberties. Yan Ling
trusted him and she had worked so hard to better herself.

HHEXP0612

He lay back on the bed and closed his eyes. There wa
too much for him to do, but he wasn't yet ready to leave thi
confinement.

There would be no afternoon lesson today. He couldn'
bear being so close to Yan Ling. He didn't know why he'
lashed out at her as well. His anger had no beginning an
no end.

There might not be a lesson tomorrow either.

MY FAIR CONCUBINE
Available June 2012 wherever books are sold.

Loving Jeannie's writing and can't wait till then?

Check out her debut duet, the award-winning
BUTTERFLY SWORDS
and THE DRAGON AND THE PEARL.